LOVE & RUIN

THE LOVE & RUIN SERIES BOOK ONE

J.A. OWENBY

EXCLUSIVE LOVE & RUIN BONUS

*Don't miss **special bonus content for the Love & Ruin series** when you sign up for J.A. Owenby's newsletter! https://www.authorjaowenby.com/newsletter*

1

I was no longer living. I was merely surviving.

Ada Lynn's worn rocking chair creaked as she rocked in a slow, steady rhythm on her front porch. She was nosy, but over the last four years, she'd become my only friend.

"Hello, Gemma." Her voice was strong, even though it shook slightly with age as it floated through the muggy, early evening air.

"Hey, Ada Lynn. How are you feeling today?" I pulled open the mailbox, the only extracurricular activity I had for the day. My eyes narrowed when I noticed a new splatter of bird crap that had graced the top of it. Reaching in, I removed the small bundle of letters.

"Well, not much has changed since yesterday. At my age, everything hurts."

The sky darkened briefly as a single white puffy cloud drifted across the late afternoon sun.

Weather permitting, she would lean on her cane, hobble outside, and sit every evening. She was one of the few people I'd spoken to in-person in five years—other than my parents. At nineteen, this would not be an easy feat for most. I found it easy after someone in the sleepy little town of Breaux Bridge, Louisiana, stole my life, turning it into a shell of what it used to be.

"Whatcha got, there?" Ada Lynn's chin tilted up with her question.

I shuffled through the mail, my shoulders tensing when Hillview University's red, black, and white logo caught my eye. Raising my arm, I tucked the remainder of the stack into my armpit.

"Not sure." I ripped off one end of the envelope, flipped opened the note, and shook it free. The thin paper rustled in the soft breeze while I read it.

"Come on now, you can talk to ol' Ada Lynn. Something's got your goat, I can tell by the look on your face."

Folding the letter up quickly, I shoved it into the back pocket of my vastly oversized denim shorts. My T-shirt hung almost to my knees, so even if my shorts slipped some, no one would notice.

"Nothing, just junk." I brushed the stray red hairs out of my face that had escaped my ponytail and approached her chain link fence, smiling.

"You got a whole lot of junk there." She nodded toward my hand holding the additional mail.

"Everyone wants you to buy something, so they pile up your box with nonsense. At least most of it's Mom and Dad's. All I get is an occasional credit card offer since I'm still at home."

Ada Lynn leaned back in her chair, her cloudy eyes critical as they traveled over me.

"When are you gonna wear some clothes that fit ya right and have some color? It's just the same drab, baggy stuff."

My gaze dropped to the cracked sidewalk beneath my sandaled feet for a moment and back to her.

"Never." My voice was strong and steady while I held her stare, challenging her to say more. Instead, her brown-eyed gaze softened.

"All right then. At least you're not prancing around like a little slut. Some of the girls these days... Well, we just never considered showing our bosoms in such a fashion." She pursed her lips in dissatisfaction and patted her recently styled gray curls.

I chewed on my thumbnail and grinned.

"Can I come up?"

"You know you don't have to ask. Come on, my blue-eyed girl," she replied, waving her hand and motioning for me to join her.

I unhooked the metal gate and strolled up the pitted and cracked walkway. I immediately made my way toward the seat next to her, as was our routine.

Ada Lynn at eighty-three was still mentally sharp. Nothing ever got by her, including me, and before I realized it, she had lifted my shirt and snatched the piece of paper out of my back pocket.

A heavy sigh escaped me as I plopped down in the chair next to her.

Ada Lynn scanned the paper, a solemn look on her face. She carefully stuffed it back in the envelope, handed it to me, and took my hand.

Silence hung in the air between us. I knew a lecture or pep talk was on the way.

"Saying it won't change anything, but it's not your business." I sighed and leaned my head back against the white rocker.

"Course it is. You're my business, Gemma Thompson."

Over the last few years, we'd grown close. Ada Lynn didn't have any children, and I didn't have any friends, so we were a perfect fit for each other.

"Someday I won't be here, so you've got to move on—keep going."

She wasn't saying anything I hadn't heard a million times from her lips. Unfortunately, my parents weren't as encouraging.

"I'm trying," I muttered.

"Try harder." Her voice sounded clipped, stern with instruction. "Go to Washington and finish your degree."

"Maybe."

I grew quiet, my mind drifting between the past and the present. Sometimes I dared to dream a little, but then the memories crashed down on me like a tidal wave, crushing me again.

"This is your chance at a new life. Take it back, girl. *Take it back*," she whispered fiercely, squeezing my hand as though she could share her inner strength with me. If it'd been that easy, I would have already left this hellhole.

An hour passed while Ada Lynn and I sat together in complete silence other than the sounds of the insects coming alive for the evening. The clouds drifted across the sun; a whisper of another day was almost over.

A little later, a soft snore escaped Ada Lynn, and she jumped, waking herself.

"Shit," she said softly. "Fell asleep again, didn't I?"

"It's okay. I'm here." I gave her a gentle smile.

"I'd better go inside, and you'd better hurry home before your parents start sniffing around looking for you. Help me in. I'll see you tomorrow." She offered a tired smile as I stood and held my hand out to her. If Ada Lynn sat too long, she struggled to get out of a chair on her own, so I always ensured she made it safely into her house.

I took her hand in mine, opened her front door, and helped her inside. Jesus extended his hand toward me, his heart glowing, as he welcomed me into her home from the obnoxious, bulky, plastic picture frame. Her living room never changed. The same bright orange and yellow colored afghan fell across the arm of the worn black leather couch. My pulse quickened while Ada Lynn turned toward me. I had a strong suspicion of what she was going to say, and I wasn't sure how I'd handle it.

"Be brave, Gemma." The thin, fragile skin of her hand felt like tissue paper as she touched my cheek. "Take the opportunity. I'll pay for your way out there and help you with some money until you're all settled. Do this for me, for an old woman with one last wish."

"I'll think about it." Tears blurred my vision, and I took a deep, shaky breath. I stepped back and attempted the best smile I had left inside me.

After locking the door behind me, my feet hurried down the porch steps and next door to my house. The yellow paint had dulled over time and was now peeling. My parents hadn't found the time to change it to a more appealing color. This was the only house I had ever lived in. My entire life, good and bad, was wrapped up in these walls. Something needed to change.

The screen door clattered closed behind me.

"Home," I called out to no one in particular. Mom and Dad were used to my schedule. I kept it like clockwork. Online college, visit next door, online college, sleep, repeat. Unlike the usual teen, I was easy to track and never left home. It wasn't always like that. Before.

"In the kitchen, honey," Mom called.

I ignored the clutter in the living room, which normally drove me crazy, and strolled toward the inviting smells of dinner.

"Got the mail." I plopped the stack on the white Corian countertop.

"How was your day?" Dad asked from the kitchen table, his work papers spread out in an unorganized mess.

"Nothing new." I closed my eyes and inhaled the familiar aroma of fresh crawdads. Comfort.

Turning toward Dad, I did a quick inventory. He looked tired, too old for his fifty-four years. His full head of gray hair accentuated his silver-blue eyes, and the laugh lines had turned to frown and worry lines. That was all my fault.

"How's Ada Lynn?" Mom busied herself with adjusting her red and white checkered apron. Her hand reached up to smooth her brown hair, now streaked with white. I didn't remember when, exactly, but Mom had long since stopped her fun routines—getting manicures, massages, and having her hair highlighted. Also, my fault. Now she just tied it in a bun and ignored the nicks in her fingernails. Shadows of my past lingered everywhere I looked.

"Same."

Awkward conversations had immersed our home in grief, held us hostage after the year we never spoke about. The year I stopped living and began to merely survive.

I wandered over to the steaming pot on the stove. The letter in my back pocket crinkled as I bent over and eyed the potatoes, mushrooms, and corn. My mind whirled with thoughts of the acceptance letter for college in Washington. I'd sent the application on an impulse. On one of the rare days I believed I could be strong enough to have a life again. Louisiana was in my blood. If I left, I'd miss everything about it. Most of all, I'd miss Ada Lynn.

Although my mind was ready, I wasn't sure I could force my body out the front door and past the dirty white picket fence. Could my feet carry me past Ada Lynn's house and to the bus stop? My shoulders tensed at the mere idea. Like I did with everything else that terrified me, I pushed the thought away and busied myself with other things.

After dinner, I washed the dishes, my mind floating back and forth between the letter from the university and my parents. Even though it had been five years since my world had shattered, the blackness still lingered. A permanent ink stain on my soul.

My mother's sudden gasp broke the silence.

"What?" I asked, drying off the last plate, placing it in the cabinet above my head, and turning toward her.

"Nothing," she replied. I didn't miss her attempt to cover up a piece of paper with her hands.

Dad's expression grew grim as he stared at her.

My spine tingled, and tension claimed the air between us.

"Are you sure?"

"I'm fine," Mom snapped.

"I have a paper to write," I mumbled and tossed the towel on the counter, walking away.

My bare feet padded lightly across the smooth wood floors as I rounded the corner and stopped, waiting for their conversation to begin.

"It's from her," Mom said in a hushed tone.

"Again?" Dad asked.

"Shh, keep your voice down. Gemma can't know."

"Even if she did, we've prayed about this, and it isn't God's will for her," Dad stated.

"Kyle don't start with me. Where was God when all of this happened?"

My skin hummed with anxiety. Who were they talking about? My brows knitted together as I wondered what I'd missed in the stack of mail today. I'd been so distracted by the acceptance letter I hadn't bothered to look through the rest.

I fiddled nervously with the hem of my T-shirt and waited.

"My God," Dad whispered, his voice breaking.

My chest tightened when I heard my mother quietly crying. I walked back toward my room. It would only be a matter of time before they fell asleep, and I could try to find out what had rattled them so much.

I slipped into my bed and stared at the white walls of my room. Stark white. Nothing. Blank. It's what my life had become. However, something deep inside me stirred, ready to be free.

THE HUM of the cicadas filled the otherwise quiet night. I kicked off the sheet, sat up, and placed my bare feet on the floor. Mom and Dad had gone to bed hours ago, but I'd waited. Sometimes Dad woke up and raided the kitchen for a late-night snack, and I didn't want to get caught rummaging around in his office. It'd been off-limits since I was a little kid. I never bothered to ask why, nor did I care, so I stayed out. Until tonight. I'd missed something important in the mail. Important and disturbing enough to make Mom cry and Dad snap at her.

I tiptoed down the hallway and peered over my shoulder while I slowly opened the door to his office. The hinges creaked, and I stopped abruptly. After a moment, when I was sure I'd not woken them, I slipped into the room and closed the door behind me. I flipped on the lamp sitting on his spacious, cherry wood desk. The tick of the wall clock seemed overtly loud in the stillness. I expelled a long sigh as my gaze traveled around the room, taking in as many details as possible. I wiped my sweaty palms on my sleep shorts and willed myself toward his desk.

Tugging on the middle drawer, I frowned as it opened. It was empty. My confusion grew as my hands traveled down each side, opening all of the drawers, but there was nothing of any significance. Only a few blank pages of paper and a pen. Uncertainty tugged at me as I chewed on my bottom lip.

My pulse quickened as my thoughts returned to my parent's conversation earlier in the evening. I was desperate to find out what they'd been talking about. The corner of an envelope sticking out from under the large desk calendar caught my attention, and I grabbed it. My eyes drifted across my mother's name and our address, written in a graceful script. The return address indicated the letter was from Washington. Seattle, Washington. Anxiety pulled and tugged at my insides. Neither of my parents had ever mentioned any friends or relatives from there.

For the second time in one day, I unfolded a thin white sheet of paper. My forehead creased as a picture fluttered to the floor. I picked the photo up, peeked at the image, and read the back, my mouth gaping open. Cold fingers of fear wrapped themselves around my neck, and I sank into Dad's office chair. How long had the letters been coming? More importantly, how long had my parents hidden this big secret from me?

Dazed, my focus scanned the room. Several boxes were stacked in the corner, hidden in the shadows of darkness. I stood and made my way to them. Each one was marked "Office." Curious, I attempted to open the one located on the top, but it was taped shut. Damn. I wondered if there more letters inside. Logically, the items from his desk were packed, but I didn't understand why.

After reading the note for the third time, I knew that no matter what had happened, it was time to leave. I shoved the contents into the envelope, folding it small enough that I could hide it in the palm of my hand if Mom or Dad caught me walking to my bedroom.

Within moments, I was tucked safely in my bed again. My brain refused to shut off. I had some planning to do.

2

When you have no life, you have even fewer items to pack. My belongings were minimal and consisted of clothes that likely wouldn't be appropriate for Washington's weather, along with my toiletries, laptop, and iPhone. Although I only bounced between my house and Ada Lynn's next door, my parents had bought me a cell phone. Honestly, it was a comfort, and I used some of the apps to stay connected with the outside world. Google really was a girl's best friend, and I *had* to have music. When I was in a full-blown panic attack, it was the only thing that calmed me. With my phone, I'd never had to worry about not having something to listen to.

Preparing to leave hadn't been difficult, and as far as I could tell, I hadn't raised any suspicions. I'd cleaned the house and taken care of my own laundry for a long time now, which helped to conceal my plan. It was finding a duffel bag or suitcase neither Mom nor Dad would miss that had been a challenge. Dad traveled for work sometimes, but Mom was typically home unless she ran a quick errand, which made sneaking around almost impossible. On beautiful days like today, however, she'd garden, and it had allowed me time to search the closets without gaining unwanted attention.

Even though I was nineteen, I was well aware leaving without telling my parents would scare the shit out of them. It certainly wasn't my intention, but my father believed it was God's will for me to continue to live here where I was safe. I'd already hidden behind his beliefs for far too long. I also knew he would stop me from walking out of the house if he caught wind of my plans.

Unfortunately, it meant Ada Lynn was my partner in crime, and my parents would be left with nothing but a note. I was a shitty person. However, I'd learned the hard way that some decisions must be based on survival, not Dad's religious beliefs. I had to decide my past would no longer hold me hostage. Refusing to allow it to have power over me and finally doing something about it were two different things. So until my ass was on the bus and too far away to turn back, my pep talks were just a load of crap.

I tucked the duffel bag in my closet and slipped out the kitchen door into the backyard. Mom's floppy, flowered hat bobbed up and down as she dug in the dirt with her spade. For whatever reason, she loved her hats, and for a change it was in my favor. I'd packed the least offensive two I'd found in the utility room and carefully arranged the remaining ones so she wouldn't notice the missing few for a while.

"How's the garden?" I approached her.

"Better this year," she responded without stopping.

"The flowers look nice. You did a great job. You've always had a green thumb."

Her hand paused mid-dig, and she glanced up at me. "Why the sudden interest?"

"No reason. It just looks nice." I fidgeted for a moment, feeling guilty for withholding my plans from her.

Her eyes narrowed, and her mouth curved into a small smile. "Thank you. It's good therapy. Would you like to join me?"

Hesitation tugged at me for a moment while I pondered the invitation. I had no idea when I would come home, so I needed to spend the time with her.

"Sure, I can help for a bit. Don't forget I'll be at Ada Lynn's for dinner tonight."

"Oh, that's right. Thanks for reminding me," she said, handing me another spade. "Grab one of my hats from the laundry room. You'll need it to protect your fair skin from the sun."

I nodded and hurried inside, taking the first one I saw. Other than Ada Lynn's porch, I'd not spent a lot of time outside and never in the direct sunlight. Placing it on my head, I adjusted it and grimaced. Regardless of how much I despised it, I'd have to get used to them.

I tucked my hair into the hat and peered into the small square mirror hanging on the wall next to the door, my shoulders slumping forward with the look. It was awful.

Thankfully, my hair had lightened to a coppery red as I'd grown older. According to Mom, the only red hair in my family was my Aunt Kim's dark red pubes, and for years I had agonized over the fact it had somehow ended up on my head. When it had lightened, it brought much-needed mental relief. Especially when Aunt Kim visited, and I could focus on spending time with her instead of staring at her in horror.

The same year my life turned upside down, Aunt Kim passed away suddenly from an aneurysm. One moment she was talking to a co-worker, and the next she had dropped dead on her office floor.

Mom had never fully recovered from the sudden loss. Maybe if I left, she would be able to move on as the constant reminder of everything she'd lost would no longer stare her in the face.

I made my way outside, inhaled the sunshine and summer air, and knelt next to Mom. For the next hour and a half, we dug in the dirt and tended the garden in silence. And for the first time since I could remember, it wasn't awkward. It was peaceful. I'd tuck this memory in my heart and cherish it forever.

ADA LYNN'S kitchen was barely large enough to hold the two of us. She sat at the small, four-person square table in the middle of the floor while I worked at the stove, boiling noodles, and making her favorite spaghetti sauce. I'd opted to use her countertop toaster for the garlic bread. Even with the air conditioning, it was too hot to turn on the oven.

"You ready for your trip?" Ada Lynn asked while I strained the noodles.

"No." My chest tightened as I placed the plate in front of her, pulled out a chair, and joined her.

"It won't be easy, but remember I'm only a phone call away."

"What if I can't do it?" I stared down at my spaghetti.

"You can do it. And when you're so scared you think you're going to puke your dinner up, you just remember if you come back, you'll never leave again. So don't. Don't come home for a long spell. Nothing ever changes 'round here anyway. So what in God's name would you miss?"

"You," I muttered, twirling noodles around my fork.

Ada Lynn's hand found mine and squeezed.

"Promise me you'll make it. There's only one thing I want to see before I pass on, Gemma. I want to see you moving forward and living your best life. Do it for an old woman. Email me updates and pictures of your beautiful smile and new friends. I'm not great on the computer, but you taught me how to email, so it will work out just fine."

My attention dropped to my plate and traveled to her again. Her eyes glistened, and tears welled in mine.

"Promise," she said sternly.

"Promise." My pulse raced with my word. She knew I'd do everything in my power to keep it.

"All right then, let's eat. I've got a bit of a treat for us." A mischievous grin spread across her face as we returned to our food for a minute.

"You know where to find my extra car key. Just lock it up and park it at the bus station. They don't know it yet, but your mom and dad will help me pick it up and bring it home. Hell, I hope it starts." She chuckled, spinning noodles around her fork.

My brows shot up. "Why wouldn't it? I started it last week and let it run."

"I know. However, the car is almost as old as I am."

"No, it's not." I rolled my eyes at her and we smiled. "I'm going to miss you most of all," I said, my heart sinking into the pit of my stomach.

"Likewise. And I'm not going anywhere yet, so I expect weekly updates."

"You got it."

We finished dinner, and Ada Lynn directed me to her top cabinet.

"Right there, the jar. Get it down and grab some glasses."

When I rejoined her at the table, I twisted the lid and opened the glass container, peeking inside. If I'd been able to see my own expression, I probably would have broken into a fit of giggles.

"What the hell?" I peered at her from the corner of my eye.

"Moonshine," she chuckled, taking it from me and pouring a little into each glass.

"Ada Lynn, are you trying to get me drunk on my last night in Louisiana?"

"You'll be fine, just don't drink it fast. Besides, I'm not giving you much."

I raised the glass and sniffed it. My focus cut over to her as she took a drink and shuddered.

"Go on now." She waved at me to hurry up.

"It's a good thing I'm leaving. You're a bad influence," I teased. Sucking in a quick breath, I took a drink. My cheeks flamed with the heat rising up my neck and ears as the alcohol burned down my throat and into my stomach. Seconds later, a fireball worked its way up, depleting my mouth of any air and moisture. A coughing fit followed, and Ada Lynn patted me on the back.

"Pretty tasty, huh?" She wiggled her eyebrows at me.

"Are you trying to kill me?" I sputtered between coughs.

"Of course not. Just a bit of toughening up before you leave. Try it again, it'll go down easier."

I took a small sip and grimaced, but I didn't hack up a lung this time. Progress.

Another hour ticked by as we talked, and she sipped her alcohol. Two tastes had been enough, and I was positive they would last me a lifetime.

The mood grew solemn, and before I realized it, it was time for me to head to the house. There were only four more hours before I slipped out the front door and drove away. Nausea swirled in the pit of my stomach, my dinner and drink churning.

"It's time," I said.

My chair scraped across the linoleum floor as I scooted away from the table, watching her while she leaned against it and stood slowly. I wrapped my arm around her and embraced her.

"Thank you," I muttered.

"Good luck." Her warm breath tickled my ear while her arms wrapped around me. I bent down and hugged her for a full minute. Letting her go had never been an option before. Tears streamed down my cheeks and into her thin hair.

"I love you, Ada Lynn. Thank you for believing in me," I whispered.

"Love you too, my blue-eyed girl. You call when you reach the school, so I don't worry myself to death."

"Yes, ma'am." We released each other, and she squeezed my hand in hers.

"Go, now. I'll talk to you soon."

Our tears flowed freely as I stepped away, grief seeping deep into my bones. I wiped my cheeks with the back of my hand, gave her a small wave, and left her standing in the kitchen—alone.

The door closed behind me, and I made sure it was locked before I sat down in my chair on her porch and quietly sobbed into my hands. How in the world would I get through each day without Ada Lynn? I hated the thought of leaving her behind. Stepping onto that bus tomorrow was going to be the hardest thing I'd ever done.

In the corner of my mind, Ada Lynn's voice broke through my whirlwind of emotions, reminding me I'd made her a promise. After everything she'd given me, I owed it to her to do the best I could—give her what she wanted before she left this world.

My body shuddered with one last cry, and I sucked in a deep breath. Standing, I squared my shoulders, walked off her porch, and to my house. The distinct aroma of Dad's cigars filled the night air. Shit, he was outside on the porch. I hoped he hadn't heard me crying. At least the darkness would hide my tear-stained cheeks.

"Hey, Gemma. How was dinner?" he asked as I hopped up the front porch steps and sat in the cedar porch swing next to him.

"It was fun. I made her favorite, spaghetti."

"That was sweet of you." He puffed on his cigar, the embers glowing brightly.

An image of the packed-up boxes flashed across my mind, and I toyed with the idea of asking him about his empty desk. It was probably no big deal. He had most likely just cleaned things out, donating the items or something. Besides, if he knew I'd been in there, he'd realize I had the letter. He couldn't know I actually did have the letter until I was far from home in another state.

"How's work?"

Dad paused for a minute. "I haven't wanted to say anything, but I lost my job."

"What? I thought you were working last night at the table." I gasped. "Why didn't you tell me?"

"Because I didn't want you to worry. You have enough on your plate, and I want you to focus on college."

The packed boxes, now I understood.

"What are you going to do?"

"Well, I'll search for another job. I have a few leads already. Most companies have an operations position or something similar, so it'll be fine. I suspect the interviews will come in next week. I mean it. Don't worry. We've got money put away in case of an emergency, so we're fine."

"Really? You're not just saying it?" I asked, chewing on my thumbnail, attempting to contain my nerves. A small part of me hoped this was my excuse to stay.

"No, we really are okay." He offered a sad, reassuring smile.

After mulling over what he'd said, I realized this was one more reason why it was time for me to leave. He'd supported me long enough. I needed to figure out how to take care of myself now.

"Okay. I trust if we were in trouble, you'd tell me. I'm going to try and get some sleep. Are you coming in soon?" I paused and waited for him to reply.

"In a bit. I'm going to finish my stogie, then I'll be on in. Night, honey."

I stood, leaned over, and kissed him on his forehead. "Night. Love you, Dad."

"You too. And Gemma, we're going to be fine, you have my word."

Our eyes locked briefly before I nodded and turned away to enter the house. Guilt nagged at me for not telling him I was leaving. If all went well, though, he'd find out in the morning. I hoped he'd see it as a positive thing, one less burden to carry, but he was a strong proponent for me never leaving and remaining tucked away for the rest of my life. If it were only that simple.

Mom's soft snore came from the couch when I entered the front door. My lips pursed, and I offered a silent prayer that she would wake up and go to bed. I watched as her chest rose and fell, my heart aching while I planned my next move. She deserved so much better than the hand she'd been dealt.

I crept down the hall and brushed my teeth for the last time in my bathroom. Tears blurred my vision as I rinsed my mouth and gazed in the mirror. My blue eyes were one of my best features, other than my now copper-red hair. I pulled on my ponytail holder, allowing my soft, loose curls to flow over my shoulder. Since it was red, I'd planned to hide it underneath Mom's hats while on the college campus in Spokane, Washington. Thank God she had a few plain denim choices instead of all that floral. There was no way I wanted to attract attention, and I assumed with the cold weather a lot of people wore hats. Honestly, I just wanted to keep my head down and concentrate on my degree. I would have enough to adjust to with sharing a room and people around me on a regular basis. Not to mention dealing with four actual seasons.

Ever since I'd made the decision to go to Spokane, my heart hadn't stopped trying to escape my chest.

I flipped off the bathroom light and walked toward my bedroom. Dad's deep tone carried down the hallway while he woke Mom up and guided her to their room. A sigh of relief escaped me. I was grateful I wouldn't have to try and sneak past her out the front door.

I peeked at my alarm clock. The countdown had officially started. One hour gave me enough time to pack the remaining items that would have caused my parents to raise an eyebrow. I had to be painfully quiet and make sure not to wake them, though. Unplugging my clock, I shoved it in my oversized duffel along with my bedspread and pillows. It amazed me how much I could stuff in the bag.

Dinner churned in my stomach. Saying I was terrified was by far an understatement. I was scared shitless. But every night I stared at these walls, I died inside a little more. Whatever it took, I had to learn to live again. Not only for me, but for Mom, Dad, and Ada Lynn.

Midnight. It was finally time to leave. With shaking hands, I shoved my toiletries into the last bit of space in my bag. The sound of the zipper echoed in my stripped clean room. I hoped like hell I could lift it. It hadn't even crossed my mind until now.

I scanned the room one last time, a single tear slipping down my face. Inhaling sharply, I grabbed my duffel, stepped out, and closed the door gently behind me. My eyes adjusted to the darkness as I glanced toward my parents' room. Thankfully, all was still. I crept my way through the hall and into the kitchen, grabbing the container of food I'd prepared with snacks for the trip. If Ada Lynn hadn't mentioned it, I would have forgotten to take any food at all.

My hand trembled as I placed the note on the kitchen table. They would see it after they poured their mugs full of coffee and sat down in the morning. My throat tightened. If I didn't leave now, I'd find myself within the safe walls of my room again, unpacking instead of walking toward a new life.

"Goodbye," I whispered.

A few minutes later, I tossed my duffel bag on the front seat of Ada Lynn's car and slipped inside.

"Please start, please start," I muttered, inserting the key and giving the ignition a turn. To my relief, the car roared to life.

Light shattered the darkness when Mrs. Brownstein's porch light flicked to life. I squinted against the brightness and remained still as she peered through her living room window in my direction. Clutching the curtains around her neck, she looked like a disembodied ghost keeping watch over the neighborhood.

With newfound courage, I shifted into reverse and backed the fifteen-year-old Cadillac out of Ada Lynn's driveway. Tears rolled down my cheeks as I slipped it into drive, my foot pressing the accelerator. I wiped at the tears, cleared my vision, turned on the radio, and drove the ten minutes to the bus station. As I focused on the dashboard clock, I realized I would barely make it. Panic shot through me.

I couldn't miss my bus! I pushed harder on the accelerator, exceeding the speed limit. Thankfully it was late, and the streets were empty.

I let out a shaky breath when I saw I'd made it in time—the bus was still at the station.

After parking the car, I quickly grabbed my bag, jumped out, and hit the lock button on the key fob. I would mail it to Ada Lynn as planned once I got settled.

"Hey!" I yelled when I saw the bus doors folding shut. "Wait! No!"

My feet pounded the pavement, but the weight of the duffel slamming into my legs was too much.

Everything moved in slow motion, right before I smacked into the asphalt face first. Pain shot through my body, but the cry which escaped my lungs was caused by the sight of the bus slowly moving forward.

I shoved myself up and waved my arm in the air, hoping someone would notice me and stop the driver.

"No! Stop!" I yelled with one last effort.

Nothing. The bus didn't slow. Instead, it continued to move forward cautiously into another lane.

A cry lodged in my throat. Shit, I'd failed. I couldn't even run away right. My head hung down with defeat.

"Hey! Come on now. Hurry up!"

"What?" My head jerked up. "I'm coming! I'm coming!" I picked up my duffel and ran, the bag banging against my shins with every step. He'd stopped. Thank God, someone had seen me. A stitch started in my side, and my breathing came in ragged bursts from the weight of my cargo.

I stumbled up the stairs of the bus and dug into my pocket for my ticket.

"Thank you," I said, gasping for air.

"Be glad someone back there saw ya." He nodded as he closed the doors, the bus jerking forward. I staggered and limped my way to an empty seat in the middle. My body collapsed in a spot next to the window. I'd made it. Covering my mouth, I choked more tears back. I took a shaky breath and attempted to regain my composure as the parking lot faded into the distance, and we pulled out onto the main road, heading toward the interstate. It was going to be a long trip, but at least I'd taken the first step.

3

Three and a half days later, I stepped onto the college campus. Spokane was a far cry from Louisiana. The sidewalks bustled with busy students, lugging boxes and suitcases toward the dorms. Parents followed behind them and picked up their dropped items. A knot twisted in my stomach. I'd never seen so many people in my life.

Dazed, I struggled to take it all in, trying not to let my nerves get the better of me. My mouth hung open slightly as I absorbed the vast buildings, the architecture, towering trees, and green grass. Everything was green here. In Louisiana, burnt and brown were the colors from July through October. Nothing compared to what was in front of me, breathtaking.

"Are you lost?" a voice asked beside me, causing me to jump. "It's okay. It can be a little overwhelming in the beginning. You'll get used to everything."

"Not sure if I will, but thanks for the vote of confidence," I muttered, and peered at the woman next to me who had obviously noticed my newbie sensibilities. My gaze connected with soft brown eyes and a gentle smile. Thankfully, my nerves calmed a bit.

"Do you have your information? I can help you." She held her hand out toward me. "I'm Savannah, by the way. I'm a senior. I volunteer to help the newbies for the first few weeks."

"Oh, yeah," I said, digging in my front pocket with my free hand. A moment later, I presented her with a piece of paper.

"Gemma," I said as I adjusted my floppy denim hat and the green-tinted glasses I'd put on before the city bus dropped me off. As much as I disliked them, they were now a permanent part of my daily attire. "Guess I'm searching for my dorm."

"Okay. Are you new to Spokane? Your accent is pretty thick," Savannah asked, her brow arching. She handed my information to me and waited for my response.

"Yeah. I just got off the Greyhound from Louisiana."

"You must be exhausted," she said, her eyes wide. "And I know exactly where your dorm is. I'm heading that way. It's close, but with your bag it would be a tough walk. I'm happy to give you a ride."

I kicked at the sidewalk with my well-worn tennis shoe. My stomach knotted. I was always wary of a stranger offering me a ride.

"It's okay, maybe if you can point me in the right direction?"

"Sure, I can. Oh, wait, I've got a better idea. I know someone else who has already moved in. Let me call her, and she can meet us here and take you. You'll like her. She's...well, she's Mackenzie," Savannah said, laughing.

I fisted my hands to stop them from shaking and forced myself to calm down. Remain aware and assess the situation, I reminded myself. The most important thing for me to remember was to listen to my instincts. My attention dropped to the sidewalk, and I inhaled slowly in order to contain the blooming fear inside me.

"Mac? Hey, I've met someone new who just arrived from Louisiana, and she's utterly lost. She's in the same dorm you are in. Can you meet us at the student center? Yeah? You're the best, thanks." Savannah disconnected the call and peered at me.

"She said she's up the road and on her way. So how did you end up here in Washington?" she asked, shoving her cell in the back pocket of her jeans.

"It was far away from Louisiana, and they offered me a full ride," I mumbled. I figured it was close enough to the truth.

"Well, welcome to the Inland Pacific Northwest," she said, her smile lighting up her face.

"Thanks." I shuffled from one foot to the other while she continued the small talk.

A car horn blared behind me, and I yelped. My hand covered my mouth as my cheeks heated.

"Mac! You scared the shit out of her," Savannah scolded.

I turned around, and a dark-haired girl with braided pigtails rolled down the passenger's window.

"Sorry!" She waved for me to come closer. "I'm Mac. Grab your stuff, I'm headed to the dorm now."

My eyebrow arched as I shot Savannah a look.

"She's harmless, I promise," Savannah said, patting me on the shoulder, reassuring me.

"Um, oh okay. Thanks for your help." Against my better judgment, I snatched up my bag and hefted it into her back seat. A moment later, I settled into the passenger's side and buckled up.

"Packed kinda light, didn't you?" Mackenzie asked as she checked her mirrors and slowly merged onto the street.

"I don't have much. Don't need it."

"That's great you keep it simple and welcome to Spokane! What's your name? Savannah didn't say, and I'm pretty sure it would be super rude not to ask you, right?"

"Gemma," I said, slipping in my name when she took a breath.

"I love it," she replied. "You don't hear that name very often. I think it's beautiful, and I bet you do, too."

Flinching from her volume, I felt terrible for her roomie if she always spoke this loudly. Chiding myself, I remembered she was being kind and driving me to the dorm.

"This is my sophomore year, and I'm getting my degree in art. That's how I met Savannah. She's majoring in art, too. What are you majoring in?"

"Criminal justice," I replied, surprised I could sneak an answer in between her incessant chatter.

I cracked my window for some fresh air. Between her energy and voice volume, the car had started closing in on me. The last few days on a cramped bus had left me eager to stretch my legs, but instead I sat in a small car with a very loud, petite human being.

"Do you like music?" she asked, her finger darting out to hit the power button. The speakers blared with heavy metal.

Oh my God. What had I done? I cringed, reminded myself to breathe, and prayed the ride would be short. Suddenly, an overwhelming pang of sadness tugged at my heart while my mind wandered to Ada Lynn. We should be on her porch right now, watching the last golden rays of the sun dip behind the hills. I hoped like hell my parents weren't angry at her for helping me leave.

"Here we are." Mackenzie pulled up to the dorm, breaking through my thoughts. I assessed the red brick building and shrank into my seat. It was huge. Surely my entire hometown could fit inside it.

"Thank you!" I yelled over the tunes while I opened the car door and grabbed my bag. With a deep sigh, I headed up the walkway. I reached into my pocket for my dorm room information and continued through the front doors. Families were filing into the building and milling around the huge lobby, bumping into me as we all made our way toward the elevator. Since I'd been sitting so much over the last several days, I opted for the stairs even with my heavy bag. Two flights and a mile-long hallway later, I stopped in front of my door. Room number 250. I sucked in a quick breath, along with some courage, and opened it.

The room was small with hardwood floors, white walls, two twin beds, and built-in dresser drawers. One side was already unpacked. Well, I wouldn't really call it unpacked. Instead, a pile of unfolded clothes and items were scattered all over one of the beds. If she kept her sloppiness to her side, I could learn to deal with it.

I dropped my bag in front of the closet and peered inside. It was small, but it would work.

My ears perked up as a group of girls ran screaming through the hallway. Startled, I jumped backward, landing on my ass. Giggles continued, so I assumed everything was okay and no one was hurt. Grateful no one had seen me overreact, I pushed myself off the floor and made quick work of unpacking.

When my stomach growled, I realized I needed to find a cafeteria somewhere to get some decent food. I'd subsisted on junk food for days—vending machine snacks and the occasional burger. And I was hungry.

First, I wanted to call Ada Lynn. I had also promised her some pictures. After I snapped a few of me in my new room, I emailed them to her.

My lips pursed as my phone screen flashed with seven missed calls, each one from my father. I'd been so wrapped up in my escape to Washington I'd refused to deal with the worry and stress I'd surely put them through. Refusing to dwell on it, I deleted the messages without listening to them. I knew him well enough to predict what they'd say.

This isn't God's will, young lady. You should be ashamed of yourself; God is.

My fingers tapped my screen, and seconds later, the line on the other end rang.

"Hello?"

"Ada Lynn, it's me."

"Gemma, you arrived in Washington safely?"

"Yes, ma'am. How are you? How are Mom and Dad?"

Ada Lynn's chuckle filled the phone. "Pissed. We didn't expect anything different, though did we?"

I smiled sadly, and my heart ached to be with her.

"I'm so proud of you. You made it. Now just don't come back," she said.

"I'm going to do my best. This place is insane, and it's huge."

"It sounds like it's a big change, but you can do this, Gemma. You call me a few times a day if you need to. I'll remind you of the big ol' nothin' you're missing down here. Your parents may be a bit upset, but they are okay, so don't use them as an excuse either."

She knew me well, and I had to keep in mind this move was good for my parents, too. They'd spent too much time hovering over me and had given up their own lives in the process.

"Yes, ma'am. How pissed are they?"

"Oh, really mad. Your dad took to yelling at me, and I had to put him in his place real fast. However, your mom, she was shocked, but she's also proud of you. Give them some time, and they'll come on around. You take care of yourself and remember your promise."

"I will."

"Love you, now you go on and find some new friends and call me tomorrow."

"Love you, too."

A tear snuck down my cheek as I ended the call and shoved my phone in my back pocket. My stomach reminded me it was past time to eat. I adjusted my hat and tinted glasses in the mirror. No one here knew I didn't need them to see. They just hid my face, and I could observe people without them seeing my eyes very well. The unique color of my hair and eyes had always brought unwelcome attention. I never used to mind it, then everything changed.

Somewhat content with my appearance, I headed out of the dorm in search of food. One of the most significant challenges I would have to deal with was the noise level. Since I'd attended an online college, I'd never dealt with other students, or the usual college antics—high-pitched girl screams, loud guys making asses of themselves around cute girls, so on and so forth.

On the bus ride to Washington, I'd memorized the essential places on campus and how to reach them from my dorm, so I had a general idea of where to find my meals.

My worn, second-hand Converses smacked against the pavement of the sidewalk as I took my time walking, cautiously taking inventory of my surroundings. Frowning, I pushed my glasses up my nose. I'd definitely have to get adjusted to them. The tint was enough to hide the color of my blue irises, but it was also more challenging to see things.

I had a few hours before the sunset, which allowed me to explore the campus a bit.

I peered at the trees, the numerous brightly colored flower baskets, and the lush, green grass. The smell of the freshly cut and manicured lawns tickled my nose. It was beautiful, and I never wanted to lose this moment of seeing everything for the first time. Nothing was skewed or ruined. It was brand new and alive.

Loud laughter jarred me from my thoughts. My head jerked toward a group of five rowdy guys approaching me.

"Hey baby, where'd you come from?" a tall, athletic dark-haired guy asked me.

Completely ignoring him, I continued to walk.

"Hey, trailer trash, I'm talking to you. Where'd you buy those clothes?"

The guys hooted and punched each other on the shoulder like the insult had been the best they'd ever heard. I ignored them and moved forward. It wasn't anything I hadn't been around before. And for whatever reason, I didn't care what they thought of my clothes.

"Why don't you take them off and let me see what you've got underneath? Maybe some perky tits? A cute little ass? Hard to tell with your cheap, shitty clothes hanging off you like that. And your fucking hat is horrible. Did you take it off your dead grandma's head?" he asked, his volume growing louder with each word.

I kept my attention straight ahead and met his insults with silence.

"Hey, bitch. I'm talking to you."

Anger dripped from his words. Fear wrapped its cold fingers around my throat, and my hand dug into my front pocket, ready, just in case he moved forward.

"Dude, come on, leave her alone. If she wants to wear a potato sack, let her," another guy piped up.

Even though I tried not to, my focus turned toward them as they grew closer. My pulse double-timed while they broke out into hysterics. One of them stared, hands shoved in his jeans' pockets, but he remained quiet. His eyes were trained on me as I walked around them, ignoring the comments and heckling. If I fed into it, they'd win.

Fortunately, the asshole had a short attention span, and moments later, when they found some other girl to harass, I ducked around the corner of a building. Knots formed in my stomach, my legs gave out from under me, and I fell to the ground on my hands and knees. Trembling and unable to support myself, I dropped flat on my tummy and breathed in the aroma of the grass and dirt. Black dots danced across my vision, and I clawed at the lush green blades, willing my heart rate to slow down.

When I felt steady enough to stand, I pushed myself off the ground. Still shaky, I placed the palm of my hand against the building, the coolness of the shaded stone comforting me. I cautiously peeked around the corner and thanked God the guys were nowhere to be seen. My eyes scanned the structure for a name and immediate relief spread through me. It was the library. I made a mad dash for the front door and pulled my phone out of my pocket, unwrapping the headphones as I hurried through the lobby.

The second I stepped inside, the familiar scent of books greeted me, and I inhaled deeply. Shoving my earbuds in my ears, I tapped my Spotify app and went to my playlist. The librarian eyed me curiously, but I ignored her and went in search of the fiction section.

After finding one of my favorite books, I plopped into a chair at a small table in the back corner and placed my forehead on the wooden surface. This was better. Books and music, minimal people around me.

Flipping the novel open, I scanned the first page and willed my body to calm. My foot began to tap to Citizen Shade's "Funk War," the music cloaking me in safety. He could sing anything and make it sound good. I'd never heard another voice like his either.

Although I'd read it multiple times, I slipped into another world as soon as I started reading *The Hunger Games*. Ten pages in, a hand snuck across the table and tapped a finger on the surface next to my book. My hand automatically jerked away, and my head snapped up at the intrusion. Folding my hands in my lap, I scowled at the guy who had settled into the chair diagonally from me. His expression was serious as he flipped his shoulder-length wavy brown hair over his shoulder. He ran a hand over his closely trimmed facial hair as his angular jaw tightened, and he motioned for me to remove my earbuds.

"What?" I asked, my tone clipped. He wasn't invited. This was my table.

"Are you okay?" His bright blue eyes flashed with concern.

My eyebrows knitted together in confusion.

"Sure," I replied. If he got his answer, maybe he would leave.

"No, I'm serious, are you okay? You almost passed out behind the library. I was there working on something," he said in a hushed tone.

My mouth gaped slightly. He'd seen me have a massive panic attack? I'd not seen anyone, but my knees had hit the ground so fast I hadn't had time to look.

"I'm fine." Heat spread across my neck and ears, giving away my emotions.

The weight of his gaze was unnerving as we stared at each other silently. Although my stomach churned, I refused to let him know how much he had unsettled me. My chin tilted up in defiance. I wasn't his problem, and I certainly didn't want him hanging around.

"There are plenty of other tables," I offered and nodded toward them.

"Okay. I just wanted to make sure you were all right. I didn't mean to bother you." He pushed his chair back and stood. "Nice glasses," he mumbled before walking away.

Was he being a smart-ass, or was he serious? Maybe the hat was awful, but the glasses weren't.

My attention lingered on him as he made his way to another table. I'd not seen a hot guy since middle school, and even though I fought it, I was intrigued. His jeans hugged his lean legs and tight ass, his white T-shirt stretched across his muscular shoulders. However, his hair was the feature that grabbed me the most. It was perfection, and I had to resist the urge to reach out and touch it.

He probably got that a lot, girls wanting to touch his hair. The color of his eyes was almost as striking. In reality, though, none of this mattered. I still wondered what he wanted from me. I'd have to be careful moving forward; no more panic attacks in front of other people.

He glanced in my direction as he sat down at another table not far away. I inserted my earbuds again and attempted to settle down into my story. However, my brain wasn't having it. After another ten minutes of struggling to focus, I gave up. I closed the book, stood, and shelved it. My finger tapped my phone screen, and I turned off my music.

I strolled by him on my way out, and his gaze followed me as I passed. Pushing through the front doors of the building, I struggled to control my breathing. Attempting to clamp down my anxiety, I leaned against the brick of the building. I hated my need to question the motives of every person who talked to me. The only people I'd had direct contact within the last five years were my parents and Ada Lynn. I was so out of practice! Inwardly I cringed as hope of ever trusting anyone again dwindled away.

My stomach growled to remind me I still needed to eat something, and I headed toward the student center. I had enough time to grab a bite and head to the dorm before it got dark.

AN HOUR LATER, with a full stomach, I pushed open the dorm room door and entered my new home. A girl sat on the floor in a lotus position with her back to me, a tan knit cap covering her head.

"Almost finished," she said so softly I struggled to hear her.

I waited patiently for her to turn around so that I could meet my new roomie.

A young woman hopped up from the floor, whirled around, and ran toward me at full speed, knocking me against the door. Her arms wrapped around me as she hugged me.

"Roomie! I'm so excited we already met."

Dear God, it was Mackenzie. I was the poor roommate who would have to put up with her loud-speaking volume and heavy metal music.

She released me, and my heart sank. She looked at me with such a hopeful expression, I immediately felt conflicted. I needed quiet and calm. She was anything but that. However, she'd been so nice and welcoming to me.

"I'm so glad it's you. I'm so sorry, if I'd known I would have walked you up here myself instead of just kicking you out of the car," she said in a rush of excitement.

Struggling to regain some sense of composure, I offered her an awkward smile. Thank God she couldn't see my expression behind my glasses. I closed my mouth and tried to form any word in the English language. I was stumped about how to handle the moment, though.

Mackenzie grabbed my hand and tugged me across the room, talking nonstop. She adjusted her blue jean overalls and turned toward me, speaking so fast I had a difficult time keeping up with her.

"Wow, you all dress a lot differently in Louisiana," she said, eyeing me. "What do people say? Never judge a book by its cover. But I totally do, so I'm apologizing now. I bet you'll be the best roomie I've ever had and we'll be best friends. And since you don't have your family here, you can share mine. I'll introduce you to everyone I know, and we can go to any classes together we might share..." Her hazel eyes widened as she jumped up and down. "Oh my God, I'm so excited."

"I can tell," I said, managing to fit in a word.

"Call me Mac, all my friends do." She flitted to her side of the room as I walked backward toward my bed and sat down in utter shock. I'd never met someone that moved and talked so fast. Was everyone here like this, or was it just Mac?

"Oh, one thing you should know about me. I'm ADHD. Do you know what that is? Attention Deficit Hyperactivity Disorder. Yup, it's me. And I tried the meds, and oh my God, they made me feel like shit, so I stopped taking them. If I can focus enough to pass my classes, I don't ever want to take them again. My mom wants me to, though. She doesn't know how to handle my ball of energy. And, like, I don't sleep a lot so do you have some noise-canceling headphones you can use in case I'm watching TV or something? Maybe an eye mask, so the light doesn't keep you awake? And enough about me, tell me all about you. I want to know everything."

Once again, my mouth gaped open as she tossed her clothes to one side and plopped down on her bed, propped herself against the wall, and honored me with a toothy grin.

"I've never met anyone who talked this much," I said.

"Oh, you'll get used to me. At least I hope you will. And sometimes, like when you need to study or whatever you *have* to tell me to shut up. If I know I'm dancing on your last nerve, I so get it, and it's not what I mean to do. Seriously, I want you to like me, I mean we're roomies for an entire year." Her voice hit a high pitch, causing me to wince. "Okay, I mean it, tell me about Louisiana, and I'll shut the hell up."

Anything to get this girl to hush sounded like a good idea to me.

The second my mouth opened to speak, she charged in again.

"Do you eat crawdads? Ew, are they disgusting? I've only read about Louisiana, I've never been to the south, but your accent is fucking amazing." She paused briefly. "Wait, oh gosh, I didn't just offend you with the F-bomb, did I? I won't use it again, if it's not okay, it's one of my most favorite words, like ever."

I held my hand up to her. "Give me a minute."

"Oh sure, you're probably super tired from the trip, and——."

"Stop," I said. "Please."

Mac frowned as she slumped forward. "Sorry," she muttered.

Oddly enough, a few moments of silence permeated the room. Something I sorely missed already.

"I only arrived a few hours ago, and I'm overwhelmed and exhausted. Yes, I have earphones, but I won't use an eye mask, or I'll have nightmares and don't want to scare you. I can tell you about Louisiana one question at a time. It's the only place I've ever lived until today, so some patience would be appreciated. I'm also adjusting to a two-hour time change. It's part of the reason I wanted to arrive a few days early, to settle in and catch my breath. And my favorite thing in the world is peace and quiet."

"Oh boy. I've scared you already. Sorry."

This time Mac stopped talking instead of running over at the mouth. Maybe I could train her with positive behavior reinforcement.

"Do you like chocolate?" I asked, working out the scenario in my head. Good behavior deserved chocolate.

"Yes, however, the sugar makes me hyper, so it's a rare treat."

Inwardly, I groaned. The last thing I wanted to do was make her more hyper. I seriously doubted it was even possible.

My pulse raced as I realized Mac would be the one person who saw me without glasses and my hat. I forced myself to remove them and tossed them on the desk next to my bed.

"Shit, why do you wear a hat? You have the most beautiful hair I've ever seen, even with it all messy," she said, hopping off her bed and peering at me, her face mere inches from mine. I flinched when her hand shot out and touched my hair. "And your eyes, you're beautiful. Why would you hide?"

I raised my hand again to stop her.

"Keep this to yourself, Mac, and we will be best friends. Obviously, we're living together, and I have to shower and stuff, but you won't see me in public without my glasses and hat. Don't ask questions, it's just the way it is. Do you understand me? Don't tell anyone, don't mention what I look like without them or anything else. It stays in this room. Are we clear?" My words carried a steel tone, and she straightened.

"Best friends if I keep your secret?" She twirled her braid around her forefinger, waiting for my answer.

"Best friends." I'd studied enough psychology to realize what Mac wanted most was to be accepted and liked. I could do that in return for her keeping my secret.

"Deal." She offered her hand to shake.

I extended mine, too.

"Welcome to Spokane, bestie." Her smile widened, and we shook on it.

"Thank you," I responded softly.

4

I cried inside myself on a regular basis as Mac and I tried to adjust to each other over the next few weeks. Although she didn't know it, I hadn't intended to make any friends at all. However, after evaluating the campus, I realized having at least one would be necessary for survival. It was also painfully obvious she needed someone to talk to. From what I could tell, Mac was just insecure. Everyone loved her no matter what nonsense she blubbered on about.

Since this was her second year at the university, I agreed to let her show me around and help me locate my classes. She chattered about everything and nothing nonstop. After I settled into my new routine, the library became my ongoing refuge. Each day, I would slip into my sanctuary to study or read, place a pair of earbuds in my ears, and form a scowl on my face to warn off potential interruptions. Like a dog marking his territory, I had officially laid claim to the same table and chair in the fiction section. It didn't take long before people got the message and left me alone.

Since I thrived on schedules, after the library and before I ate dinner, I'd call Ada Lynn. It was the best part of my day. Talking to her continued to provide me the courage to give Washington a chance. She laughed until she cried as I told her about Mac. Savannah was right. Mac was, well, Mac. I'd never met anyone like her and doubted I ever would again.

"Are Mom and Dad calming down any with your daily updates?" I asked Ada Lynn.

"Your mom is. Your dad demands you hurry home immediately and stay in God's perfect will. Don't you worry, though. I let him know if he doesn't knock that crap off, I won't tell him anything about you at all. It tends to shut him up pretty fast."

I grinned at her feistiness. It was more than her stories, it was also the fact my parents knew I was safe, and they weren't as worried as they would have been if no one was providing daily information. Maybe it soothed my concerns more than it did theirs.

Ada Lynn brought me up to date on the neighborhood and city gossip. Our conversations were rarely of any real importance other than us talking, but it was our routine. Regardless if I was there or here, I didn't want to lose the time with her.

"How are classes going?" she asked.

"Good, I basically hide in the back corner of the room. I have gone to every one of my classes. You would be so proud of me. I haven't missed one."

"Maybe soon you'll inch forward a bit. Now, don't get me wrong, I can't imagine how difficult this has been for you, but I'm so proud of you I could burst."

"I might be a little proud of myself, too." I hadn't mentioned the episode with the group of guys, or that I'd nearly passed out behind the library in front of some random dude who had happened to be studying. There was no need to worry her, and I hadn't seen him again. It was just a one-time fluke he'd even been around anyway.

"Well, you get your studies done and call me tomorrow. Love you, girl."

"Love you too, Ada Lynn."

I tapped the phone, disconnecting the call. The time flashed on the screen, reminding me I only had a few hours left to spend at the library before it got dark. I grabbed my earbuds and backpack and headed out.

Since Mac was glued to me as much as possible, I was rarely alone unless we had a separate class, or I was in the library. Although my ears and brain got tired of her chattiness, she was growing on me, and I was grateful she was by my side most of the time. Not to mention I'd developed the uncanny ability to tune her out but still respond to her in a way, so she had no idea I was mentally elsewhere.

The soothing scent of books engulfed me as I strolled through the doors and to my corner table in the fiction section. I glanced around and observed my surroundings before I settled in.

An hour and a half later, even though I was dialed in to my music and my studies, I didn't miss when the chair diagonal from me moved.

I pulled one headphone out, my eyes traveling up. It was him. My heart stuttered. We'd had this conversation three weeks ago when he'd invited himself to sit down with me. What did he not understand about leaving me alone when other seats were available? Maybe I needed to draw a big sign for him that read, "Go Away!"

He flashed me a panty-dropping smile as I stared at him, deadpan, mentally willing him to get up, turn around, and walk away. Ignoring me, he settled into his chair, scooted up to the table, grabbed a book out of his backpack, and nonchalantly began his homework. Although he was no longer looking at me, I continued to glare at him.

After a long minute, I put my earbud back in and turned my music on. No matter how hard I tried, I knew he was there, and it was throwing me off. I stopped my music again and smacked my phone and headphones on my book.

His gaze shot up to me.

"Fine, what do you want?" I asked, my voice thin with impatience.

His blue eyes traveled slowly over me. I felt the gravity of his gaze, and an uncomfortable tightness gripped my chest.

"Can't a person study? I'm sure you've noticed how noisy the dorms are," he said matter-of-factly while he tucked his hair behind his ear.

"Yeah, I have. Sit somewhere else. This is my spot. It's the only time I have to myself and don't have to share a space with someone."

"Other than the shower," he added dryly.

Great. This guy was the ultimate smartass. No, thank you.

"My showers or lack thereof are none of your business." Maybe if he thought I didn't shower every day, he'd leave. Unfortunately it didn't faze him.

"I like it here. I'll study, and I promise I won't try to talk to you."

My nostrils flared with his resistance. I knew he was right, but there were literally five other tables with no one sitting at them. What the hell?

I slammed my book closed and huffed loudly, earning a dirty stare from the librarian, while I gathered my belongings. He glanced up from his book, frowning.

"Hope you enjoy your night," I spat before I walked away.

My body slammed against the door bar as I threw it open and stomped across the lobby, making a beeline for the front door of the building. Stepping outside, I noticed the sun had begun its descent, and the temperature had already cooled from when I'd arrived at the library.

My feet came to an abrupt halt while I encountered the same group of guys who had given me shit my first day on campus.

The group's loud mouth peered at me, and a nasty grin pulled at the corner of his mouth. "Hey, baby, did you miss me? I've been keeping my eye on you. Not that you're difficult to spot, just look for the sloppy clothes and grandma hat." His buddies laughed as my cheeks flushed.

"Leave me alone," I said, attempting to act braver than I felt.

"Aww, how cute. It talks." He cracked his neck, his stare traveling up and down my body.

I quickly scanned the area around us, but his group had effectively positioned themselves to take up the majority of the space that led to the stairs, not just at the top but at the bottom as well. I wasn't sure I could move safely around them. Not to mention there were four of them and only one of me.

My heart pounded, and I stepped forward, testing their motives.

"Now, now, don't run off so soon. We have all night to get acquainted." He sauntered toward me, blocking my way, and crushing my hopes of getting around him. My head throbbed with fear. I knew his type, and most of the time it was about intimidation. However, I had a bad feeling he would take it further, and I wasn't interested in finding out. I'd had more than my fair share of crap from men.

"Leave her alone," someone demanded from behind me.

The shit-eating grin dropped off my harasser's face.

"Aw, how cute, pretty boy came to save his girl."

"Shut the hell up, Brandon. Leave her alone."

The guy from the library moved in front of me, shoulders squared. He wasn't a huge guy, but something about him commanded the space.

"Fuck you, Hendrix," Brandon said, spitting on Hendrix's shoes.

I couldn't see Hendrix's facial expression, but there was no way he wasn't pissed right now.

My eyebrows shot up as Brandon stepped forward and the two stood toe-to-toe. Shit, they were about to fight over me. I froze, unable to breathe.

Hendrix waited patiently until Brandon backed down.

"Next time," he said, sneering at me. "You won't have your body-guard with you. This isn't over, and I'm watching you. *Everywhere* you go," Brandon hissed.

My resolve withered as he and his group of asshats walked away. A cry escaped me, and I slapped my hand over my mouth.

Hendrix turned to me slowly, worry lines creased his forehead as my body betrayed me, and I visibly trembled in front of him.

"Here, sit down," he said, guiding me by my elbow to the stone wall near the steps.

"Thank you," I croaked. "Not sure what I did to him. He harassed me on my first day here."

"He feeds on it, you're not the only one."

I searched his face and only found compassion and concern. Even though he'd saved me, he'd pushed me too, by getting in my space in the library. And now...now he sat so close to me our shoulders touched. I couldn't be this close to him. He couldn't touch me again.

"I have to go," I said, suddenly jumping up from my seat and darting down the stairs.

"Wait, what's your name?" Hendrix called after me.

I didn't respond. Instead, I ran as fast as my feet would take me all the way to my dorm. By the time I'd ran up the stairs and burst through the door, tears were streaming down my face, my breaths coming in short, jagged bursts.

"Whoa!" Mac cried, her voice filled with surprise.

I slammed the door behind me, crawled into bed, and shrank in the corner. Sobs shook my shoulders while my mind taunted me and replayed Brandon's words over and over.

"Hey, hey," Mac said, crawling in my bed next to me. "Shh," she said and patted my arm.

I flinched at her touch, then grabbed her hand, welcoming my new friend into my dark world even if it was only briefly.

Slipping off my glasses and hat, I placed them on my desk as I regained a bit of my composure. Mac remained wide-eyed and—for the first time since I'd met her—quiet.

"I'm sorry," I sniffled, wiping the tears away.

"No, Gemma. Are you okay?" Her dark eyebrows rose with her question.

I wasn't okay, but how could I tell her?

"Mac, I don't think this is going to work," I muttered.

"What? You don't want to be my roomie anymore?" she squeaked out.

"No, it's not that." I squeezed her hand in reassurance. "This. College. Washington. I don't know what I was thinking. I don't belong here."

"Wait, now, back it up a minute. What happened? Talk to me."

Another sob choked off my words, and Mac's arm slipped gently around my shoulder.

"It's okay, Gemma. I'll help you in any way I can," she assured me.

"Brandon," I managed to say.

There was no way I could miss the sudden tension in Mac's body as I spoke his name.

"Brandon Montgomery?" she asked, her tone barely floating above a whisper.

"Don't know his last name," I mumbled through my tears.

"About six-foot-tall, wears a constant sneer, and lives to torment girls?"

"Sounds about right."

"Oh, Gemma. I'm so sorry." She reached for a tissue from the desk and handed it to me. "I can't tell you how many of my friends have had to deal with him, including me. If we'd had proof—," Mac trailed off, unable to finish her sentence.

"You've dealt with him?" My attention drifted up, watching the fear and sadness flicker across her expression.

Mac nodded and took my hand. "Stay away from him, Gemma. If he's following you, please, let's go to campus security or even the police."

"Did you go?" I asked and rubbed the tears from my eyes.

Mac nodded and sighed deeply. "I did, and it helped, but I had to spray him with pepper spray to get him off me. Do you have some?"

I frowned. "Yes, it's in my pocket. I was so scared I forgot. Like, what the hell? What good will it do me if I forget I have it, Mac?" My pitch rose a notch as the fear returned.

"Don't. Don't beat yourself up. When you're alone, keep it in your hand instead of your pocket. If he messes with you again, spray the son of a bitch right in the face," she said, her voice laced with venom.

"I'm out of my element, Mac. I'm a small-town girl. I've never been anywhere outside of Breaux Bridges, Louisiana until now. I was homeschooled for years, and I took online college classes. All this...college, the people, it's too much. I should go home."

Mac shook her head so hard I worried her neck would snap.

"No, please. Don't give up yet. I can't imagine how hard this has been, but look at what you did! You came all this way on your own. You should really be proud of yourself. We will stick together everywhere we go, and when I can't be around, carry your spray in your hand. How did you get away from Brandon this time? I mean, you're here and not drugged out somewhere naked with him."

My eyes popped open. "Mac," I whispered. "Did he?" I paused, not wanting to speak it aloud.

"No, not me." Her head hung down, and her shoulders slumped forward, signaling she wasn't open to discussing it yet. "How did you get past him?" she asked again.

A ragged breath escaped me, and I told her about Hendrix.

"No one fucks with Hendrix Harrington, Gemma. We went to high school together, and he was the state boxing champion for three years in a row. In fact, he still boxes. He was popular. I wasn't. No one wanted a hyper chatterbox like me around." She twirled her braid around her finger, her attention dropping to her lap as she fell silent again.

Sadness seeped through me. I knew how loneliness could suffocate someone, its frigid hands wrapped around your neck, unwilling to let go. I didn't want that for her, too.

"I do," I said softly.

"Really? You'll stay? We can figure this out and keep you safe."

"I'll stay for a little bit longer and see if I can deal with this."

"Thank you," Mac said shyly. "Thank you for not giving up." Her eyes softened with a gentle smile. "Wait...now, don't get mad." She hopped off the bed and walked to her dresser. She returned with the same tan knit cap she'd worn the day I moved in. "Wear this. Like, get rid of the ugly ass denim hat. All it does is make you more of a target for people like Brandon. Plus, it's getting cold, and you'll need to keep your ears warm since you wear your hair tucked up in it." She extended it toward me and waited to see if I would accept her idea or not.

"Thank you," I said softly, taking the hat from her hands.

And for the first time, I saw past Mac's incessant talk and straight to her heart.

5

Intro to Criminal Justice had quickly become one of my favorite classes. Despite the fact I preferred to stay in the background, my parents and Ada Lynn weren't surprised when I expressed an interest in the field. So far, the professor had left me alone in my corner, close to the door, and never called on me. There were so many other students, I wasn't even sure he noticed me. I also appreciated the fact he made the classes exciting and didn't just spit out factual data. It was evident he was passionate about the topics and enjoyed teaching his students.

After class, I packed up my belongings and headed to the library. I customarily called Ada Lynn beforehand, but I had an exam to study for and had let her know I would call tomorrow, instead. My body had finally adjusted to the time difference, but my brain hadn't. I still had to remind myself she was two hours ahead and was asleep by around nine-thirty.

The gawking was bothering me less, too. The new knit hat and glasses offered me something to hide behind without being too obvious. And mentally, it made things easier to deal with when snickers followed after I walked by. Truth be told, although I'd worn clothes that hung off me for a long time, it was rare others had seen me in

them other than my parents and Ada Lynn. Only occasionally would
I even leave the house to go out in public. I'd told myself it wouldn't
bother me when I attended the university, but it had. However, I
wasn't going to change my appearance to make someone like me.
Screw them. Besides, I had Mac and Ada Lynn. I didn't need anyone
else.

I inwardly groaned as I slipped into the library and spotted the
back of Hendrix's head at my table. Honestly, I wasn't sure if I wanted
to pull his pretty hair out of his head or run my hands through it.
He'd been good to his word so far and had sat quietly at the table. On
occasion, I'd catch him peeking at me. The only reason I caught him,
though, was I'd glance his way as well. His insistence on sitting at my
table had started as a battle of wills, and some days I didn't mind him
being there. However, today wasn't one of them.

My books smacked against the table as I huffed and slumped into
my chair. Hendrix ignored me, his head low, hair hanging over whatever he was working on. Maybe he had headphones in and couldn't
hear me. I'd had every intention of asking him to move today, to let
me breathe for a few minutes and focus on my notes for the
upcoming exam. There was only one problem. I didn't want to touch
him to get his attention and tell him to go somewhere else. Tapping
on the table, like he'd done to get my attention the first time, was also
not an option because his damned hair was hanging down over his
face. I refused to move. This was my table, and I wasn't the one
invading someone else's space.

The minutes ticked by and the more I told myself to ignore him,
the more his presence taunted me. He never looked up. Why the hell
I gave a rat's ass was beyond me.

Flipping through Spotify, I landed on some music I hoped would
help me concentrate on the task at hand, studying for my test
tomorrow.

Finally, his head lifted slowly, his face solemn. My gaze lifted from
my biology book enough to peek over at him, but not enough he
would realize what I was up to.

My mouth dropped open slightly when I realized what it was he'd been working on. His blue eyes lifted from the pages he'd been writing, his expression softening as he caught my stare. He flashed that damned smile at me and motioned for me to take my headphones out.

"Yes?" I asked, injecting as much irritation as possible into that one word.

"You're not curious?" he asked, his eyebrows rising. "I saw you looking."

"Maybe." My chin tilted slightly. "What are you working on?"

"A new song." He laid the pencil down by the sheet music covered with notes and lyrics.

"What kind?" I inwardly groaned at my inability to hide my interest any longer.

"I don't want to say pop. It's not accurate." He hesitated and ran his hand along his chin. "I'm more along the lines of a singer-songwriter."

"You sing, too?" There was no more hiding behind my wall. He had my undivided attention.

"If that's what you want to call it," he chuckled. His laugh was a low rumble that sent a thrill through my body, making my cheeks hot.

"You okay?" he asked, examining me intently.

Oh. My. God. My face grew hotter with his scrutiny. I didn't think I'd blushed as much in my entire life as I had since meeting Hendrix. I'd also forgotten how red my fair skin got when I was embarrassed. People actually thought I was sick with a fever. Shit.

"Mm-hmm." I tugged my hat down farther over my ears and returned to my book, hoping the redness would calm down.

"You listen to music a lot," he said. "I can hear it sometimes."

I stared at him. "Yeah. All the time. Music and books are my thing I guess. People—not so much," I said, my nose wrinkling in disdain.

He nodded as though he understood exactly what I was talking about, but he didn't. Couldn't. Not really. From what Mac had told me, he knew a lot of people and was very popular. Why he chose to sit at this table every day with me was beyond my comprehension, unless he wanted something. I quickly brushed the thought away and reminded myself he was the one who had kept me safe from Brandon that day. A part of me wanted to believe he was different and was a good person, but I hadn't met many of those.

"Tell me what you like to listen to," he said and nodded toward my iPhone.

His words were soft, and I swiped through a few of the songs on one of my favorite playlists.

"There's a *small* possibility I might have a Spotify addiction. However, I'll deny it if you ever bring it up." My eyes narrowed in case he wanted to laugh, but he didn't. Instead, he tapped the screen of his phone, pulled up the multiple playlists on his Spotify app, and turned it toward me. His made mine look like a hobby.

"Shit," I said and scooted forward in my chair to get a better look. They were all over the board from pop to classical. "Can I?" My voice was barely above a whisper.

"Yeah. Can I see yours?"

I nodded, and we exchanged phones.

My brow raised as I recognized Citizen Shade, Billy Raffoul, P!nk, Alexander Jean, and some others I wasn't familiar with. I'd officially met my match.

"You should try this one." Hendrix made a few taps on my phone. "And really listen to the lyrics," he said, his gaze intense as he handed my phone to me. Reluctantly, I returned his, too. If I could, I'd have spent the rest of the evening scrolling through his tunes and sampling.

I looked at the screen. "Church with No Ceiling" by Lostboycrow. I'd never heard of this artist. I started the music and slipped in one earbud. As soon as the singer's silky tone drifted into my ear, my soul sighed with happiness. As Hendrix instructed, I listened carefully to the lyrics and the message they imparted. This song had just officially landed on my playlist. Plus I would look up every other one by this guy.

After it finished, I set my phone down on the table and peered at Hendrix. A familiar fear crept up my spine.

"What do you want from me?" I asked, remembering my past, how people hid behind a façade until it was too late. Nothing was ever what it seemed.

Hendrix's eyes widened. "What do you mean?"

"Cut the shit. No one sits at the same table as someone else, day in and day out, and doesn't want something. Thank you for what you did for me concerning Brandon. I don't need anything from you, though, and I sure as hell don't owe you anything." My nostrils flared, my anger escalating.

He relaxed in his seat, a gentle smile easing across his handsome face.

"I don't want anything from you. Well, that's a lie. Your name would be nice."

"Why should I tell you my name? What. Do. You. Want?"

Hendrix leaned over the table slowly.

"Honestly? I want to know who the girl underneath the new hat and glasses is, and I want her to feel safe enough to have a friend. I don't know what you've been through or anything about you for that matter. There's something...captivating I can't ignore. Something special."

My breath hitched in my throat. He was lying. He wanted to gain my trust so my walls would drop and he could move in and hurt me. His approach was just smoother than Brandon's.

"Stay away from me." I jumped out of my chair and gathered my belongings.

His mouth hung open in shock. "Wait, no. Dammit, I didn't mean to scare you. Let's talk. Come to the fundraiser tonight. It's outside the student center."

"No. Don't sit at my table again or come anywhere near me," I demanded, my voice cracking and tears threatening my vision. I darted past him and out of the library.

Once again, I found myself running as fast as I could to my dorm room. Slamming the door closed behind me, the tears spilled down my cheeks. How in the world could I have thought he might, just might, have been a decent person? Seriously, who the fuck did he think he was? He needed to stick to writing music and stop analyzing people. What I chose to wear or anything else about me was none of his damned business.

Exhaustion washed over me, and I settled into my bed, wishing I was at home with Ada Lynn, rocking together on her porch. Safe.

With fun memories of Ada Lynn, I drifted off to sleep.

"Yo, BESTIE ROOMIE," Mac said, shaking my shoulder gently.

"Huh?" I sat up and peered at her through hazy, sleep-filled eyes.

"We're going out tonight," she announced while she shed her clothes and rifled through her stack of clean ones piled on the floor.

"No." My body collapsed on my bed again.

"Sorry, no isn't in the English language tonight. Up you go."

I rolled away from her and hoped she'd take the hint and leave, but no such luck.

"You're in a funk, and I need my bestie, so get your ass up, put on your hat, and let's go."

"Now that I only have one hat, I had planned on staying in and washing it. Figured I'd wrap my hair in a towel like I'd just stepped out of the shower so that no one would see it."

"Nice try, but no. I have another one you can borrow if you're going to give me that nonsense. I'm so not kidding, I will tug you out of bed, and it won't feel too great when your body hits the hardwood floor. Trust me."

Groaning loudly, I rolled back over to see her dressed in jeans and a bright pink long-sleeved shirt. Her hands rested on her hips as she tapped her foot incessantly, waiting for me to get out of bed. Although I hated to admit it, I'd met my match with Mac. Fighting her was a lost cause.

I ran a brush through my long hair and twisted it up, bunching it underneath my newly borrowed knit hat.

"Where are we going that's so important?" I asked, slipping on my glasses.

"There's an event outside the student center tonight. I'll cover your admittance fee. Besides, it goes to the local children's hospital. It's for a great cause, and the entire campus will be there."

My pulse quickened as I realized Hendrix would be there. At least it was highly unlikely I'd run into him if the entire campus would be there.

"Mac, you know I don't do well in crowds." I gulped.

"We will stay together. You have your phone and pepper spray, right?"

I nodded.

"Great! We're all set. If we, for some odd reason, get separated, just meet me by the eagle statue near the south side of the building. Got it?"

I hesitated.

This didn't sound like a good idea to me.

"I don't know," I muttered.

"What? Gemma, come on. You never leave the room unless it's for a class or the library. I've had a shit day, and I need a break. Like, I'd even hookup tonight with some rando dude."

"Mac!" I gasped.

"What? A girl's got needs, and I'm too damned busy to have a committed relationship, so sometimes ya gotta do whatcha gotta do. I mean, don't you?"

"No!"

"Like never? You've never had a booty call? A hookup? A one-nighter? A slut fest? What do you guys call it down south?"

"Inappropriate," I said, instinctively grabbing the collar of my shirt, pulling it tighter around my neck.

"Okay, totally get it, but we're going. And don't forget your jacket. I need my bestie tonight, not you making excuses to return to the room and hide."

Until Mac, I hadn't had a best friend since I was fourteen. And Fae had turned out to be the exact opposite of a best friend. Unfortunately, by the time I figured her out, the damage had already been done.

After five weeks of spending virtually every day with Mac, I knew she wasn't mad at me. This forcefulness was just part of her unique personality. Despite the fact it was against my better judgment to go out tonight, she'd admitted she'd had a shit day. I wanted to be there for her.

"Fine." I stood, gathered my belongings, and begrudgingly followed her out the door.

TO OTHER PEOPLE, it wasn't chilly yet. But after sunset, I froze. Louisiana never cooled off this much in early October. We took our time and strolled toward the student center. The crisp air was a nice change after being inside all day. I wouldn't admit it to Mac, though.

"Thanks for reminding me to grab a jacket," I said, pulling it tighter around me.

She grinned. "I realize I can be difficult, but I appreciate you coming with me. I know other people here, but I think it's good for you to get out some, too. Besides, you put up with me better than others do. I'm always worried I'm going to say the wrong thing or never shut the hell up." She sighed, her shoulders slumping forward, a tic I had noticed whenever she was unsure of herself. "They get mad at me. You're not like that. I mean, at least I don't think so."

"Mac, you don't 'put up' with friends," I said, smiling shyly. Not once had she pried about my clothes, hat, or anything else. She'd simply accepted me for me. The least I could do was return the favor.

The flare of a snare drum rang through the night as we approached the busy lawn. We edged our way through the crowd and settled somewhere in the middle. Everyone was standing, and the group gave an ear-splitting scream when several people strolled out onto the stage.

I grimaced and shot Mac a look as she jumped up and down, clapping.

"Can you see?" she asked.

"Yeah!"

She frowned at me, cupping her ear, so I nodded at her instead. She pointed toward the front of the large group.

"Hello, Spokane!"

The crowd went nuts. I'd never seen or been in the middle of anything like this before. My stomach clenched, and I inched closer to Mac. She smiled and looped her arm through mine. She knew. She realized I was already freaking out.

"Could you be mine?" a raspy male voice asked.

The girls went ballistic. You'd think we were watching Charlie Puth or something.

"Did you see?" Mac asked, pointing again.

I frowned and pushed up on my toes to get a better look over the sea of people. The moment the song started, my mouth dropped.

Hendrix.

Holy shit. This couldn't be real. I shot Mac a wide-eyed look. His voice could melt butter! He totally lied to me in the library when he said he couldn't sing.

"Right? He's so amazing. Oh, my God, I could listen to him twenty-four hours a day—"

Although I was angry with him for not being honest with me, Mac was right. I'd happily listen to him all day long.

Regardless of the fact I tried to fight it, my toe tapped, and I held onto Mac's arm and lost myself in the music. I'd never attended a concert before, much less something like this. I fought the part of myself that told me to run and hide. Instead, I stood straighter, my attention trained on Hendrix, my arm looped with Mac's.

It was okay.

I was okay.

And for the first time in years, I allowed myself to have a little bit of fun.

Hendrix talked to the crowd and introduced the band members before the keyboard began again, and he slipped into Citizen Shade's "Forfeit Tomorrow." My heart almost stopped. This song was on both of our Spotify lists. I knew what it meant to me, and I couldn't help but wonder if it held a special meaning for him as well. Regardless, the song was hauntingly beautiful.

Another hour flew by as I listened to every word that slipped from his lips. He'd catch shit from me the next time I saw him. Sort of sing? This dude needed to step away from the pot brownies. He was one of the best singers I'd ever heard.

I felt a little guilty for biting his head off earlier today. But a moment later, suspicion and anger took over. There was no way someone like him wanted to get to know someone like me. Shit didn't go down that way.

"Thanks, everyone! Have a great night!" Hendrix waved to the crowd as he slid his mic into place and strolled off the stage.

People went wild, pushing and pulling in every direction. What was going on? Were the girls trying to get to him? Panic shot through me as Mac and I were pulled in opposite directions. She opened her mouth, but all I could understand were the words *spray* and *eagle*.

My eyes widened as I was wedged between other students and Mac disappeared from sight. Bodies were tightly squeezed together, my arms pinned to my side, and I was unable to reach my phone or the pepper spray in the front pocket of my jeans. Anxiety fought to take over as I thought about Mac. She was so petite, and I hoped like hell she was okay.

The strength of the crowd lessened a bit, then the yelling started.

"Fuck you, bitch. Keep your snatch away from my man!" The shorter blonde-haired girl yelled, jabbing her finger in the air toward the athletically built girl.

"Your man? I've been fucking him the entire six months you've been dating. Don't think I'd call him *your* man."

Holy hell. I couldn't believe all of this was about a guy. What was wrong with people?

"Break it up!" Someone yelled over the anxious, angry crowd. "This is campus police!"

Everyone backed away, allowing them a path to the fight. From the chatter around me, I gathered the girls were throwing drunken punches, and the shouting continued.

"A little more excitement than I'd counted on," a girl next to me muttered as she rubbed her arm.

"Me too," I replied, eyeing her. She stood about five-seven, long brown hair with blonde highlights. Worry lines creased her forehead.

"Things should calm down now. Are you okay?" she asked, nodding toward me.

"Other than being scared shitless, I'm okay. You?"

"Yeah, I'm okay. Your cheek, though. You have blood on it." She pointed to the right side of my face.

Frowning, I raised my hand and touched it. Red streaked my fingers.

"It's not too bad. You probably got scratched when everyone got a little crazy. Just clean it up and make sure it doesn't get infected," she said.

"Thank you," I responded.

"Nursing. I mean, I'm attending college for nursing."

"Oh, okay. Thank you. I appreciate it," I said, readjusting my hat.

Pushing up on my tiptoes, I tried to see over the top of everyone and identify the direction of the statue. The noise had calmed some, and I was finally able to talk at an almost normal volume.

"Where's the eagle statue? I'm lost," I said.

"Over there," she replied, pointing toward the side of the crowd. "Be careful getting out of here." She gave me a small wave and worked her way through the people in the opposite direction.

"You too," I said, and began to politely move through the group myself. All I wanted was to find Mac and go to the dorm.

The angry events had stripped away all the fun from the evening, which pissed me off since I couldn't remember the last time I'd relaxed a little and enjoyed myself.

Finally, I slipped my hand into my pocket and grabbed the pepper spray like Mac had told me to. A small amount of comfort swelled inside of me while my fingers wrapped around it tightly. Grabbing my phone from my other pocket, I checked for missed calls. There weren't any. My pulse quickened as I wondered if Mac was okay.

6

Nearly twenty minutes later, I reached the statue located near the stage. I frantically searched for Mac, but she wasn't anywhere to be seen. Not wanting to get caught up in the crowd again, I took a few steps backward and huddled against the safety of the building.

I searched the group one more time and tried to call her. Nothing. A tremble traveled through me as I called her again. She had to be okay. At least the mass of people had thinned out and calmed down some. Where was she, though? She specifically told me to meet her here if we got separated.

The loud clang of the drum set's cymbal startled me, and I yelped while I peered up at the stage. A part of me had hoped I would see Hendrix so that I could wait for Mac with him. He was better than standing alone in the middle of the night.

The crowd had cleared to make way for the campus cops, who were escorting the handcuffed girls away. I stepped forward after they passed, scanning the remaining people for Mac.

"There she is!" a male voice boomed.

My head snapped toward the sound.

"Are you Gemma Thompson?" A tall, heavy-set officer sauntered toward me.

"Yes?" I took in the scene in front of me. Brandon and his minions were standing to the side of the officer. Panic rose in my chest.

What in the hell was going on?

"This young man said you started the fight," he said, pointing toward Brandon.

"What?" I gasped. "No, I was pushed around in the crowd with everyone else. How would I even have started a fight?"

"She's lying," Brandon said, moving closer. "She pushed the girl in the red shirt. See the scratch on her cheek? I'm telling you, she started all of this crap tonight."

"No! I didn't!" My pitch climbed a notch as the officer took my arm.

"Miss, come with us so we can clear all of this up. Instigation of a fight is grounds for dismissal from the university."

Wide-eyed, I shook my head. There was no way they could possibly believe this shit. It didn't make sense.

Was Brandon trying to get back at me for Hendrix standing up to him on my behalf?

As the officers escorted me across the lawn of the school, I caught a glimpse of Brandon laughing. The bastard thought this was funny.

"Gemma!"

I turned around. "Mac! They think I started the fight. Help me."

"Seriously?" She hauled ass across the freshly mowed lawn and caught up to us. "What the hell?" she asked, gasping for breath.

"Brandon. He lied to them, and now they won't listen. What am I going to do?"

Mac bent over, resting her hands on her knees briefly. A moment later, she straightened, her expression solemn.

"I'll meet you there," she yelled.

My brows shot up while she took off running again in the opposite direction.

Shit. Where was she going?

My shoulders slumped in defeat as I walked with the officers toward the building. If the girls from the fight were already there, then maybe they would clear my name. Neither of them would even recognize me, so it should help swing things in my favor.

We entered the building, and they ushered me to a desk and chair. I scanned the room for the other girls and noticed they were talking with another person in the department.

"Ask them," I said and nodded toward the girl in the red shirt. "Ask if they have seen me before and if I started the fight."

"Gemma, we have an eyewitness already."

"Brandon? He's been harassing me. I should be here filing a restraining order on him!" I squeaked out.

"Actually, he filed a complaint against you, and there's a restraining order as well. You're not allowed to be within three-hundred feet of him. If you break this order, you'll be arrested."

My mouth hit the floor. There was no way this was really happening. At any moment, someone was going to hop out from behind a desk and tell me I was on *Candid Camera* or some other reality TV show, and all of this nonsense was one big joke.

"Gemma!"

I turned to see Mac hurrying across the room toward me, and I groaned. The night had just gotten worse. She'd brought Hendrix with her. Mac had just invited one more person to watch my sideshow of humiliation. If I got out of this mess, she had some explaining to do.

"Hey," Hendrix said as he approached the desk.

Mac bent over and whispered in my ear. "It's going to be okay. Be quiet and listen."

"Officer, there's been a misunderstanding," Hendrix stated.

"I doubt it but go ahead." The officer slumped in his chair and crossed his arms over his bulging stomach.

"She wasn't even in the crowd. She was side stage. I could see her the entire time and so could my band members."

"And what was she doing there?" he asked impatiently.

"Waiting for me. I invited her tonight and said she could hang out until the show was over. She was never even in the crowd."

This time I had the sense not to allow my mouth to gape open at the lie. Apparently everyone was immune to telling the truth around here.

Mac gently squeezed my shoulder as we listened to Hendrix give every detail of my whereabouts tonight. I played along since I had no other choice. I mean, Brandon had already talked the cops into a restraining order. I bit my lower lip.

"Anyone else in the band willing to vouch for her?" The cop's expression grew stern while he looked Hendrix up and down.

"Yup. Everyone will tell you the same thing."

My shoulders tensed. It was one thing to lie for a friend, but I'd never met his band before. There was no way they would tell security I was there.

"Fine, we'll call them tonight. If they tell me the same thing you did, we'll drop the charges against Gemma for starting the fight. However, the restraining order sticks."

"What restraining order?" Hendrix asked, his jaw clenching as he waited for an explanation.

"Brandon Montgomery. She's been harassing him, and he filed against her tonight."

"You're screwing with me, right?" Hendrix ran a hand through his hair and attempted to remain calm.

"Wouldn't do that, son. We're done here, so if you all want to leave, then go on. Otherwise I'll find another reason to keep your friend."

"Nope, we're good," Mac said, grabbing me by the arm and hauling me out as fast as she could.

"Dammit!" I yelled the moment we exited the building. "Mac, what just happened? How did this night turn to total shit?" I groaned and pulled on the sides of my hat with both hands.

The sound of the front door opening pulled my attention away from her.

"Thank you," I muttered as Hendrix approached.

"Sorry," he said.

"For what? You didn't do anything other than invade my library space. And you've actually been nice to me," I mumbled shyly.

"If I'd been there sooner, Brandon wouldn't have gotten away with the restraining order. Do you know why they believed him?"

"Not. One. Damned. Clue." My focus bounced between Mac and Hendrix, waiting for a response.

Mac snickered, and I shot her a look. She held her hands up in surrender and muttered something about the ADHD causing her to have untimely outbursts. No shit. I'd lived with her for over a month now and had already figured that out.

"He's the dean's son, Gemma. He's very well connected and has a lot of pull with important people. That's the only reason he got away with the restraining order." Hendrix's jaw tightened again.

For the second time in the same night, my mouth hit the ground.

Stunned, I slapped my hands over my face, only managing to smash my glasses into my nose. My hands dropped to my sides, defeat nudging at me with the new information.

"What? No! This is why he gets away with tormenting people? Oh my God. I didn't harass him or follow him or whatever else he said. It's the opposite. You know that, right? You were there," I gushed.

"Yeah, I know," Hendrix said, running his hand over his hair.

From what I'd seen, Brandon and Hendrix had a severe dislike for each other. Maybe I'd work up the nerve to ask about it sometime, but for now I had to figure out how to get out of this mess. Not to mention this was the most I'd ever said to Hendrix.

My pulse sped up, and I tried to wrap my addled brain around the night's events.

"Come on. I'm walking you two back to your dorm," Hendrix said.

Mac wiggled her eyebrows at me as he moved forward, and we fell into step next to him. I mustered up the best nasty glare I had in me and shot it at her. She giggled, and I tossed my hands up in mock surrender.

"Talk to him," she mouthed, motioning wildly with her hand.

I frowned and crossed my arms over my chest, trying to steady my nerves.

"You lied to me," I said softly. "Like, not a tiny white lie, but a big fucking fat one."

"I did?" he asked, looking perplexed and shoving his hands into the front pockets of his jeans.

"Mm-hmm. You said you couldn't sing."

"Aww," he said, his chin tilting up toward the night sky and grinning. "I didn't lie."

"Yes, you did. You looked right at me and said you couldn't sing."

"Technically I didn't. I said I was a singer-songwriter and then you asked if I could sing, and I responded with 'If you could call it that.'"

"Seriously? You're throwing a technicality at me? Are you pre-law or something?"

A soft chuckle escaped him. "No, I'm majoring in music. However, my dad is an attorney. He's just not practicing right now."

"Retired?" Suddenly, I was super curious about his background.

"Something like that," he said, tucking his hair behind his ear and glancing at me. Even in the darkness, his blue eyes were captivating. There was no question why the girls screamed over him. He was dangerous in a sexy, panty-dropping way. No matter what he looked like or what he sounded like, though, my panties and everything inside them were off-limits. I mentally chided myself as I realized what I was thinking. There was no way he'd ever want in them anyway.

"You okay?" he asked, pulling a hairband from his pocket.

"Yeah," I responded while I watched him gather his hair and pull it into a low ponytail. "No. No, actually I'm not. I'm a small-town girl. I don't do drama. I've been homeschooled most of my life, and all of a sudden, I have a restraining order against me. I've never even toilet papered someone's house, much less harassed anyone. All I want is to attend college, mind my own business, and graduate. Is that too much to ask?"

"I'm not sure how yet, but we will get it taken care of. Give me some time."

I eyed him for any hint he was screwing with me. As far as I could tell, he seemed honestly legit.

"Well we're already in trouble since you told the police your band would confirm your story." I huffed at the possibility they'd stand up for me.

"Oh no, they will. The moment Mac told me what happened, I told the band to confirm you were on the side of the stage. It was already taken care of before Mac and I even showed up. Right, Mac?"

"Yup," she said, two-stepping to catch up with us.

"Thank you both," I muttered. "I'm so sorry you're involved."

"Don't worry about it. Besides, I finally got your name," Hendrix smirked.

My lips pursed when I realized he was right. There had been no way around it. The second Mac involved him he'd found out.

"Well, *Gemma*, here we are." Hendrix waved his arm toward the dorm, emphasizing my name. "It's been an unforgettable night for sure. I look forward to more." He flashed me his smile, and despite the fact I'd willed it not to happen, my pulse quickened.

"Thanks, Hendrix," Mac said, beaming up at him.

My attention bounced between them. I was missing something. Mac had mentioned they had attended the same high school, and now that they were standing next to each other, it was apparent they knew each other...and well.

I adjusted my hat and stared at the ground, unwilling to let them see my expression as things began to fall into place. They were obviously friends, but there was more to their relationship. I just wasn't sure why she hadn't told me.

"Sing. Please, something quick," Mac begged Hendrix, clapping her hands like a little kid.

I bit my lip in anticipation, focusing on him again.

"Mac, this probably isn't the place." He raised a brow and crossed his arms over his chest.

"Who cares! Do you understand what this will do for Gemma's and my cred? Like, every girl in the dorm will want to be my new best friend. No offense Gemma, I won't replace you. You're still my bestie, but this could do amazeball things for our social life."

"I don't want a social life," I groaned at her idea.

"Oh, you don't? Okay, I'll sing," Hendrix laughed. The air stood still as his raspy voice broke through the night and he sang "I Can't Breathe" by Bea Miller. Chill bumps danced down my spine. I was pretty sure I could listen to him for hours. Out of nowhere, something stirred inside me, and I found myself softly harmonizing with him. His eyes widened as my voice blended with his. Mac gawked and covered her mouth with both of her hands, remaining quiet while we sang.

And just for a minute, I stepped out of this hellhole called my life and into a beautiful place enriched with melody, his deep, smooth tone allowing me to hope, for a fleeting second, things might be okay.

Our song ended, our voices fading into the quiet of the night. His eyes found mine, and I returned his gaze, wrapped up in the moment.

Clapping broke the silence, and my cheeks flushed as I realized how many people were surrounding us. A crowd had gathered, but I hadn't noticed. My only focus had been Hendrix and the music.

"Give me your phone," Hendrix said, smiling down at me.

Without hesitation, I handed it to him and watched him enter his number on my screen.

"Your turn." I did as he requested. Speechless, I handed his back to him.

"I'll see you in the library tomorrow," he said to me. "Night, Mac." He gave a little wave and strolled away.

"What in the hell just happened?" Mac asked me.

I stood there, completely befuddled. "No damned clue," I said. The girl's chatter brought me out of my daze. "You have some serious explaining to do." I grabbed her arm and made our way to the dorm room.

"What do you mean?" Mac asked, innocently.

"There are too many people around right now. We'll talk in our room," I said as we ran up the stairs to our floor.

As soon as we were in our room, I flopped onto my bed.

"Spill, like right now."

"I don't understand what you want, Gemma." She hopped onto her bed and rooted around, attempting to straighten her blankets.

"How do you know Hendrix, other than school I mean? Why did you bring him to help me?" I demanded.

"Totally obvi, Gemma. The moment the cops showed up, I could smell it in the air. Ya know, the shit you were steppin' in. I knew something was off. You're a wallflower, not a rabble-rouser."

"A what?" The description floored me.

"Troublemaker, instigator, rabble-rouser," she repeated for me slowly.

I laughed as she over accentuated each word. "Shit, it's really not funny."

"No, it's not. It will be okay, though. You're not getting suspended or in any trouble. Hendrix will think of something."

"He mentioned his dad was an attorney?"

Mac leaned against the wall and released a huge breath, sinking into her bed. "Yeah, he is," she muttered. "He's just not practicing now."

"Retired?"

"Something like that."

She'd given me the same response Hendrix had. How could I not be curious about it?

"So, yes, I grabbed him because when I saw him, I realized if anyone could help, it would be him. He'd be able to stand up to Brandon and the dean without any real consequences. Hendrix is very well known around Spokane, Gemma. His dad was a big shot lawyer at one time, and he holds some major clout in the city."

"Oh." Suddenly I felt small and insignificant.

"But what the hell! You've been totally holding out on me. Gurl! You can fucking sing!"

"What? No, no, I was only having a little bit of fun. Honestly, I didn't mean to start singing. He's just so damned good, and I knew the song. It sorta happened. And did you know he could sing like that? Oh. My. God."

"Mm-hmm. I also saw some digits being exchanged."

"Digits?" I asked. Where in the world did this girl come up with this shit to say?

"I saw him put his phone number in your phone! Gah! You're driving me nuts, catch up already."

"You're overreacting, Mac. Calm down."

"Nu-uh. You have Hendrix's phone number, and he has yours."

"So what? We sang together. We like music. Besides," I paused, rolling my eyes for extra emphasis so she would calm down, "he sits at my library table every day."

"What?" Mac gasped and hopped off her bed and over to mine.

"Why are you acting all—" I stammered for the right words. "Like this is a big deal. I guess we're friends!" I shrugged and held up my hands in question.

"Umm, why haven't you told me he's been sitting with you every day at the library? This is super important info, Gemma!" She pointed at me for extra emphasis.

"Mac, we've barely spoken until today. And all we did was search through each other's playlists on Spotify. He was writing his own song, and I saw it. We chatted for like sixty seconds. Nothing else. You're trying to make this into something it isn't." At that moment, fear shot through me as I realized I was letting a guy get close to me. I couldn't allow this. We couldn't be friends. It didn't matter if he was able to help me with Brandon. It was not happening.

"I disagree. I think he likes you. Consider it, Gemma."

"No! I don't want to. Don't you understand it, Mac? I don't want to be around any guys. Not nice ones, not mean ones, none. Zilch. Nada."

Mac's forehead tightened in a frown. "Take off your glasses and the damned hat. It's just me."

"Why?" I asked, adjusting the hat lower over my forehead.

"Take it off," she said sternly.

I huffed and placed the items on my desk. "Better?"

"Yes, much. Now I can see your eyes and read your face. So, let me get this straight. You're telling me you don't want to be friends or anything else with Hendrix?" she questioned.

"No, it's not what I'm saying. I don't want to be friends with Hendrix or *any* guy for that matter. None. Got it?"

We both went silent for a moment, and my breath hitched in my throat.

"Something happened, didn't it?" she asked softly, grabbing my hand and holding it firmly.

I attempted to jerk it away from her, but her grip was too strong. "Mac, we have an agreement, so I'm going to kindly remind you of said agreement. I'm your bestie, and in return, you agreed not to ask questions."

Mac blew out a breath and released my hand.

"Yup, I remember, sorry." She nervously rubbed her hands up and down her jeans and glanced down at her lap. "I'm sorry, I didn't mean to push. Shit just flies out of my mouth sometimes."

"Sometimes? How about all the time," I said, irritated. "It's fine. Let's drop it, okay?" A sigh escaped me as I let it go.

"Yeah."

"Besides, you still haven't answered my question," I reminded her as I twisted my long hair around a finger.

"Which question?" she asked, peering at me.

"How do you know Hendrix? I mean, it's obvious you are more than acquaintances. There's definitely something between the two of you. Did you used to date or something?"

A loud giggle escaped her tiny body.

"No, nothing like that," she insisted.

"So, what gives? I would assume since you went to the same school that you knew each other, but you two really know each other."

Mac closed her eyes for a minute. "You're right," she said, opening them again. "We have a past."

"What kind of past?" I asked, my curiosity peaking.

"We didn't date." She paused and wrinkled her nose at me.

"What? I thought you liked him or something."

"Eww, no!" She cowered down and tugged on her braid. "No! I mean I do like him, he's a great guy. And he's got substance, he's not just an amazing voice and hot body. And since I do know him so well, I can totally say it in a non-sexual way."

"Mac! Stop. Quit rambling and focus. How do you know Hendrix?"

"Shit," she said, sighing loudly.

Silence hung in the air while I waited for her to respond.

"He's my older brother."

7

For the *third* time that night, my mouth hit the floor.

"What?" I screeched. "And you left out this information...why?"

Floored by the news, I fell back onto my bed, grabbed my pillow, and placed it over my head.

"Well I didn't realize he was your library buddy for starters. The only time you've mentioned him was when he stood up to Brandon for you. I only share the info about Hendrix and me on a need-to-know basis."

I tossed the pillow off me and bolted upright. "Tell me. All of it. Now," I demanded.

Mac's shoulders slumped forward. "Fine." Her lips formed a pout as she shot me a look. "You can't tell anyone this. It was hard enough living in his shadow in high school. I'm not interested in putting that part of my life on repeat."

"Agreed." She had kept my secret, and now I would repay the favor and keep hers.

"We're step-siblings, actually."

My forehead creased as I wrapped my head around what she'd just told me. "Okay. Keep going." I motioned for her to continue. For all the times Mac ran off at the mouth, this story should be flowing off her tongue. Why was she struggling?

"My mom was married to his dad, Franklin. She was his second marriage, and Franklin had Hendrix from his first marriage. After eight years, Mom left because he worked too much. I was in elementary school at the time. Anyway, Hendrix's dad remarried, and it's a long story. What I will say is when his dad's career went into the shitter, he started drinking, and Hendrix took care of him."

"Oh," I said. "That's a lot for a kid to take on," I whispered and imagined Hendrix taking care of a drunk father. My insides cringed with regret for him.

"Things turned to shit real fast, though, and Hendrix came to live with Mom and me. We were in junior high by that time. Everyone knew he was my brother, and it sucked. He was popular, and everyone loved him. I was the younger sister that wouldn't shut up and was a constant annoyance."

"Did he say those things to you, Mac?"

"No," she mumbled. "I could tell from how everyone acted around me. Like, I would be in mid-conversation, and his friends would just walk off. Hendrix would frown and leave with them. He didn't know how to handle it, I guess. It didn't take long before we ignored each other at school, and eventually, everyone forgot about me and moved on," she said, her voice sharp with pain.

"Including him?"

"At school, yes. At home we were fine. He was my best friend, but the moment we stepped outside, we had different worlds. I accepted it and realized it was the easiest thing for both of us. It seemed to bother me less if he and his friends weren't around."

"Shit. I'm sorry, Mac. It had to have been difficult. And everyone seems to really like you."

"They do, I guess. It's better here than it used to be. I think since it's a big campus, people can avoid me if they want to."

"Mac," I scolded. "Don't be ridiculous. Savannah had great things to say about you. Hendrix was there the second you needed him, and I'm here every day. We're not going anywhere. Sometimes having a small group of loyal friends is way better than a big group of acquaintances and never knowing who you can trust or where you fit in. Shit, we all feel like that sometimes. Look at me. I don't fit in at all, but I'm not whining about it. I just want to be left alone."

Mac searched my face, her expression growing serious.

"Are you going to tell me someday, Gemma?" she asked softly.

"No. I'm not. We protect each other's secrets, and that's it. I owe you nothing, and you owe me nothing."

Her gaze narrowed. I knew Mac well enough to realize the wheels in her head were turning a million miles an hour, attempting to figure out my hat, glasses, and clothes.

"Fine," she said and shot me a dirty look.

"Fine," I snapped as she hopped off my bed and to hers.

Silence settled into the room. This was the first time Mac and I had argued, and it sucked. I'd not realized how close we'd gotten.

"Thank you for not telling anyone about Hendrix," she muttered with her back to me as she snuggled underneath her blankets.

My heart softened. Mac seemed as lost and alone as I was. "It's what friends are for," I replied, attempting to make up for my earlier rudeness.

She rustled around, turning toward me. "Yeah?" Hope flickered in her eyes.

"Yeah," I responded.

A smile eased across her pretty features, and we both snuggled into our beds. I willed my body to relax in the hope that I would drift off to sleep. As hard as I tried, I couldn't rid my thoughts of the night's events.

"I WENT TO AN ON-CAMPUS CONCERT. Can you believe it?" I asked, squealing into my phone.

"What? Gemma, that's wonderful. Tell me everything," Ada Lynn said.

I propped myself against my pillow and updated her on everything—Mac, Hendrix, the concert. I could practically hear her smiling. I purposely left out my run-ins with Brandon. Ada Lynn was on blood pressure and heart medication. No need for her to get worked up when there was nothing she could do about that asswipe. Besides, she'd be on the next plane to club him with her purse and cane.

I loved Ada Lynn with all my heart, and if anything were to happen to her, I would be on the first bus to Louisiana.

I was surprised to admit it, but I didn't want to leave Spokane just yet.

"This Mac sounds like a character, but in a good way," Ada Lynn piped in once I finished updating her on my simple life at college.

"How are the folks?" I asked, steering the conversation away from dangerous territory. "Has Dad found a job?"

"No, he hasn't." Ada Lynn's tone dropped an octave. "I was going to tell you at the end of the conversation. Now will do fine, I suppose."

Fear shot through me and my body stiffened. "What is it?"

"Your mom is going to call you tonight. Gemma, you need to pick up the phone and talk with her."

"What? Why? What aren't you telling me?" My pulse raced.

"I'll be here for you after your mom talks to you, but Gemma, it's not my place to tell you anything. She'll be calling you shortly. In fact, as soon as we hang up, I'll have her call you, okay?"

"You're scaring me. Do I need to come home?"

"No. Don't you dare," she said sternly.

My shoulders relaxed a little bit. Maybe I'd jumped to the wrong conclusion. "Okay, let's hang up so she can call. I've got about thirty minutes before my roommate returns, and I won't have any privacy."

"All right. You call me after you talk to her, okay?"

"I will."

Pulling the phone away from my ear, I ended the call and stood. The small room didn't afford much space for pacing, but I managed. Back and forth, back and forth. My mind sped along with different scenarios as I waited for Mom to call.

Finally, my phone buzzed in my hand.

"Mom?" I asked.

"Hi, honey. It's so nice to hear your voice."

I sank into a sitting position on the edge of my bed. Hearing her voice after so many weeks filled me with sadness and regret for leaving the way I did. I missed her. Them.

"Ada Lynn says you're doing really well," she said, continuing with the small talk.

"I am, Mom. I'm doing great."

"That's good, honey." Mom took a shaky breath. "Gemma, your dad..."

"He can't find a job?" I asked, interrupting her. I scolded myself. I had to be careful not to pick up Mac's bad habits.

"Well, he's not searching right now."

Puzzled, I waited for her to continue.

"He's sick, hon."

"What do you mean sick?" I asked, jumping off my bed and pacing again.

"He's got lymphoma. He had his first chemo treatment today."

Silence lingered over the line while I struggled to understand what she'd just told me.

"I'll come home," I said, barely above a whisper.

"No. You will not come home. We're getting it treated, and there is nothing you can do here. You stay put, and you have my word if I need you, I'll let you know. Until then—don't you dare. All I ask is that you talk to him. He misses you so much."

A lump formed in my throat as tears threatened my eyes.

"Yeah. I'll talk to him, but Mom, if he starts in with how I'm not in God's will, I'm done. Those are his beliefs. They're not mine." I cringed. I'd never stood up to my parents about their religious views. My heart pounded against my chest, waiting for her reaction.

"I understand, and I'll talk to him. Will you at least say hi to him right now? His spirits are pretty low, and I think hearing from you will help."

Hesitation nipped at me, but I pushed it away. This wasn't the time for my personal feelings to stand in the way. I needed to be an adult. Besides, I missed him.

"Okay."

Sound rustled through the phone, and then, "Gemma?"

"Dad," I said, my voice thick with emotion. "Are you still mad at me for leaving like that?" I blurted out.

"No, not anymore. It was a shock, but I understand. How are you doing? Ada Lynn keeps us up to date on most things. It's not the same as hearing it from you, though."

"I know. At least you've had her updates, so you didn't worry. Maybe I can call you and Mom once a week."

"I would really like that," he said, sounding exhausted.

"Are you in pain?"

"No, I'm just tired all the time. I'll be fine, Gemma. They caught it in time, so with the treatment I'll be back to normal in no time."

"Promise?" I asked, quietly.

"Yeah. I'm going to be fine. And so are you. We've had some big changes, but we're Thompsons and nothing keeps us down for long, right?"

I smiled. Here he was sick and trying to make me feel better.

"I'd better get some rest. I love you, Gemma."

"Love you too, Dad."

I should be there. They were sugar-coating the seriousness of the issue. I could tell in their tones.

Walking over to my closet, I yanked the door open and started to clean it out. In a minute flat, everything I owned was on my bed. My attention landed on my bag, and I grabbed it, stuffing it with clothes. The door swung open, breaking my train of thought.

"What the hell?" Mac asked, approaching me. "What's all of this?" Her eyes widened, and fear flickered across her features. She fidgeted with the braid draped over her shoulder and adjusted her bright green top while she waited for an explanation.

"I'm leaving, Mac. My dad has cancer. They need me in Louisiana."

"Wait, what?" She grabbed my hands and turned me toward her. "Look at me. What happened?"

A tear slipped down my cheek, and my throat was thick with fear and grief.

"Did he ask you to come home?" Her brows knitted together as she tried to figure out what had happened.

"No, the opposite."

Mac squeezed my hands. "Start from the beginning and tell me everything."

I repeated my phone conversations with Ada Lynn, Mom, and Dad while I sank down onto the side of my bed.

"Gemma, he said to stay, are you sure you want to go?" she asked, her fingers steepled together, her expression pleading with me.

My chest ached as a waterfall of emotions washed over me. I didn't want to leave Washington at all.

"No, I don't want to. But what kind of daughter am I if I stay?"

"A good one. And your mom promised if things got worse, she would tell you. Plus, from what you've shared with me, Ada Lynn would definitely talk to you about it."

"Shit, I'm supposed to call her again."

"Okay, you do that, and I'm going to make a call myself. Afterward, we're going to put your things away."

"I'll put my stuff back as long as Ada Lynn says I don't need to hop on a bus."

"Well hurry up and call her then. You've made the room one big mess." Mac smiled while she grabbed her phone and left the room, allowing me some privacy.

I chewed anxiously on my thumbnail while I waited for Ada Lynn to pick up my call.

"Hello?"

"It's Gemma."

"Well it took you long enough," she said, chuckling.

"I had started packing to come home." I sniffled and sat on the edge of my bed.

"Don't you do it, now. Your mom, Dad, and I have told you to stay put. I promise I'll tell you if your dad gets worse and they need your help."

Silence hovered between us.

"How long?" I asked. "How long have you all known?"

"Well, I found out today when he had his first treatment. Obviously, your mom has known for longer."

"Yeah, it makes sense," I said, pausing for a minute. "Are you sure Dad and Mom don't need me there? I feel like I'm an awful daughter, and I should be there for my family." I groaned while I stood and began pacing again.

"Listen to me, my blue-eyed girl. Your family bonded over tragedy, and it has to learn to thrive again. The longer you're away and learning to stand on your own feet and moving forward, the more your family as a whole will get better. It's the trickle-down effect. So you stay and continue to heal unless you hear out of my mouth otherwise. Don't you show up here. You have my word that I'll tell you if you need to," she said, pausing for a second. "Promise me." Her sharp words stung. She wasn't playing with me.

"Promise." I sighed, giving in. Mac would be thrilled, and as awful as I felt about staying, I was also relieved. If I went back to Louisiana, I wasn't sure I would ever make it out again.

"All right, it's late here, so I'm going to try and get some sleep. You should, too. Call me tomorrow, and I'll keep you up to date on your dad, okay?"

"Thank you, Ada Lynn. Love you."

"You too, honey. Talk to you tomorrow."

8

_____

F ive minutes after I hung up with Ada Lynn, my clothes were
put away, and Mac returned.

"Oh. My. God," she whispered, flinging herself against
the closed door. "You're staying." Her shoulders sagged with relief.

"Yup, you're not getting rid of me yet," I said, attempting a
smile.

"Well Hendrix said to meet him at the library." ·

I whirled around toward her. "You told him about my dad?" My
hands fisted at my sides.

Mac full-on cringed. "I'm sorry, Gemma. But I needed help
convincing you to stay if your parents said to go home."

"Hendrix is your backup?"

"I'm sorry," Mac pleaded. "I didn't know what else to do, and
you're upset, and I'm not great with knowing how to help people. He's
super good at it, like it comes naturally to him."

"Enough." Mac jumped when I stomped my foot. "You had no
right to share my business."

My words seemed to echo in the now silent room. We stood
frozen, me with my hands on my hips, Mac with both hands covering
her mouth. The wide-eyed look of remorse on Mac's face melted my

anger. I let out a defeated sigh. "It was a lot to dump on you, so I'm sorry. I understand why you wanted Hendrix's help."

"No, no, I'm sorry," she said, lunging at me and pulling me into a hug.

Startled, it took me a minute to hug her in return. And for the first time in a long time, I felt as though I really did have a friend my age.

"Okay, you need to hurry. Hendrix is waiting for you. Shoo, go," she said, waving her arms toward the door. "Grab your shit and don't keep the man waiting."

I barked out a laugh at her dramatics. My heart sped up a little at the thought of him waiting for me. I wasn't naïve enough to think he was anything other than a friend who shared an interest in music and my safety from Brandon, but both he and Mac were growing on me. And if my circle expanded a little, I would be okay with that. One thing at a time. I still wasn't sure of his motives. Although, he was her brother and if Mac vouched for him, he had to be okay.

I smiled with the realization I trusted her, even when she did stupid shit like calling Hendrix and sharing my business. At least I knew where her heart was.

"Okay, fine," I said, grabbing my stuff. "I'll be back by dark."

"What? *No*, just have Hendrix walk with you. Then you can take your time and relax instead of watching the clock."

"Mac, I can't ask him to do that." I frowned at the idea. I'd relied on myself so much over the last few years I'd forgotten how to ask anyone for help.

"Why? He knows the deal with Brandon. Besides, if Hendrix opens the door and sees it's dark, he's going to offer anyway. It's who he is."

Unease gnawed at me while I considered being out at night, allowing myself to be an easy target for Brandon and his assholes.

"You're fine. If for some strange reason Hendrix can't, then call me, and I'll meet you. Deal?"

I nodded. I liked how Mac's mind worked—with backup plans.

"Okay, I'll see you tonight." I skipped down the stairs and hurried toward the library.

I PULLED out my chair at our table. A smile lit up his face as I settled in.

"Hey," he said, his voice low.

My stomach clenched with butterflies at the sound of it.

"Mac told me about your dad. You all right? Are you leaving?" he asked, worry lines creasing his forehead.

"No, I'm staying for now at least. Mom promised she'd tell me to come home if it got worse. She wants me to stay here. Even Dad said to stay. So...I will." Guilt flooded me, and I swallowed the ball of emotions that threatened to erupt.

Hendrix released a slow breath, his body visibly relaxing.

"You seem relieved," I said, tilting my head and studying him. Something had shifted between us since we'd sung together. I just couldn't put my finger on it. He seemed more at ease talking to me, and maybe I was with him, too.

"I'm glad you're staying." He reached his hand across the table, placing it over mine. Heat shot through me, and I snatched it away.

"Please don't do that," I whispered, my cheeks burning with embarrassment.

"Sorry, I was trying to—"

I raised my hand to stop him from saying anything else. A heavy silence fell between us, and I inhaled a shaky breath. How could I be so childish as to not want a friend to touch my hand? Mac did. So what was the difference with Hendrix? I already knew the answer, though.

"I," he paused as I stared at him. "I wrote a new song and wondered if you'd be interested in hearing it."

"Me?" I asked, confused.

"Well, yeah, is it okay?" He tucked his hair behind his ear, his attention never leaving me.

I shrugged. "I don't understand why me is all."

"Shit, really? Gemma—" He sat up straighter in his chair. "Your voice is unlike any I've ever heard, and I listen to a ton of music."

I couldn't help but giggle. I'd seen his Spotify lists, he wasn't joking. My shoulders relaxed, and I settled into my chair.

"So what does that have to do with you wanting me to hear it?"

"Everything. Before I say anything else, though, will you come with me to listen to it?"

My guard immediately went up. "Where?"

"The campus studio. I recorded it earlier today."

My brows shot up in surprise. I'd never seen the inside of a real studio, but I'd always wanted to. It would also mean we'd be in a small room together. Alone. No one else would be around, no librarian, no other students. And although my emotions and logic played tug of war with each other, my curiosity won the battle. Music was my weak spot, and I wanted to hear his song.

"Okay, but only for a little bit."

A smile spread across his face as he stood and studied me for a long moment.

"Now I'm nervous. I hope you like it." A flush dusted his cheeks.

"I'm sure I will," I said, trying to reassure him. I stood, pushed my chair in, and walked toward him. He extended his hand to me, and I hesitated. My eyes held his, then my gaze dropped down. He wanted to hold my hand, but I wasn't sure I would be comfortable with it.

"I won't bite," he said softly. "Unless you like that sort of thing." His low chuckle filled the space between us as I slowly reached out and took his hand. Shivers shot through me at his touch. One I'd willingly consented to. His fingers intertwined with mine, and he gently pulled me toward him, giving my hand a little squeeze.

"This okay?" he asked, tilting his head toward our hands.

I nodded, unable to articulate a yes or no.

"Good. Let's go." I didn't pay any attention to the campus or where we were going. My brain was still trying to process the fact Hendrix was holding my hand, and I was allowing it to happen. Every time I wanted to take off running, reminders of what Mac had shared with me helped ease the panic. They were stepsiblings, and if she trusted him, I could too. Regardless of my pep talk, my entire body tensed with anxiety. I was well aware that people weren't always who they said they were, and Mac might not know him as well as she thought.

"Here we are," Hendrix said, smiling.

My fingers slipped from his as he ushered me into the building, the door clanging shut behind us. I jumped when it clicked closed, the finality ringing through the empty hallway.

"You okay?" Hendrix asked, concern flickering across his expression.

"Yeah. I don't know the campus well yet, and I'm a bit jumpy. Where are we?"

Hendrix took my hand again and led me toward the large windows near the door we'd just entered.

"See over there?" I looked where he was pointing to the right of us. "Your dorm is over there. If you glance up, you'll see the roof."

"Oh," I said and leaned closer to the window. He was right. I could actually see the dorm from here. A little bit of tension eased from my neck.

"Better?" he asked, giving my hand a little squeeze.

"Yes, thank you." A small smile pulled at the corners of my mouth as my focus dropped to the floor.

"All right, let's go to the studio."

As we walked down a long hall, I took note of every door and exit, committing them to memory in case I needed to escape.

Hendrix opened a door marked Studio C and stood aside for me to enter first. It wasn't a large room, and it was empty except for a couple of chairs and a mic hanging from the ceiling. When he opened the door next to a large glass observation window, I gasped.

"Pretty awesome, huh?" he asked and dropped my hand. He inspected the mixing console and pulled out a chair for me. "Here ya go."

He flipped some switches, then sat down next to me. The next thing I knew, the studio was saturated with a soft melody. His rich tone rang in my ears, and moments later my body relaxed into the music. He was amazing. Everything about his tone and execution was perfect. The song finished, and I looked at him with awe.

"Well?" He stared at me in anticipation.

"I love it," I said, my words cracking with emotion.

"Did you like the lyrics? I can change anything. I wasn't sure about the hook, actually."

"What do you mean?" I asked.

"I think it's still missing something." He frowned, cued the music, and played it again. "Here."

Leaning forward, I listened intently, tuning in to what my instincts were telling me.

"What if you took it up half a step here, like this," I said, singing softly.

"Again?"

I sang it a few times, and he joined in, our voices blending together effortlessly.

"Yeah, that's it." He smiled as he cued the music to another spot, asking for my opinion. We continued for another few hours, collaborating and singing together.

For the first time in years, I completely lost myself in the moment. I was no longer tangled in the terror of my past or the fear of my future. I allowed the joy of music and being with Hendrix to fully encompass me, and it felt—peaceful.

I relaxed in my chair and smiled, really smiled at him.

He grinned at me as he sank into his chair. "You have a beautiful smile," he said. "I can physically see the change in you when you're lost in the music. You light up."

Heat rushed to my cheeks. Not only with his comment about my smile, but the fact I'd been so easy to read. I self-consciously tugged on my hat and pushed my glasses up farther on my nose.

"Sing it with me," he said, clapping his hands together like it was the best idea he'd ever had in his life.

"*No*," I said, waving my hands in front of me for extra emphasis. "No way. This is your thing, not mine."

"You're amazing, Gemma. You're what this song needs. What I need." He placed his hand on mine.

What did he mean by what he needed? My heart skipped a few

beats and raced full speed ahead while his touch sent shockwaves through me. I was so confused. There was no way that Hendrix was interested in me. He didn't even know what I looked like beneath my oversized, drab-colored clothes, hat, and tinted glasses. He couldn't even tell what color my eyes were.

"Please," he whispered.

Any reservations melted with his plea. Suddenly, I was putty in his hands, stripped of my own will. Shit, how was this happening?

"What if we record here and when I sing live, you can sing with me backstage?"

"What?" I almost giggled at his suggestion. "Live? No, Hendrix. Hell no."

"Hear me out before you go into full panic mode on me. Stages have curtains, and you can stay backstage completely concealed, and we will mic you up. No biggie. No pressure, just your beautiful tone," he said, his eyes pleading with me.

I chewed on my bottom lip as his idea sank into my head. I couldn't commit to singing on stage, but I could with him here in the studio.

"How about one thing at a time? The studio first, and that's all I can agree to right now."

He searched my face, a smile easing across his handsome features.

"Deal."

"Okay," I said, unable to hide my grin.

"Let's book some studio time, then."

I nodded, the impact of my decision weighing on me. So far, he'd been a perfect gentleman, and now I understood the reason for his kindness. He wanted my voice, not really me. And somehow it was a huge relief. If he was genuinely trustworthy, I could give him that.

Hendrix's cell phone rang, the sudden and loud intrusion making me jump. His chuckle filled the room as he squeezed my hand before letting it go and answering his cell.

Snapped out of my daze, I pulled my phone out of my pocket and checked the time. Shit. It was after nine, which meant it would be almost dark. I jumped out of my chair and headed for the door.

"Hang on, man," Hendrix said into his phone. "Gemma, are you leaving? Let me walk you to the dorm."

"Yeah, I gotta run," I replied anxiously. "You don't need to go with me. It's not dark yet." I gave him a small wave and darted out the door.

The second I was out of the studio, my survival instinct kicked in, overruling any logic, and I hauled ass out of the building.

"Gemma!" Hendrix called after me as my feet pounded down the sidewalk. I ignored him and kept running.

9

My arms pumped at my sides as I ran across campus, the semi-darkness of twilight hindering my visibility. I knew it was irrational to bolt out of the studio like a lunatic. I'd need to come up with a good excuse for Hendrix later. Just as I rounded the corner of the building next to my dorm, I slammed into someone. My body reeled backward, and I landed with a hard thud on my ass. A sharp pain stabbed my side as I peered up at the person I'd run into. I froze. The survival instinct I'd relied on for four years had just led me to my personal hell.

Nausea swelled inside my stomach while Brandon kneeled next to me.

"Where you off to in such a hurry, *Gemma*?" he asked, his words like ice in my veins.

"You're not supposed to be near me," I choked out.

"No, you're not supposed to be around me," he said, sneering.

And yet I'd managed to land right in front of Brandon. What the hell? I frantically looked around me, but the only people I saw were far away.

His hands gripped my shoulders, his bony fingers digging into my skin. He jerked me into a standing position, a startled squeal escaping me.

"Screaming won't help you. As you can see, there's no one around." He laughed.

"Why?" I stuttered. "Why would you put a restraining order on me? You know I'm not the one harassing people."

He laughed as he pulled me forward and around the corner to the back of the building, entirely out of sight. My eyes brimmed with tears while he slammed my body against the wall and his hand covered my mouth.

"Maybe you're more stupid than you look," he said, his breath tickling my cheek. "The restraining order is to cover my ass from any lies you might try to spread about me. You know, any bullshit about rape or assault. As far as the cops are concerned, you've harassed me. So after I'm balls deep in your tight pussy, who would ever believe I'd hurt you? Besides, I know you want me pumping in and out of you. And I can't wait to get under those ugly, baggy clothes and see what you're hiding." He shoved his hips into me, his erection pushing against his jeans.

I screamed against his hand, but only muffled cries came out. His hand cupped my breast through my clothes, my nipple betraying me, hardening against his touch.

"Told you. I knew you wanted me." He slid his hand beneath my shirt, his fingers brushing my bare skin. His body pinned me against the side of the building, and my brain scrambled for a way to get him off me. The bricks bit into my skin and broke through the thick wall of fear. My fingers slipped cautiously into the pocket of my jeans, and I pulled out my pepper spray. He was too involved with kissing my neck and grinding against me to even notice.

The next thing I realized, his fingers slipped into my bra and pinched my nipple. I yelped against his hand as the pain shot through me. Without thinking, I stomped on his foot. He automatically stepped away, and I took my chance, pushing him away and gaining several feet between us. I raised my arm, sprayed him in the face, and turned my head away quickly, trying to avoid any of it myself.

"You bitch!" he yelled, clawing at his eyes and walking backward, coughing.

Without hesitation, I bolted around the corner and ran toward the dorm. I'd been so damned close to safety when I'd run into him. My tears stung, the remnants of the spray burning my eyes. I'd been so terrified I'd not realized I'd caught a little bit of it myself.

I took two stairs at a time and hurried into my dorm as the burning intensified. I struggled to see through the tears and find the main floor bathroom. Hugging the wall, I managed to find it and slipped through the door, groping for a sink. The squeak of the faucet handles broke the silence of the bathroom. I splashed cold water on my face. It didn't help. Smacking my hand against the sink, I recalled water didn't help remove pepper spray. My jaw clenched, and the real tears started while the horror sank in, my skin pebbling with goosebumps as I realized how close he'd gotten to me. His hands on my bare skin.

Before I knew it, I was crouched over the toilet, the contents of my dinner rushing out of my stomach. I puked until there was nothing left. My head rested on the toilet seat, and I gasped for air as my body shook with sobs. I wasn't sure how long I sat there, hugging the toilet before it dawned on me; I needed to call Mac. Fumbling for my phone, I attempted to see through the haze and tapped her number on my screen.

"Yo, bestie, you ready to come to the dorm? Where are you at? I'll meet you."

"Mac." My throat cracked with emotion.

"Gemma? Are you okay?" she asked, her tone hiking up in pitch.

"I'm in the bathroom on the main floor of our dorm. I need your help," I whispered.

"Fuck. On my way, but don't hang up. I'm on my way. What happened? No, it's okay, you don't need to tell me yet. I'm running down the stairs now. You don't sound good. You're scaring me. Say something, dammit."

"I can't. You won't shut the hell up."

"Oh my God. You're okay," she said loudly while she released a nervous laugh.

Her voice burst through the bathroom door as it sounded through the phone at the same time.

"I'm hanging up, now." My phone clattered to the tile floor.

Footsteps echoed across the bathroom, then she spotted me.

"You're sick?" She knelt down, inspecting me. "Take that ugly ass hat off for shit's sake."

I remained still as she removed my hat. My head hung down, and I took my glasses off and peered at her.

"What the hell?" she gasped.

From her reaction, I'd caught more of the pepper spray than I'd realized.

"Brandon," I croaked. "Pepper spray."

"Jesus help me. The motherfucker," she spat.

She stood and wrapped her arm underneath one of mine and helped pull me to my feet.

"Hang on, let me guide you to the sink. We need to get to a nurse or—wait. I have baby shampoo. We have to rinse your eyes out. I'll be right back. No, come with me. No, wait. Dammit!"

Although my vision was blurry, I didn't miss Mac starting toward the door and coming back to me multiple times as she tried to decide what to do. If the circumstances hadn't sucked so much, it would have been comical.

"Go, I'll hang out here," I assured her.

"Right!" She hurried out the door.

I'm not sure how fast she could run, but she returned more quickly than I'd anticipated.

"Okay, this won't feel good, but it's all we can do for now."

I nodded and let her help me.

"OH MY GOD. ARE YOU OKAY?" Mac sat next to me on my bed and examined me.

I covered my face with trembling hands and crumpled against the wall.

"Oh, Gemma," Mac whispered and wrapped her arms around me while I cried.

My stomach suddenly cramped, the sour taste of bile rising in my throat. I bolted off the bed and barely made it to the trash can before I dry heaved, Brandon's face sneering at me the second my eyes closed. When I was sure I was finished, I climbed in bed.

"I'm gonna kill that motherfucker," she muttered, stroking my hair, attempting to calm me. "And wait till I tell Hendrix."

I straightened and stared at her with swollen eyes.

"You. Can. Not. Tell. Him. Mac! You don't even know what happened."

"Yeah, I do. The only reason Brandon didn't rape you is because you got away."

I had no response because she was right.

"At least you remembered the pepper spray, though. How are you feeling?"

"Honestly, I don't know," I mumbled embarrassed. "What are the chances I'd run into Brandon? Like what the hell, Mac?"

"Dammit, Gemma. Why were you even alone? Why didn't you call me like we talked about?" Mac asked, bouncing on my bed as she tucked her feet beneath her.

"I panicked. Shit, I was so stupid." I covered my face with my hands as the earlier events played through my mind; Brandon pushing against me, his hot breath on my neck, the sheer terror that ripped through me. "We were at the studio and Hendrix got a call. I'd totally lost track of time, so when I realized it was almost dark, I bolted and ran. We weren't far away—" My words trailed off.

"Wait, back it up a minute," Mac said, pointing at me. "What were you doing at the studio? I thought you were meeting at the library."

A heavy sigh shook my body. "He wanted me to hear a new song he'd recorded."

Mac gawked at me.

"Holy hell," she muttered after I updated her about the music and Hendrix wanting me to sing with him.

"Somehow, and it's just a guess—I don't think hell can be holy."

"Ugh, you're so...so logical sometimes." She rolled her eyes at me, her lower lip jutting out slightly.

"Are you pouting right now?" I asked incredulously, trying not to rub at my burning eyes. "I was attacked tonight, and you're focusing on petty details?"

"No. Shit, maybe. Like what the hell happened tonight?" She tossed her hands up in surrender, staring at me.

My attention remained on her while she processed her emotions. She was trying to digest everything like I was.

"You sang with him on a new song?" she asked, peering at me.

I nodded. I'd gotten used to her jumping from one topic to the next.

"And?" She leaned toward me, waiting for my response.

"It's a beautiful song and he's—musically, he's amazing. I..."

"You what?" she asked eagerly.

"I'm starting to consider him a friend." My neck and ears flushed, remembering the soft touch of his hand and how it was the exact opposite of Brandon's.

"Friend?" Mac burst into laughter. "Gemma, come on now. Hendrix likes you."

"No. You're wrong. It's the music, that's all."

"Oh Gemma, what am I going to do with you?" she asked, smacking herself on the forehead with the palm of her hand.

"You know what? Fine," I said, my nostrils flaring with sudden irritation. Sometimes Mac pushed too much, especially tonight after my encounter with Brandon. I needed to shut this shit down now. "Let's play with this for a minute." I inhaled sharply, suddenly secretly grateful for the distraction.

"Fine," she said, copping an attitude and folding her hands over her chest.

"Facts only, no emotion." I'd found if I set parameters, Mac stayed more focused.

"Agreed." Her eyebrows rose as she waited for me. We were going head to head, determined to prove the other wrong. I would never admit it, but Mac had crossed the friendship line and was more like my sister now.

"Here are the facts, Mac. I wear an ugly hat, oversized clothes, and tinted glasses. He has no idea what I really look like, so there's no way he'd be interested in what he can't see. Guys are visual. They want a gorgeous blonde, boobs, and a curvy ass. Fact, Hendrix is the hottest guy I've ever seen, which means he's used to having girls fall all over him. I won't do that. Fact, he can sing a girl right out of her clothes, but not me. He can't even see past mine. So why in the hell would you think he's interested in me other than for my voice and as a friend?"

Mac's lips pursed together, and her expression grew stern.

"Fact, he's my brother, and I know him better than anyone else. Fact, he's not a shallow douchebag that just wants to get laid. He actually cares about people, and I don't appreciate you insulting him, implying he's only after a quick piece of ass. Fact, he can have any girl he wants, but I saw him grab *your* phone and put his number in it. You're the girl he's singing with and spending studio time with. Do you have any idea how much he pays for studio time? A. Fucking. Lot. So if he wrote this song and wanted you to hear it, it's because you inspired him. There's something about you that's different than anyone else he's ever met, and he likes everything about you. Please don't insult him again to me. He's not shallow." She hopped off my bed, opened the door, walked out, and slammed it behind her.

I was left sitting on my bed with my mouth hanging open. What the hell had just happened? Had I really insulted Hendrix to his sister?

My heart sank as I realized I'd done precisely that. I snuggled into my bed, pulled the covers up over my head, and cried myself to sleep.

THE AROMA of coffee tickled my nose the next morning. Although I rarely drank it, I loved the smell, and it always reminded me of home with Mom and Dad.

Bleary-eyed, I sat up and rubbed my face. A chill shot through me when the memory of Brandon's assault the night before crushed me like a tidal wave, and my pulse rang in my ears. As soon as I saw Mac place a cup of coffee on my desk, a shy smile on her face, my fear immediately subsided.

"How ya doing?"

Unable to form any words yet, I reached for the coffee and took a sip. "Okay, after some sleep." I searched her face to see if she was still angry with me.

"I'm sorry," we said in unison.

I smiled at her while she sat down on her bed and sipped her coffee. "It was a shit day yesterday, and I didn't mean to imply Hendrix was an asshole like Brandon. I just think you're mistaken about him being interested in me for anything more than my singing."

"I know." She twirled her newly braided hair around her finger. "He likes you, Gemma. Some guys want more than a hot body. They want some substance, even the hot ones."

My cheeks warmed. "I don't have a lot of experience with guys, Mac. I—I don't even know how I feel about him except he's been kind to me."

"He's kind because it's who he is. I don't know if it was everything with Kendra or what, but he's—" She stopped mid-sentence.

"Who's Kendra?" I asked, my brows pulling together in confusion.

"Shit. I shouldn't have let it slip." She smacked her hand over her mouth.

I leaned forward on my bed and assessed her. Whatever it was, she'd slipped up big time.

"Kendra?" I asked, impatiently motioning for her to fill me in.

"I can't tell you. I'm sorry! I hate it when someone does that to me. Hendrix would kill me, though. You'll need to talk to him."

She cringed and grabbed her pillow, hugging it tightly to her chest.

"I get it. I guess I'll talk to him about it myself."

My phone buzzed, interrupting our conversation. I picked it up quickly.

"Dad? Everything okay?"

"Yeah, honey. I'm fine, just tired, and I wanted to say hi."

"Guess it has been several weeks since we've really talked," I said, biting my lip, guilt washing over me. I'd had no idea he was ill when I left. I would have never made it to Spokane if he'd told me. "How's mom handling you being sick?"

A soft chuckle answered me. I couldn't help but smile. I missed him. As long as he kept his religious beliefs to himself, I could deal with him and enjoy our conversations.

"You know your mother, fixing everything she can. The house has been cleaned with organic cleaners. Our laundry detergent has been changed, wool balls for dryer sheets, organic food, shampoo, and even shaving cream. She's convinced it'll help."

Tears filled my eyes as I envisioned mom tossing all the products saturated with chemicals into the trash. I glanced at Mac, embarrassed to be on such an emotional overload around her over the last twenty-four hours.

"She's a ball of action when the shit hits the fan, huh?"

He laughed in agreement.

"Well, tell me how things are going. How's Washington? Do you like it? Have you settled in okay?"

"I do like it," I replied. "It's very different. It's beautiful, and the people are nice. My classes are packed and huge, but it's okay. And—my roomie is pretty damned awesome. Her name is Mackenzie. We all call her Mac, though. I'm friends with her and her brother, Hendrix."

"Hendrix?" he asked, without skipping a beat.

I didn't miss the tone in his question.

"We're just friends, Dad. I have some news," I said, changing the topic. "I'm singing a little bit again." I held my breath, waiting for his response. I hadn't even told Ada Lynn yet.

Mac's bed squeaked, and I glanced up at her. She was at full attention and eavesdropping on my conversation. I shot her a dirty look and pointed toward the door. She shook her head.

"You are? I wasn't sure if you would again. I'm—I'm speechless."

"Is it a good speechless?" I asked and motioned for her to get out again, staring at Mac until she got up and left the room. I wouldn't be surprised if she was on the other side of the door with her ear pinned against it.

"You're an incredible singer, and my heart broke when you stopped, but I understood why."

"It's amazing actually, like I've come back home in a way. I'm not sure if it makes any sense."

"It does, and I couldn't be happier. Although I don't agree with how you left, Gemma—I understand. You have your mom's, Ada Lynn's, and my full support in making it work there. In fact, now that I've had some time to think about things, I agree with Ada Lynn. Stay in Washington unless you have no other choice. You deserve to have your own life."

"Dad?" I hiccuped through the tears that had slipped silently down my cheeks. "You know I'm on the first bus to Louisiana if you need me. All you have to do is pick up the phone and say the words."

"I know, honey. I don't think it will come to that. Try not to worry."

"You promise you'll tell me if it does?" I wiped the tears away, my nose growing stuffy.

"I promise. Besides, your mom will call you before I will."

"Okay. I don't want a call when or if it's too late—" I whispered, my voice trailing off.

"Now, you listen to me. I'm not dying. We caught it in time, the doctor's assured me, so no more of this nonsense. Do you understand me?" Dad's tone was firm, like when I was younger. "One more thing, clean up your mouth. It's not appropriate for a young lady to swear."

A giggle escaped me. "Dad, I'm grown, and I've cussed for a long time. I'll try and be more mindful around you, though."

"All right. Well, your mother wants me to go to the lake with her today and get some air, so I need to go. I'll call in a few days, okay?"

"Yeah. Have a great time, and hug mom for me." I tapped the end call button and flopped into my bed.

"You can come in now, Mac." I didn't even have to yell. I knew damned well she was on the other side of the door, hoping to hear something that would give her a clue about my past.

The door creaked open slowly, and she slipped in, wearing a guilty expression.

"Rude," I said.

"Yeah, I know. How can we be best friends and you dating my brother if I don't know about your past?"

One eyebrow shot up in denial. "I am not dating your brother. End of discussion."

She kicked through her pile of clothes on the floor and changed from her plaid pajamas into clean jeans and a red shirt. She might not know it, but she looked amazing in anything she wore. "Are you meeting him after classes?"

"I haven't heard anything from him. I rarely do. We typically just see each other at the library."

"Tell him I said, 'hi'." She grinned, gave me a wave, and slipped out the door.

It was nearly nine, and I needed to hurry if I didn't want to be late for my class.

10

The day crawled by, and I found myself excited about going to the library. I never knew if Hendrix would be there or not. However, I found myself hoping he would be today. The idea of singing with him again sent a shiver of excitement through me.

I'd hurried across the campus and almost skipped through the front doors. I inhaled sharply when I saw him. Today he wasn't across from my usual seat. He was next to it. My hands trembled, and I clutched my books closer to my chest in order to calm them. It made sense he wanted to sit next to me so we could look at the music together. I willed my feet forward, my pulse racing as I approached him.

"Hey." He smiled widely as he stood and pulled my chair out for me. He'd never done that before, and I had a sinking feeling he and Mac had talked. I'd kill her if she'd spilled our conversation to him. Dread taunted me as I realized I would need to tell him about Brandon and the attack anyway.

"Thanks," I said, sitting in the chair he offered.

Butterflies fluttered inside my stomach as his smile softened and he squeezed my hand. Heat traveled up my arm and through my body. His touch excited and terrified me at the same time. Mac's earlier conversation swirled around in my head, and I began to wonder if her words had validity. Maybe she was right, and I did inspire him. Even if it were true, if he knew...I slammed the door shut on the thought and glanced at what he was working on.

His fingers tapped incessantly on the table, his eyes traveling over my face, his expression suddenly growing grim. I frowned. Something was off. A strong suspicion nudged me.

"Mac told you about Brandon, didn't she?" I released his hand.

He hesitated briefly. "Yes, but don't be upset with her. Gemma, her heart was in the right place. She was scared. She is scared."

"I know," I said, my voice hovering above a whisper. My gaze dropped to the floor, my hands wringing together in my lap. I didn't want to talk about this. The entire situation with Brandon just needed to disappear, but I knew better.

"Gemma, he's dangerous," he whispered fiercely. He glanced at the floor for a moment, his hand clenching into a tight fist on the table. His eyes traveled up again, his stare intense. "I kicked myself all damn day for not walking you to the dorm last night. It won't happen again, so I don't want you to worry about it. I'm here..." he said, his words trailing off. "But I have to be honest with you. I was so fucking pissed I looked for Brandon. I searched for him, ready to pound my fists into his face. The son of a bitch is lucky I never found him."

A chill shot through me, flickers of the attack bombarding my thoughts again.

"You did?"

Hendrix took a deep breath and gently rubbed my arms with his hands, reassuring me it was okay.

"I'll be waiting for him. This isn't over. I want to see your eyes, so I can make sure you're okay, too. This whole damned thing is messed up." Anger flickered across his face.

"Mac told you about the pepper spray?" I asked, panicked.

His hands moved toward me slowly.

"No! I'm fine." I cringed and pulled away quickly, my outburst drawing unwanted attention from other people in the library, but no way would I allow him to see me without my glasses. "Mac helped last night, but thanks."

He nodded, a twinge of hurt in his expression. "I met with Mac earlier and gave her another pepper spray. One for you and one for her."

"Thank you," I said softly. Hendrix must have sensed I was at capacity with the conversation and let it go for the time being.

"How's your Dad?" he asked.

"Okay. I talked to him again this morning. He sounds exhausted. From what I've heard, it's pretty normal, though. He assured me again he was fine, and I didn't need to come home. So I guess you're stuck with me unless something changes."

"Good. I just found you; you can't leave me."

My eyes grew wide at his words.

"Yeah, but you're just interested in me for my singing voice," I blurted.

"What?" he asked, confused. "Why would you say that?"

"Because it's true?" My pitch climbed an octave, revealing the nerves I was trying so hard to hide.

Before I realized it, Hendrix leaned forward and brushed his lips against mine. His fingers trailed down my face gently as he smiled and sank back into his chair.

"You remember the day you asked me what I wanted from you?"

I nodded, speechless.

"Over the last few months of seeing you every day, sitting across from you, and the tiny pieces you've allowed me to see...I want more, Gemma." He paused, studying me for a reaction. "Go out with me."

My breath hitched in my throat, and I struggled for a response.

"Time," I whispered. "I need some more time."

Hendrix's jaw tightened briefly, and then he recovered.

"Okay, but I'm not going to stop holding your hand," he said, grinning.

"I'm okay with that," I replied shyly. My head throbbed with fear and excitement. "What do you have?" I nodded toward the papers in front of him, deliberately changing the direction of our conversation.

"I made adjustments and worked in some additional places for you specifically."

"You did?" I was unable to hide my surprise.

"Yeah, and I have some time in the studio if you want to go?"

"Oh my God, that was so much fun!" My shoulders tensed the moment the words left my mouth, recalling the encounter with Brandon.

"What's the matter?"

"I'm fine," I muttered, refusing to allow Brandon to stop me from enjoying the music. "Let's go." Hendrix took my hand and led the way out of the library, completely ignoring the stares focused on us.

The crisp fall air greeted us, and Hendrix held the door open for me. Once outside, he took both my hands in his and placed a soft kiss on each of my palms. My heart skidded to a stop, my world spinning as he smiled and began walking toward the studio again.

"Mac has a big mouth," I said, falling into place next to him.

He smiled and looked down at me. "You have no idea."

"Yeah, speaking of…" I cleared my throat, working up the nerve to ask him. "Who is Kendra?"

Hendrix stopped mid-step, his face clouding with so many emotions I couldn't get a read on what he was thinking.

He dropped my hand and ran his across his jawline.

"I'm not mad at her for bringing Kendra up. It's a shitty thing all the way around." His stare fell to the grass, and he kicked at the ground. "Tell you what. When you go out with me, I'll tell you about Kendra. Like you, I need some time before I open that box. Deal?"

His attention traveled up to me, his eyes questioning. I tilted my head as I considered his offer. Obviously this Kendra girl meant something significant to him, or he wouldn't have reacted so strongly. I figured if he was patient with me, I could show him the same courtesy. Besides, if I was honest with myself, I wasn't sure I wanted to know who she was. I didn't think learning about an ex would be easy, and I was in no hurry to find out. At the same time, I needed to understand him. I wanted him to be a part of my life.

"Deal," I said. "Until then, we can hang onto our secrets."

He nodded, intertwined his fingers through mine, and we strolled toward the studio.

Goosebumps prickled down my arms as I realized I'd agreed to go out with him. Did he really not care what I looked like under my frumpy clothes and hat? Maybe Hendrix was different, and he was interested in me for who I was. Fear bloomed to life inside me, but I shoved it down.

I thought back to my conversation with Mac last night. I believed everything she told me about Hendrix. Whether she knew it or not, she'd become my safety net where he was concerned. She knew and trusted him and apparently ran to him when she felt scared, and some part of me was able to find some solace in that. If I trusted Mac, I could learn to trust Hendrix one step at a time. I mindlessly reached up and touched my mouth where his lips had been. Heat traveled through me, and I immediately squelched any desire for him. Not until I knew for sure what his intentions were. Even then, my past might have fucked me up so bad I wouldn't be able to move on.

"Here we go," Hendrix said, opening the door for me and breaking through my thoughts. Oddly enough, he had allowed me my silence. It was almost as though he was content just being next to me and holding my hand. This entire situation was boggling.

"Thanks." I gave him a small smile as I entered the building.

"You're thinking pretty hard over there," he teased as he guided me toward the studio.

"Processing. I mean, I tend to take situations and analyze them from multiple angles and try and break things down so they make sense."

"What doesn't make sense?" Hendrix looked at me curiously, waiting for an answer.

"Um, this," I said, raising our still linked hands. "It's almost like there's an us?" My voice squeaked with the question, my heart pounding against my chest.

"You don't have to question it, Gemma," he replied softly. "I do like you. Otherwise I wouldn't have asked you out. And as I said earlier, take your time, and when you're ready, we'll go somewhere nice, then I'll tell you about Kendra. For now, we are just us. Two people who like each other, sing together, and have some fun. That's it. Let's keep it simple and let the rest fall into place."

I gawked at his words. "You're okay with it being like this?" I asked, skepticism lacing my words.

"Why wouldn't I be?"

I shrugged, unwilling to answer him. A heavy silence hung in the air between us, our eyes locked as though we were searching inside of each other for the answers we needed in order to take the next step.

"You ready?" he asked, pulling out a chair at the mixing console for me.

"Yeah, I'm eager to hear everything." I bounced in my chair with excitement.

He flipped some switches, and suddenly music floated through the air, surrounding us. His deep voice, with its sensual tone, melted me and caused tingles throughout my entire body. I had to will myself not to turn into a blob of jelly. Even though it made me weak, my heart felt stronger—alive. Every emotion possible flooded through me as the song ended.

"So in the hook, maybe you could take it up an octave?" His eyebrows raised in question.

I nodded. "Can I hear that part?" I scooted forward on the edge of my seat, ready to work.

For the next few hours, we broke down the music, layered in my parts, and recorded. As much as I'd intended to keep Hendrix at arm's length, he'd not only slipped behind my walls, but he was slowly working his way into my heart. Regardless of how much I'd tried to hide it from myself, the fact that he wrote music and sang was the main thing that lured me toward him. It was almost as though he was the pied piper, and I followed along in a daze. Mac did her part to put my mind at ease, with her incessant talk about what a great guy he was and how much she trusted him, whenever I had the urge to bolt out the door.

"So what do you think?" he asked after playing the new version all the way through. "Are you willing to perform it live?" His lips twitched in a small smile.

I sank into my chair, dread ripping through me at the mere idea. "Don't push your luck."

"Dammit, I figured it was worth a try." He grinned and winked at me.

My eyes narrowed as an idea formed in my head. "How much is it worth to you?"

His eyebrows shot up. "Are we bartering?"

"Maybe. I don't want to push too hard, though. If you want me to perform live, I'll do it on two conditions."

"Yeah? And what are those?" He reached for my hand, his thumb gently tracing circles along the back of it.

"Ah, no cheating," I tsked, grinning and removing my hand from his.

A low chuckle filled the room while he shifted in his seat and propped his long legs up on another chair.

"Give it to me." He motioned for me to continue.

"First, I'll sing with you only behind the curtain. Second, I want to know about Kendra." My lips pursed as his face fell. If anyone understood secrets, I did, and I'd just cornered him. What in the hell had I been thinking? It was never okay for my curiosity to overrule my manners. "Shit, I'm sorry. I shouldn't have said that. It was dumb, forget it." Apparently spending time with Hendrix and writing music left me stupid.

I stood, my shoulders sagging, my focus on the beige carpeted floor.

"Sit."

My head snapped up, and I frowned. "No, Hendrix, you don't have to say anything."

"Sit," he said firmly, pointing toward my chair.

I swallowed hard as I slid into my seat. Did I really want to learn about his ex? My heart told me that I wasn't prepared to hear about someone he had loved.

"Deal. You sing with me on this song. I don't care if you're on stage or behind the curtain, as long as I hear your voice with mine."

My head throbbed. What had I agreed to? And for what? Information that would only make me feel more insecure than I already did. I'd officially lost my fucking mind.

Hendrix's expression grew serious, and he leaned forward slowly, the chair creaking with his movement.

"After Dad's third marriage—Well, I guess I need to back up a little bit. You already know Mac's mom and my dad were married. It was his second. And honestly, I felt bad for Janice. Dad worked constantly, and when he did come home, his breath reeked of alcohol. They yelled at each other all the time, which left Mac and I hiding in one of our bedrooms together. Sometimes we'd talk about stupid shit, and sometimes we'd make up games—anything to keep our minds off the arguments. One day, I came home from school, and all of their stuff was gone. Mac's room was empty. Janice had reached her limit and they'd left. Dad's drinking got worse, but he was still fully functioning most of the time." Hendrix paused, laced his fingers together, and ran his hands over his hair. "It was bad enough I'd lost Mac, but Janice had been a mom to me, too. My world fell apart, and a year or so later, he married Marion. She got pregnant, and they had a daughter."

My mouth gaped slightly. This wasn't what I'd expected. Tension tightened my shoulders as I waited for him to continue.

"Her name was Kendra," he whispered.

At the moment he spoke her name, my heart shattered. Was. Past tense. I blinked the tears away as I silently cursed at myself for pushing the topic.

"After a few years, the marriage fell apart, and Dad lost his law practice. He sat at home every day and drank until he passed out. Even though he wasn't very attentive, he had visitation with Kendra, and she came over every other weekend. She was four, and I was thirteen at the time."

Hendrix rubbed his palms along his jeans, head bowed, his hair falling around his face. I wanted to reach out and wrap him up in my arms. I hadn't even heard the entire story yet, but I had a guess, and my heart ached for him.

"One afternoon, Marion was called into work, and she asked if Dad and I could come over to help with Kendra. Dad started drinking as soon as we got there, he refused to listen to me, and he eventually passed out. I'd turned on some cartoons for Kendra and told her to stay put while I made dinner. I hurried like I always did when she was around. She was a good kid, but she still got into stuff."

He cleared his throat. "When I was finished, I went to check on her, but she wasn't in front of the TV where I'd left her. The front door was wide open. She'd gone outside and was playing with her ball in the front yard. I ran outside just as the ball rolled into the street." Hendrix swallowed hard, and my body shook with dread at what he was about to say. Somehow, he managed to choke out his next words. "She never saw it coming, and the doctors said she never felt a thing." He squeezed his eyes closed, tears hanging on his long, dark lashes. "A car came flying down the hill. Kendra never had a chance," he said, struggling with his words.

My hand flew up to cover my mouth. "You saw it all?" Tears slipped down my cheeks. "Hendrix," I whispered. "I'm so sorry. I would have never asked," I said softly, my words thick with shame for making a deal with him for this information.

"After everything, I moved in with Mac and Janice. They helped me get my shit together and into music. Janice treated me like her own son, and Mac and I were inseparable. They are my real family."

I wiped the tears away and inhaled a shaky breath. "I'm so sorry. I had no idea. I thought Kendra was an ex-girlfriend. It makes sense now, why you and Mac are so close."

Hendrix nodded, took a deep breath, standing slowly. "The accident haunts me every day. I should have never left her, how I failed her, and how fast that goddamned car was going. They never stopped." His hands fisted while the pain etched across his face. "Her little body flew up and over the hood. They. Never. Fucking. Stopped," he said, his words sharp with anger. He rubbed his palms over his cheeks and stared at the ceiling before returning his gaze to mine.

I stopped breathing and watched helplessly as he relived the most horrifying minutes of his life. My attention never left him as I stood, my heart broken for him, and the young man who saw his sister die. I shut my eyes against the racing thoughts, realizing how much he blamed himself for what happened.

"I'm sorry," he said breathlessly.

My eyelids fluttered open in time to see him step toward me. He rested his hands gently on my shoulders and placed his warm lips on mine.

Shock sparked through me and quickly transformed into a delicious warmth I'd never experienced before. His soft mouth remained on mine, and I slowly lifted my hand and threaded my fingers through his hair. Inwardly I sighed. This was my first real kiss. And although my emotions were running amuck, I sank into him, and for a second, I allowed myself to be happy.

He stepped back, worry lines creasing his forehead while he studied me.

"Sorry. I couldn't wait." His shoulders tensed as he waited for me to say something. Instead, I stood still and stared at him. "I shouldn't have done that without asking first. I guess the music, being alone with you, and Kendra—I just lost it."

"Don't. Don't apologize," I said quietly. "I'm the one who should be apologizing for being an insensitive brat."

"You didn't know. It's not something I talk about, so if you have any questions, you should ask them now." He leaned against the console and folded his arms across his chest, his bicep muscles bulging against his sleeves. I knew this had to be beyond difficult for him. And the fact he trusted me with this part of himself blew my mind a little.

I nodded. "Where was your mom?" I sat back down, never taking my attention off him.

"She left Dad, but she also left me. I haven't seen her since I was two. In fact, I don't even know where she is or what she looks like now. I have pictures of her from before I was born, nothing else. Eventually, you give up hope of someone ever coming home, ya know? So I finally packed her belongings. Janice became my mom after that, and it stayed that way."

"Oh," I whispered. What in the world was I supposed to say about any of it?

"I realize it's a lot to take in. It still screws me up."

"Yeah, I think some things change you for life, and bits and pieces of it linger in the corners of your mind, haunting you no matter what you do to move on." I tugged on the side of my hat.

"Sounds like you know something about that," he said, shoving his hands in his jean pockets.

"Unfortunately, yes—" My voice trailed off as the memories came rushing back. "Why did you tell me all of this, Hendrix? You didn't have to. Ever." I tilted my head, carefully watching emotions play out on his face, waiting for his answer.

"Well, I want you to sing with me, but more than that, Gemma, I want you to trust me. In order for you to really do that, I have to show you everything. Not just the good parts, or only the pieces I think you should see. You need to see my scars, too. If you really know who I am, as a man, then maybe—" He paused, hope flickering in his expression.

"Maybe?" I asked softly.

"Maybe we can both stop being afraid to love someone. I'm as afraid as you are to take a chance, but I can't stay away, Gemma. I've been waiting for someone like you for a very long time."

"Hendrix," I whispered, unsure of what to say. No one had ever said anything like that to me before. A ball of emotions exploded inside my chest, and I shoved them aside until I had more time to process what he'd just said.

"All I ask is that you think about it. The more time I spend with you, the harder I'm falling, and I needed to tell you. I don't expect anything to change or for you to even feel the same. Just please don't stop singing with me and hanging out. You're the best part of my day."

I nodded. "Okay, I can at least give you that, hanging out and singing." My heart split me in two. One part of me wanted to hug and kiss him, and the other part of me wanted to run right back to Louisiana and pretend none of this was happening. Regardless, I was afraid it was too late. He'd reached me in a way I'd never thought was possible, and even then, I wasn't sure if I could fully accept what he was offering.

"It's late, and I need to go back to the dorm." I knew the moment I said it he'd see right through me, but if I stayed any longer, I would do something stupid. I would break down and kiss him. Between him trusting me enough to share Kendra's story and admitting he cared about me, I was on emotional overload. Again. My cheeks flushed, and I bit my lip where his had been minutes before.

"At least we got some music written. And now you're singing with me live, so this is a good thing." A smile cracked through his sadness as he stood and held his hand out to mine.

"Mm, I set myself up for that one. Now I'm going to sing live in front of a ton of people." I wrinkled my nose. "But we won't be singing it for a while, right?"

"We still have some things to work out, so yeah, you have a bit of time."

I nodded.

Neither one of us found it necessary to talk as he walked me to the dorm. My mind churned through everything he'd shared with me. And the kiss. I groaned inwardly. Nineteen and never been kissed —until tonight.

We stopped in front of the steps that led to the front door of my building. Although I needed to sift through everything, for the first time, I didn't want him to leave.

I turned toward Hendrix as he moved closer, only mere inches between us.

"Can I kiss you again?" His voice was deep and husky, making me tremble with...so many feelings.

I nodded, unable to find any words.

My eyelids fluttered closed as his lips brushed gently against mine, his hand stroking my face. I struggled to keep my feet planted and not stumble backward or drop to the ground from my knees turning into jelly.

He pressed his mouth to mine again, then allowed some space between us.

"I realize it was a lot, but I did have a good time tonight," he said. "My favorite part was kissing you, though." He flashed me his damned panty-dropping smile, and for the first time, I wondered if my panties might drop next.

Heat permeated my cheeks, and I thanked God it was dark, and maybe he wouldn't be able to tell how much he'd affected me.

"Mine too," I whispered.

Hendrix kissed me one more time before he gave my hand a gentle squeeze and slipped away. Lightheaded, I strolled into my dorm. Unable to hide my smile, my hand touched my lips. His mouth had been so soft, gentle. He hadn't rushed anything, just a sweet lingering kiss. Perfection.

11

"Oh my God," Mac's voice echoed through the hall. "You're going to be my sister-in-law!"

She bounded toward me and hugged me until I couldn't breathe.

"Mac!" I scolded and pushed her away. "What are you doing down here?"

"I'm so excited. How was it? I told you he liked you, but no, you didn't believe me. Oh my God, this is going to be so awesome!" She bounced up and down on her tiptoes, her smile nearly splitting her pretty face.

"He told me about Kendra," I said.

Mac's mouth gaped open, and she stopped bouncing. "Shit."

"Yeah, it was intense, and I'm trying to wrap my head around it."

"So double whammy tonight," she said, looping her hand through my arm as we strolled past a few other girls and made our way up the stairs to our room.

"Double?" I asked, confused.

"Yeah, first Hendrix told you about Kendra, and then he kissed you," she responded, wiggling her eyebrows at me.

"Oh no, it was a triple whammy night, Mac." I sighed as we opened our door and both plunked down on my bed.

"If you cleaned your side of the room and made your bed on occasion, we would sit on your side, too," I mentioned, pointing to the mess of junk scattered everywhere.

"I like yours better. Besides, I don't have to keep mine clean since you take care of yours. I know there's always a place to sit." She beamed at me.

Removing my hat and glasses, I rolled my eyes at her. "So glad I could help," I said with a hint of snark.

"Now tell me what else happened, sis."

My brows knitted at the reference. "Slow your roll, Mac. One kiss does not make me your sister-in-law. Besides, you might be planning my funeral soon."

"What?" Mac gasped. "Why would you say such a shitty thing?"

"Because..." I chewed my bottom lip as I struggled for the words. "Because I bribed Hendrix, and I'm pretty sure I'm going to hell now."

"Dramatic much?" Mac asked, tapping her fingers on her leg. "Get to the point."

"Dammit, I was having fun screwing with you." I was unable to hide my smile. "However, I might be somewhat serious about the funeral. Ugh, I can't believe what I did." I settled against the wall and closed my eyes.

"Spit. It. Out," Mac demanded impatiently.

"I agreed to sing live with Hendrix and the band," I blurted in one breath.

To my surprise, Mac was speechless, but it didn't last long.

"I'm sorry, you did what?" She shifted and sat on her knees, facing me. "How in shit's name did he get you to agree to that?"

"I know, right?" My nose wrinkled as I glanced at her. "We kind of bribed each other. Well, wait, let me start at the beginning. He asked me out first, then I asked about Kendra."

"Oh. My. God. You're going out with my brother!" She bounced on the bed, squealing.

"Mac! Wait, there's more."

She peered at me with one eye. "More?"

"Do you want the whole story or not?"

"Yeah," she said, settling down again.

"When Hendrix asked me out, I said I needed more time. When I asked him about Kendra, he said he needed more time as well. But he would tell me about her when I went out with him. I thought Kendra was an ex, though. I was super curious, so...I pushed him into talking about her. I told him if he shared with me about Kendra right then, I'd sing with him on the song we're working on—behind the curtain, but not on the stage."

Mac gasped. "You agreed to sing in front of people? Holy shit, does this get any better? I mean, Hendrix does realize what a major deal this is, right?"

I frowned at her. "Uh, yeah?"

"No, I mean of course he does, but you're the shyest person I've ever known. Not to mention you don't like people from what I can tell, and you hide yourself. Am I the only person who knows what you look like without the hat and glasses?" Her voice softened with the last question.

I hesitated. "Yeah," I whispered. "Hendrix hasn't ever seen me without them."

"Oh, Gemma." Mac reached for my hand. "Don't you understand?"

I stared at her, our gazes locked while I waited for her to explain. "He likes you for you. Not what you wear or what you look like. Gemma, he sees your heart, who you are beyond everything else. Like I do."

My chin quivered, and my eyes brimmed with tears. Did I dare to hope he was the real thing? That maybe, just maybe, there was a chance that I could pick up enough of the pieces left of my shattered life and live again.

"Don't take my word for it, though. Go out with him."

"I have taken your word for it. It's the only reason I've even been alone with him, much less let him hold my hand or kiss me." I reached up and touched my lips, my attention dropping to the floor, my cheeks flushing with the memory.

"Wait, how did I not guess this before? Gemma, was Hendrix your first kiss?"

I shot her an angry glance as I jumped off the bed and turned my back on her. "I'm not discussing this with you or anyone else," I huffed. Dammit, how had I been so transparent with her? I missed my hat and glasses already.

"Wait, don't be mad. There's no judgment. None. I just, I mean, best friends talk about guys, dates, and clothes." Mac got up from my bed and turned me around to look at her. "Now that I think about it, it makes sense. You're shy and don't let anyone get close to you. Well, other than me. But it's beside the point. You've never had a boyfriend?" she asked, her question gentle and compassionate.

"Fine. No, Mac, I haven't. Hendrix was my first. Like the first guy to hold my hand, the first guy to ask me out, and the first guy to kiss me. Happy?" I stomped off toward my bed and flopped down on the side of it.

"Thank you."

"For what?" I picked at my nails, frustration rising inside me.

"For trusting me."

My head snapped up. She'd somehow turned into my best friend, and even though she blurted shit out sometimes unintentionally, I trusted her.

"Do *not* share this with Hendrix. I mean it, Mac. I will never speak to you again. This is for me to share with him."

"I understand. I won't say a word, not even in a blubbering idiot moment. I promise." She sat down next to me. "I've only had one boyfriend if it makes you feel any better."

"Really?" I asked, shocked. "You're so pretty, funny, and so nice. I don't understand."

"Have you met me?" She giggled.

I couldn't hide my smile.

"Not everyone loves my ball of energy. And, oh my God, can I be a first date mess."

A giggle burst out of me as I imagined her eating dinner and never shutting up, the poor guy on the other side of the table cringing and checking his watch.

"What was his name?"

Mac hesitated briefly. "Asher. We were together for over two years in high school. He was my first everything, too. So I understand the nerves, fear, excitement, and overthinking everything, Gemma. I swear to you, you're in good hands with Hendrix."

"Promise?" I asked, fear threading through me.

"You have my word that if he hurts you, I'll make sure he can never have children," she said, placing her fisted hands on her hips.

I barked out a laugh. "Let's not go to extremes but thank you. Since you know him so well, I do feel safer." I paused, biting my thumbnail. "I think I might want to go out with him, but I'm terrified, Mac. I'm so fucking terrified." Tears slipped down my cheeks at the thought of being in public with him, but alone at the same time. He'd pick me up and bring me back to the dorm, plus we would have time alone in the Uber. Nausea turned my stomach as my mind raced with the possibilities. At least with an Uber we would have a driver, and nothing could go wrong, right?

"Hey, wow. That was intense for a minute. Where'd you go?" She waved her hand in front of my face.

I blinked away the tears, my head hanging down while I took a deep breath.

"Whatever happened in the past, it's not Hendrix."

Mac and I sat silently, both knowing what I couldn't verbalize.

"I'm proud of you for trying," she said and reached for my hand.

I nodded and attempted to regain my composure. "How am I going to do this?" I asked, looking at her.

"Well, let's make an exit plan for your date. We will go over every detail of what to do if you suddenly feel unsafe. Okay? So, by the time you walk out of here, you'll feel great about everything. We can do this."

"Yeah? You'd do that for me?"

"Hell yeah, bestie!" She yelled and engulfed me in a bear hug.

I laughed through my tears and returned her hug.

For the next few hours, Mac and I planned my first date with Hendrix—every possible scenario and escape route. By the time we finished, we were both exhausted and a little punch drunk.

"Are you doing better now?" Mac asked, stifling a yawn and crawling into her bed.

"I think so. I feel like I'm planning a special ops mission instead of a date," I said, laughing. "Thank you for all the help."

"Please, if anyone is going to be with my brother, I'd rather it be you. There are so many girls after him, ugh, it's disgusting. Just because he's good looking and can sing, every female goes into spontaneous heat when they see him. You're different, though. You don't want anything from him, and it was all so innocent. I mean, how you fell for him."

"What?" I choked. "I have not fallen for him."

"Girl, please, keep lying to yourself. We just sat here for two hours planning your first date with him. A date that he doesn't even know about. It's after two in the morning. You've never stayed up this late with me."

My lips pursed as I realized she was right. "Sorry," I muttered. "I'm a bit rattled."

"Don't be. Besides, he doesn't know you're going out with him yet, so there's no need to stress about it."

"Yeah, guess you're right. You and I are the only two who know anything, right? I told him I needed more time, which means I can take however long I need."

"Nice try, Gemma, but you'll just keep putting it off, though. Tomorrow. Tomorrow, you'll tell Hendrix you're going out with him. We've figured everything out, including back up plans. You've got this. And if you find yourself scared on the date, just start singing, he'll join in, and everything else will fade into the background."

"You're probably right. Nothing seems to matter when the music starts."

"Tomorrow then?" she asked, staring at me expectantly.

"Sure."

"You gotta say it. You don't get to be all ho-hum and brush me off." Mac pointed at me for emphasis.

"Fine. Mac, I'll tell Hendrix that I'll go out with him on a date tomorrow if I see him."

"Ha! You're so full of shit. You'll see him," she said, bouncing on her bed.

I laughed. "I wondered if you would catch that."

"Caught. Now, I'm glad we have this settled. My ass is tired."

"Mine too."

Feeling somewhat pacified, I slipped under my covers and fell into a fitful sleep.

12

The rain came down in a windy torrent as I sprinted from my dorm to my first class. My hat clung to my head, soaked with water. I slipped into the somewhat crowded bathroom and attempted to dry off before I went to class. Thunder rumbled through the sky while I grabbed some paper towels and blotted the drops from my skin.

Slipping off my glasses, I wiped them off and put them back on before anyone else noticed. I cursed as lightning flashed through the sky, and the rain pelted against the bathroom windows.

I wondered if it would stop by the time I was finished with classes and on my way to the library. Even though things had shifted with Hendrix and we'd grown closer, we still met there every day. Maybe he didn't want to assume I'd want to go to the studio. Strangely enough, I felt safer there with him. Maybe it was because people stared at us in the library. I'd caught the librarian watching us multiple times, especially since Hendrix no longer sat across the table from me, but next to me, holding my hand on top of the table for everyone to see. He didn't seem to care or even acknowledge the looks, and I liked him even more for it. What he saw in me was a mystery. My heart knew better, but my mind still had me fearful he'd turn into another Brandon.

Humming to myself, I opened the library door and smiled when I saw Hendrix. My heart fluttered but for a different reason now. I almost laughed out loud at how mad he made me when he first sat at my table. Now I was glad he didn't leave.

Mac's promise rang through my mind as I pulled out a chair and sat next to him, leaving my backpack on my shoulder in case we were headed to the studio.

"Hi," he said, his eyes lighting up with his smile. He leaned over and kissed me on my cheek.

A giggle erupted from a few tables away, and I shot the girls a dirty look as they pointed at me and snickered.

"Ignore them," he whispered. "We have music to write and don't have time for petty bullshit."

A smile crept across my face. "Okay, but it's pouring outside. We'll be drenched if we try to make it to the studio."

"I parked right outside."

"What?" I asked, taken aback. "You have a car?"

"I do," he responded as he took my hand in his.

"Why haven't you ever mentioned it before?" I eyed him questioningly as I waited for his answer.

"I like to walk on campus until it turns too cold or it's raining."

"Oh." My forehead creased as I processed everything. This meant no Uber, just Hendrix and me in the car. Panic threatened me, but then my brain went in another direction, and my alarm stepped up a notch, my ears ringing for a minute.

"Hey, what's wrong?" Hendrix asked.

My breaths came in short bursts as he lifted my chin up toward him.

"You're okay, Gemma," he whispered. "You're safe with me, right now, at this moment. You're okay. Nothing and no one can hurt you. Listen to my voice. Do you hear me?"

I nodded, staring at him while his thumb stroked my cheek.

"Take a deep breath for me," he said in a soft tone.

I did as he asked, my body finally relaxing a little. "I'm sorry." I grabbed his hand and squeezed it. "I'm so sorry, Hendrix."

"Let's get you out of here." He stood and pulled me to my feet. "I think some air will do us both good. It stinks in here anyway," he said, shooting the girls a nasty glare.

He squeezed my hand and led me outside. The chill in the air and the rain broke through my panic, and I stood next to the door and inhaled deeply.

"How did you know this would help?" I asked as we tucked ourselves under the small overhang and hugged the wall. I peered up at him.

"I went to a lot of counseling, and my therapist recommended meditation classes after I lost Kendra."

I nodded. He didn't need to say anything else. Hendrix obviously recognized my panic attacks. He'd seen the one I'd had my first day on campus.

"Do you trust me?" he asked, peering down at me.

My gaze shifted away from him. What a shitty question to ask me right now.

"Let me ask a different way. Can you, right now, trust me for a little bit?"

I hesitated briefly and nodded. "Yeah. I can do that."

"Good, come on."

Hendrix bolted out into the pouring rain, and I ran after him. Our shoes splashed through puddles on the sidewalk as we ran toward the parking lot. A beep beep sounded as he darted toward a newer maroon Toyota Camry, and he opened the passenger's door.

"Get in," he yelled as he ran around and slipped into the driver's side.

I didn't hesitate and slid into the leather seat. Soaking wet, I stuffed my backpack next to my feet on the floorboard. I was so focused on all of the rain, I didn't realize we were alone in his car.

He reached behind him and pulled a couple of towels out of the backseat. "Here ya go," he said, handing me one and running the other over his hair.

I attempted to dry off the best I could, turning away from him to remove my glasses, clean them, and slip them back into place before I faced him again.

He silently looked at me, a hint of sadness in his eyes. My heart sank. Hendrix had been nothing but kind to me, and he didn't even know the color of my eyes. How screwed up was that? I chewed my bottom lip as a mix of fear and sadness swirled inside me. I inhaled sharply.

"Yes," I said, my voice barely above a whisper.

"Yes?" he asked, strands of his wet hair sticking to his jawline.

I mentally thanked God for my hat, or I'd look like a drowned redheaded rat.

"Yes, I'll go out with you."

His brow arched, and he gave me his charming smile. My heart jumped. He was sincerely happy.

"Before we go any further, I need something first," I added.

"Okay, whatever you want," he said, still grinning.

"I need you to take me here." I fumbled around in my backpack and pulled out a sheet of paper and a pen, scribbling down an address and handing it to him.

His expression filled with a deep frown, and I sank into the seat. He wasn't going to do it.

"Seattle?"

I nodded.

"If I take you, will you explain it to me? I mean, why you need to go?"

"Yes."

"You're okay being in the car alone with me for a day?"

I swallowed hard. I'd have to be. What other choice did I have?

"Yes."

He peered out of the car window, the fat drops of rain splattering against the windshield.

"If I do this, are we planning a date when we get back? Like a real date, Gemma, not studio or library time, but a going out to a nice dinner kind of date."

"Yes," I answered, knowing we probably wouldn't make it that far. I had to do this, and I couldn't do it without him. It was time.

"Tomorrow is Friday, does it work for you?"

I paused, mentally reviewing my schedule and the information I'd researched. "Yeah, it works."

"I'll meet you at seven tomorrow morning in front of your dorm. Let's get this over with, whatever it is so that we can move forward."

"Okay, thank you." We'd arrive around twelve-thirty. The timing would be perfect. My head hung down while I worked to regain my composure. He'd agreed. I never thought he would. Shit, what was I about to do?

He reached over and took my hand. "Is your playlist ready? It's a four-and-a-half-hour drive one way."

"Yeah, I Googled the trip already. I'll give you some gas money, too," I said, glancing at him and then to our joined hands.

"Don't worry about the gas. I'm just happy to spend the time with you."

I fell silent. This trip could be the end of us before we even really began. Sadness filled me with the idea.

"Kiss me," I said before I talked myself out of everything.

Hendrix didn't hesitate. Reaching over, he tilted my chin up and brushed his lips softly against mine. My hand threaded through his wet hair as I responded. I inhaled him, every beautiful thing about him, and allowed myself to get lost in the moment, lost in him. For a fleeting second, I took the opportunity to believe someone might really care about me, not because they wanted something in return.

Our lips parted slightly, and his tongue tentatively caressed mine. I moaned into his mouth as our kiss deepened. Heat shot through me, my body suddenly awakening. I needed air, but the only air I wanted was his. I never wanted to let him go, and for the first time in my life, I wanted more. I wanted to experience all my firsts with him.

I gasped and pulled away. The unwanted flush traveled through my cheeks and down my neck while I struggled to regain my composure. Was it normal to feel so lightheaded after a kiss?

"Shit," Hendrix said, placing his forehead and hands on his steering wheel.

"Did I do something wrong?" I asked, alarmed.

He turned his head to look at me. "No," he said. "You did every-thing right," he whispered and shifted in his seat.

"Okay," I muttered, embarrassed as I realized his body had reacted to our kiss. "Can we pass on the studio tonight? I guess I'd better get back to the dorm. We have a long day ahead of us tomorrow."

"Yeah, we do." He hesitated briefly. "Gemma?"

"Yeah?" I asked, tilting my head.

"Can we kiss like that again?"

I giggled. "Yeah, I'd love it."

"Good, because I'm pretty sure that kiss was song worthy."

"Oh my God," I said, cringing and sinking into my seat, my cheeks flaming with embarrassment as he chuckled and started the car.

We drove in silence, grins on both of our faces, his hand holding mine tightly until we reached my dorm.

"You don't need to walk me to the door, maybe just watch me until I step inside?"

"Don't be silly. I'm already wet."

He turned off the car, ran around to my side, and opened the door for me. We ran through the rain, hand in hand, laughing.

"Your hat is soaked," he said as we stopped in front of the entrance to the building.

"Yup," I said, smiling up at him. "Thank you."

"I'll text you in the morning when I'm here, okay?"

"Sounds good."

A few girls passed us, and Hendrix moved me away from the front door to allow them in. Suddenly, his mouth was on mine, and he was pulling me into his body. I gasped, feeling him against me. Every other time he'd kissed me, there'd been space between us. Not this time. His hand traveled slowly up my back, causing me to arch into him. Butterflies swirled inside my stomach while my brain registered every single inch of him through his jeans.

I quickly pulled away, shaking. His face fell as he realized he'd scared me.

"I'm sorry, it was too fast," Hendrix said, tossing his hands up in the air. "Shit, sorry."

"It's okay. I...slow. I need to take things slow."

He nodded, unwilling to touch me. I wondered if he thought I would break. Hell, I wondered if I might. He was the first guy I'd met that might be worth the risk, though.

"Still on for tomorrow?" he asked, his look hesitant as he rubbed his jawline.

"Yes," I replied, giving him a shy smile. "I'll see you in the morning."

His shoulders relaxed as he gave a small wave and ran through the rain toward his car.

Still shaking, I opened the doors and walked into the dorm. A dozen or so students occupied the main floor. No one wanted to be out in this weather. I scanned the girls and turned toward the stairs.

"It fucking kills me," a loud voice rang through the hallway.

I stopped mid-step and slowly turned. Was she talking to me?

A tall brunette with a resting bitch-face expression sauntered toward me. "Like, how did this even happen?" she asked, pointing at me. If I'd had any question about who she was referring to before, it was gone. She stopped a few feet away from me.

My chin jutted up as she surveyed me.

"You must give one hell of a blow job. I mean, seriously, how Hendrix could even touch something like you is beyond me, and not to mention disgusting." The other girls giggled behind her.

"It's none of your business," I said, determined to hold my ground.

"Oh, but it is my business. I just fucked his brains out last month, and tonight he had his tongue in *your* mouth?"

"You what?" I asked, the words sticking in my throat.

Her dark eyebrows wiggled at me. "You heard me, I have fucked his brains out on multiple occasions."

"Oh, for shit's sake. Seriously Gigi? You've never slept with

Hendrix, so shut your pie hole," Mac said, descending the stairs and placing her hand on my shoulder. "Go find someone else to harass," she said, shooing her away like she was a pesky bug.

If I weren't afraid Gigi would kick my ass, I'd have laughed out loud—hard. I wasn't searching for a fight, though.

"Take her shopping for some real clothes that fit her and burn that hat," Gigi barked.

My eyes widened. How could people be so rude?

"I'll catch you later, Mac." Gigi sneered as she turned around and strolled over to her group of haters.

"Let's go," Mac said, pulling on my hand and leading us up the stairs.

"Who is she?" I asked, stammering.

"A bitch," Mac said, laughing. "Seriously, she's kind of like the little chihuahua who has a big bark but never bites. At least that's been my experience with her. She's all about the intimidation factor."

"She's rude for damned sure." I closed the door behind me while Mac sank onto her bed. I heaved a sigh, my shoulders slumping as I removed my wet clothes. After I was in dry pajamas, I sat on the edge of my bed.

"I need to call Ada Lynn this weekend. She's going to worry."

"Nice topic change. I saved your ass, and you talk about Ada Lynn?" Mac smiled, letting me know she was teasing.

"Did you hear Gigi? What she said to me?" I asked her, frowning.

"Part of it. I was actually headed down to check the washing machines so that I could do some laundry. Hell, I'd recognize her voice from anywhere. We've gone to the same school since we were in the third grade. She's a bully, but she's harmless for the most part. Most importantly, she's not one of the brightest bulbs in the box."

"Mac! That's not nice," I chided her.

"Nope, but it's true. I'm not sure she could piece together a believable lie even if she tried really hard. Blow it off."

"She's really never slept with Hendrix?" I asked softly.

"Nope, not that he's ever told me about," she replied. "And we do talk to each other about stuff, including who we've slept with."

My nose wrinkled. "Not anymore."

"Nope, I'm going to get all the deets from you now." She smiled, leaned forward, and wiggled her eyebrows at me.

I shook my head and laughed. "No deets here."

I quickly thought about it and decided against telling Mac about the Seattle trip tomorrow. For now, I needed to keep it to myself.

"I have an early day tomorrow, and I'm tired," I said, glancing at the clock. I slipped underneath the covers and got comfortable.

"Me too. I have a big test tomorrow. I'm actually tired too, so the laundry can wait." Mac settled in as well, and the room grew silent.

13

As tired as I was, I couldn't sleep. My covers were in a twisted mess, so I finally sat up on the edge of my bed and peered out the window. The sun would be up soon, and Hendrix would meet me outside. My stomach churned with nerves. Honestly, I wasn't sure I could even go through with it. Maybe I would text him that I was sick and couldn't go. My mind raced through the possibilities, but deep inside, I knew. I knew I had to do this.

A few hours later, my phone vibrated with a rare text. I looked at the screen and grabbed my backpack. Mac had already left for Starbucks and class. At least I didn't have to explain anything to her. She was always full of questions.

My head throbbed with anxiety, and black dots floated in my vision with every step I took toward Hendrix and Seattle. I placed the palm of my hand against the wall and breathed. The memory of Hendrix's kiss last night broke through my fear, and I straightened. With every step I gained strength, and before I knew it, I was settled into his front seat.

"Morning," he said, smiling.

I leaned over and gave him a quick kiss. "Thank you for doing this."

"I have a date to plan," he said, chuckling. "Are you ready?"

I took a deep breath and nodded. The scent of his woodsy aftershave filled the car.

"Okay," he reached over and took my hand. "I put the address in the phone, and we'll arrive in about four hours. Sleep if you can. I have a sneaking suspicion you didn't get a lot last night."

"How did you know?" I asked, shocked.

"Just a feeling. Whatever this trip is about, it's important." He shifted the car into drive and pulled out of the dorm parking lot.

"I've never been to Seattle before," I announced once we were heading west on I-90.

"I've performed there several times. We can plan another trip if you'd like to. I mean, I know you have something in mind for today so we can visit again. I'm pretty familiar with the area."

"I'd like to," I said, and meant it.

A comfortable silence settled between us in the car. One of the things I appreciated about Hendrix was there was never any pressure to make conversation. He was perfectly content sitting next to me, holding my hand. It didn't take long before I slipped into the safety of his touch, and my eyelids fluttered closed.

"Hey, Gemma."

"Huh?" I asked, sitting up in my seat. "Where are we?" I searched my surroundings frantically.

"We're about five minutes away from the address you gave me, so I wanted to pull over and wake you."

"Thanks," I mumbled, a bit embarrassed I'd slept the entire way here. My heart skipped a beat as I glanced around. "Let's go." I nodded at him, and he pulled on to the road.

I swallowed the ball of emotions that threatened to strangle me and glanced at the clock on the dash. Our timing would be critical.

In less than a mile, we reached our destination. Hendrix pulled into a public parking lot, took the ticket the machine spit out, and quickly found a spot since the lot was only half full.

Once we parked, he turned to me, a solemn expression on his handsome face. "Ready?"

My throat was so tight all I could do was nod.

We stepped out of the car and into the warm sunshine. Hendrix stretched his long legs while I searched for which direction we needed to go. He took my hand, and I silently led him down a walkway lined with multiple restaurants, and a coffee and ice cream shop.

Once we reached the landmark I recognized from my research—a tall fountain, its water cascading into a surrounding pond—we left the sidewalk and climbed a steep, grassy hill. I hadn't uttered a word, still struggling to wrap my head around where I was and what I was about to do.

"Whatever is going on, I'm here," Hendrix said, attempting a smile.

I looked up into his blue eyes and swallowed hard. He was nervous, too. This poor guy had no idea of what was about to happen.

Rays of sunshine peeked through the clouds, and I released Hendrix's hand, walking a few steps ahead of him. Guilt wrecked me as I approached a chain-link fence, wrapped my fingers through it, and focused on the light breeze. I stared at the people in front of me, searching. The sound of children's shouts and laughter swirled around me almost as if I were in a dream. But it wasn't. It was my worst nightmare.

Hendrix quietly joined me. Tears slipped down my cheeks while I waited—struggled to form the words I needed to say to him.

"Gemma, you're shaking. Whatever is going on, we don't have to do this." Pain flickered across his features as he watched me.

"I need to," I whispered. My fingers had turned red from holding onto the fence so hard. Somehow, I managed to pry my hand loose.

"See?" I asked, pointing toward a group of kids. "See?" I asked again, choking on my word. I cleared my throat as a teacher stood and blew her whistle. Twenty or so little kids lined up to go inside. "His hair is red like mine."

"What? Gemma?" Hendrix asked, his words thick with shock. "You have a kid?" Strain pulled at his eyes, the seconds ticking by as he waited for me to answer.

"Yes. His name is Jordan, and he's four. He's wearing the gray and red jersey."

Hendrix ran his hands through his hair and searched the kids. "He looks like you," he mumbled.

I gasped and took off, running in the opposite direction. I'd screwed up. I'd lost my life all over again and ruined my future with Hendrix. There was no way he would want me after this.

"Gemma!" Hendrix called after me.

I didn't slow down. I'd just seen a happy little boy. The same little boy with big brown eyes and red curly hair who'd stared at me from the photo I'd found in the letter on my dad's desk. My son. The son I hated and loved all in the same breath.

Trees flew by me as I left the sidewalk and stumbled onto the grassy field, gasping for air.

"Gemma," Hendrix said, catching up with me and touching my shoulder. His breathing was heavy.

Sobs wracked my body, forcing me to my knees. My vision turned black as the memories crashed through me. Emotions I'd worked so hard to bury—guilt, shame, and fear rose up and ripped me to pieces. Nothing else existed. Not Hendrix, not Jordan, not Seattle. Only my wrecked and broken soul.

"Jesus," Hendrix whispered, wrapping me in his arms. "Gemma, if I'd known, I would never have agreed to this. Watching you is tearing me the fuck up. Please, what can I do?" he asked, rocking me as I cried.

Oblivious to everything but Hendrix holding me tight, my mind revisited every twist and turn of the horrific event five years ago. I had no idea how long Hendrix sat there on the ground and rocked me. He had to have a million questions. I was ready to reveal the whole story, but for one more minute, I wanted time to stand still, fearless in the safety of his arms and confident that he cared deeply about me. Not because of my looks or what I could give him, but for me—and all of my ugly.

I lifted my head and wiggled out of his lap. I would need some space to tell him my story.

"I got pregnant when I was fourteen," I whispered.

"Gemma, don't," Hendrix said, holding his hand up. "You don't have to do this. Just tell me what you need."

"I need to tell you, see your reaction, and if you handle it without judgment, okay...I will know the truth," I said.

"What are you talking about?" he asked, a hint of confusion in his eyes.

"Guys like you, they don't like girls like me," I started. "My clothes, my hat, I hear everyone talking, but not you. From day one, you sat at my table, asking nothing of me in return. Each day, you worked your way into my heart. Your presence was a comfort even though I hated you for making me feel anything but emptiness again." I paused. "It was the year I was in choir and had my first solo," I said, smiling with the memory, my gaze remaining straight ahead on the water fountain, unwilling to look at Hendrix.

I took a deep breath and continued. "We were almost ready for the concert, and we had an extra practice one evening. Mom had some committee meeting, and Dad was working late, so I walked home. It was dark. I shouldn't have—" My words trailed off. "The insane thing? I was almost home, Hendrix. I was three blocks away when he came up from behind me. He covered my mouth so I couldn't scream and dragged me behind an abandoned store. I kicked and fought with everything I had, but he overpowered me easily." I dared a glance at Hendrix while tears streamed down my cheeks. His expression twisted with horror as I continued. "He took everything from me that night. My innocence, my virginity, my life—my voice." Shame washed over me, and I broke down sobbing, reliving the nightmare.

A few minutes later, I sucked in another deep breath and kept going, keeping my attention trained on the water fountain so I wouldn't have to see his disappointment in me. This was harder than I had imagined.

"Do you have any clue of what it's like living in the South with super religious parents? They refused to let the doctor give me the morning after pill. My father said if I was pregnant, then it was God's will." I spat. "God's will? Rape was God's will? Where was God when this happened? Where was he when I was lying lifeless on the pavement, my dress torn, and blood between my legs?" I gasped, glancing at him quickly and hiding my face again while he remained silent.

"There were complications with the birth, and I had to have a c-section. I gave him up for adoption. Before I came out to Spokane, the lady that adopted him mailed my parents a letter with Jordan's picture. It was the first time I'd seen him. Right after delivery, they took him away, which was fine. I didn't want to see him. I didn't want anything to do with him, and if it'd been my choice, I would have taken the morning after pill."

The silence grew as I waited for Hendrix to say something. He never did.

"I'm sorry. I thought if you could handle the truth, you really did care about me...you would still want to go out with me. This is too much for anyone, though. I'm so sorry. You can take me home now," I whispered, rising.

Hendrix stood slowly, staring at me, his eyes like lasers. I turned my back on him and walked away, wishing with all my heart he would stop me, tell me he really did care, and that none of this mattered. I screamed inside as all of the hope that he was different, shattered to pieces. How had I been so stupid? How could I have even dared to believe Mac? How would she even know what he was like with girls he dated? She was a sister.

Reaching the car, I glanced over my shoulder to see if he was anywhere near me, or if he was going to leave me here while he got his shit together enough to drive, but he hadn't moved. I placed my palms on the passenger window and bowed my head against it. Tears flowed freely as I scolded myself for my naiveté and for allowing him into my heart. Hendrix would be what finally broke me beyond repair.

"Gem," he said from behind me. "I can handle it. This doesn't change how I feel about you." He reached for my hand. "It's a lot to think about, and seeing you torn up like that, imagining what you went through, it really hit me hard. It all makes sense now. I need some time to digest everything, but I don't need time away from you. As far as I'm concerned, we still have a date to plan," he said gently.

Shocked, I whirled around to face him and looked up. "What? Hendrix, I'm ruined. You can't possibly want to be with me."

"Not true. From the moment I saw you, I knew you were special. I had to figure out how to get beyond your walls. You were so hard to reach, but I understand why now."

A mixture of disbelief and hope began to swell inside me as he talked, and I searched his face for signs he might not be telling the truth. He'd passed the test, though and was still here when I needed him the most.

My head bowed down as I attempted to wrap my mind around his words along with the facts. He stood here in front of me. He hadn't run.

I slipped off my glasses and shoved them into my jeans pocket. Slowly, I removed my hat and shook out my long, wavy hair. It cascaded over my shoulders, and I peered up at him shyly. "Here I am," I whispered, and for the first time, I allowed him to see behind the tinted lenses.

His eyebrows shot up, and his mouth gaped slightly as he took it all in.

"Jesus, you're beautiful," he said softly, reaching out and touching my hair. "Your clothes, hat, and glasses. All this time you've tried to hide how beautiful you really are."

My shoulders tensed with the unwanted attention. "I thought it would protect me from people like Brandon. I can't live through the nightmare again, Hendrix."

He nodded as he pulled me into him and wrapped his arms

around me. "Never again, Gem. Never again," he said, placing a kiss on the top of my head.

I nestled into him, allowing the warmth of his body to break through all the years of loneliness, all the heartache, and all of the crippling fear.

He kissed my head one more time, then reached for my hand. "We have a lot to talk about, but if you're ready, let's take you home."

I nodded and let him open my door and help me into the car. Once he'd settled into the driver's seat, he looked over at me and grinned.

"What?" I asked, puzzled.

"I get my date," he said, chuckling. "I'm one happy guy."

I paused for a moment, then kissed him. "You're the reason I'm singing again, Hendrix," I admitted quietly. I settled into my seat and buckled up, my focus never leaving him.

His eyebrows shot up as he stared at me. "Really?"

"The evening you walked Mac and me to our dorm when I harmonized with you outside...it was the first time I'd sung since that night. You gave me my voice back."

His fingers trailed down my neck and threaded through my hair around my shoulders. "And you gave me my heart back. After Kendra, I never thought I'd truly feel again. I'm more alive than ever when you're next to me. And when you're not, it's as though a part of me is missing. My heart isn't able to beat on its own anymore. You own me, and you have had no idea."

Hendrix tilted my chin up, his lips almost touching mine while he searched my face. His mouth was gentle as he kissed me, and everything we'd run from, every horrible nightmare that had haunted us up to this moment, shattered into a million pieces.

14

"Can you talk about it?" he asked, reaching for my hand.

"Yeah, I think so. I've remained quiet for so long, maybe it will help to tell you."

"Did they catch the guy? They obviously had DNA." His knuckles tightened on the steering wheel, whitening with what I assumed was anger.

"There was no match in the system. My parents took me in for a rape kit the moment they saw me. I was such a mess. My dress was torn, and tears stained my dirty cheeks. The medical process afterward was almost as intrusive. By that time, I don't even think I was really in my body anymore. I was in so much pain physically and emotionally, I just checked out. From what Mom and Dad told me, I didn't speak for a few weeks afterward. The morning sickness started about five weeks later. Dad had refused to allow me to take the morning after pill, and I was angry, but I was still in shock from the rape. When I discovered I was pregnant, something inside me woke up to the harsh reality, and I hated him. I'd never felt hate that strong before."

Hendrix kept focused on the interstate as we headed toward Spokane.

"I can't imagine allowing religious views to dictate a decision like that for your own daughter. I can't even wrap my head around it," Hendrix said, shaking his head.

"I was fourteen, weeks away from turning fifteen. I had no rights of my own. I had no transportation or a way out of the house." I paused and stared out the window, collecting my thoughts.

"I was finally able to see past the hatred for my dad and realized I was carrying a rapist's child. With all of the insanity—this baby was also mine. A part of me. And how could I turn my back on it? The child was an innocent in all of the darkness. I tried to talk myself into keeping it, but I couldn't. There wasn't a single day that went by that I didn't wonder if he would hurt others like his father had harmed me. How could I bring a child into the world, knowing he might have that part of his father's DNA? Finally, I pulled my mother into my room one night while Dad was watching TV in the living room, and I asked her to take me for an abortion. I was sobbing, literally clutching at her clothes as I sank to my knees, begging her to help me. She actually agreed. Mom said she'd have to talk to Dad first since she couldn't keep a secret that big from him, even though she supported me under the circumstances. She left to speak with him, and minutes later, Dad rushed through my bedroom door and found me curled in a fetal position in the corner of my bedroom. He scooped me up in his arms, carried me to my bed, sat down on the edge, and sobbed with me. It broke him, Hendrix. It broke all of us. I wrapped my arms around his neck, and he held me for what felt like hours. I've never seen my father cry like that ever again. And when I finally raised my head, knowing he would do everything in his power to help, he told me he'd failed and not protected me—how sorry he was for letting his little girl down. And in the next breath, he said that as much as he loved me, he couldn't go against God's commandment and allow me to murder my unborn child."

Without warning, Hendrix pulled off on the nearest exit, took a quick turn, and pulled behind a gas station, the car coming to an abrupt screeching halt. My lips pursed while he slipped off his seat belt, opened the door, and got out of the car. He took several long steps away and threw his head back. Terror shot through me as he released a desperate, gut-wrenching yell that ripped from his throat toward the sky, his hands clenched into fists.

"Hendrix?" I asked, jumping out of the car and running to him. "I'm so sorry. I'm so sorry," I whimpered. My hands shook as I reached toward him.

In one quick movement, he pulled me into him and wrapped his arms around me. His hands threaded through my hair, gripping tight while he took a deep, shaky breath. "Never again, Gem. Never fucking again. As long as I have breath in me, no one will ever hurt you again."

His body trembled against mine, and unwanted tears streamed down my cheeks. I wrapped my arms around his waist, holding him in return.

Eventually he calmed down and placed a kiss on the top of my head. I pulled away just enough to tilt my chin up, finding his beautiful, gentle eyes staring at me.

"I'm sorry I lost my shit. I just don't understand how your father could have done that to you." He sighed and paused. "I think it would be a good idea if we find a place to eat and talked some more there. I don't want to put us in danger. My reaction was a little stronger than I anticipated, and I shouldn't be behind the wheel like that again," he said.

"I understand."

His strong hands cupped my chin, and he placed a gentle kiss on the tip of my nose. "Let's go," he said, taking my hand and leading me to the car.

We found a burger joint not far away and were sitting across from each other in a corner booth, our food having just arrived. I picked at my fries, realizing I needed to eat something. My nerves were frayed, though, and I didn't want to hurl my dinner on the floor of his car on the way home.

"How are you feeling?" I asked him.

His brows knitted as he ran his hand through his hair. "I think I'm supposed to be asking you that instead."

I attempted a smile, still reeling from the day's events and his reactions. The magnitude of what I'd done suddenly hitting me. Holy shit, I'd just seen my son and exposed my soul to Hendrix. Even though it broke my heart, seeing him lose his shit in the parking lot, I knew he really cared about me, and he was still willingly sitting across from me.

"Did you go back to school?" He popped a fry in his mouth, waiting for my response.

"I tried. My best friend at the time, Fae—I understand we were young, but she refused to have anything to do with me after I started showing." I shook my head at the memory. "She spread vicious lies about me getting pregnant and how I'd asked for it. I didn't understand. We'd been inseparable since we were six, but I guess tragedy changes people in unexpected ways. Or maybe she'd always been a bitch and it took horrible circumstances for me to finally see who she really was. I came home sobbing one day after school, and I never went back. My parents homeschooled me from that point on. I stayed at home my entire pregnancy and refused to go anywhere. Plus they hadn't caught the guy, and I was having nightmares of him crawling through my window at night. I was exhausted, hormonal, and dying a slow, torturous death inside myself."

His jaw clenched as he listened.

"Ada Lynn is my best friend," I said, smiling sadly. "She's eighty-three, but she was the light during my darkest days. I miss her so much." I leaned against the booth and stared at the ceiling, fighting the tears again. I took a deep breath and continued.

"Right after I had the baby, no one could get me out of bed. I was hormonal, and I'd carried a child who I was afraid of, but at the same time I'd felt him kicking and growing inside me. I didn't know how to handle it all. A part of me loved him and marveled at how my body protected and nourished him. The other part of me hated him. It was too much under the circumstances. Anyway, Ada Lynn got her cane one day and walked right into my room without knocking. She stopped short when she saw me. My hair hadn't been washed or brushed in weeks, and my room smelled like someone had died in it.

And in a way I had, but she wouldn't take no for an answer. She hauled me out of bed and got me into a shower, clothes and all. I stood there motionless, letting her lean on the shower door washing and conditioning my hair. She left me alone under the spray, and as she was about to leave, she turned to me and said, 'You get your butt up tomorrow, make your bed, and come over to my house. We don't have to talk, and I expect nothing from you except for you to show up and be clean. That's all you have to do.' And she left."

A slow grin broke through his serious features. "Wow. I like her already."

"I miss her so much. She—she saved me. I was suicidal, and she became this strong, stable force of tough love. And for whatever reason, I did what she told me to. It was just enough not to push me over the edge, but got me moving toward living again, no matter how little of a life it was."

"I had someone like that, too. Janice and Mac." Hendrix paused for a moment and took a bite of his burger. "I realize you're processing a shit load of information right now, but please take a few bites of your hamburger. For me. When you let me hold you earlier today, it was the first time I noticed how tiny you are. You need to eat more," he said, smiling.

I could feel the rush of heat with his comment. No one else knew my size other than Mac and my family in Louisiana. Hell, I didn't even know what size I really wore. I always reached for the baggiest, blandest colored clothes I could find to hide behind.

I cut my burger in half and managed to take a bite. Although I wasn't hungry, I had to admit it was delicious.

"Oh my God, this is so good," I said, covering my mouth with my hand and chewing.

"It's these little Ma and Pa places that have the best food," he said, chuckling at my reaction. "I can't tell you how amazing it is to see your eyes," he said softly, looking at me as if for the first time.

My focus dropped down to my food, realizing I'd unveiled myself to him after he'd accepted my past. It would take some time to adjust to him really seeing me.

"The green tint to the glasses hid them well. I have to say it was a bit difficult getting used to them. Everything looked different, and when it was dark, I really struggled to see. They did the job, though. They kept me concealed, so no one could really see my expression or what I was thinking."

"Which was what you wanted."

"Yeah, until now." I dared a glance at him.

He flashed that damned beautiful smile at me and my stomach flipped.

"Why?" I asked, taking another bite of my burger.

He took a long drink of his water and waited for me to chew.

"Why me, Hendrix? Like, we're beyond all the bullshit. We've crawled into the darkest places of our lives with each other, and we're still here. You knew nothing about me the first time you sat down at my library table, and I told you to leave. Why did you come back?"

A smile pulled at the corner of his mouth as he wiped his hands with his napkin, then took my hand.

"The first time I saw you, I didn't realize you were running from Brandon. I would have beaten his ass right then, but you fell apart in front of me. Your pain was so raw and broken. You didn't stay down, though. After a minute, you got to your feet, held your head high, and walked to the front of the building. This quiet strength took over, and I've not been able to forget you since."

"Oh, I'd almost forgotten you were behind the library when I had my meltdown," I whispered, embarrassed again.

"I saw all your vulnerability at that moment, Gem. You left me breathless and inspired the song we're now singing together."

"What?" I screeched. My hands covered my face as I sank into my seat. "What the hell, Hendrix?" I asked, peeking between my fingers.

When he chuckled, I relaxed a little bit and sighed.

"I don't care about what you wear, or the stupid hat and stuff. It's just stuff. It's you I saw that day, your heart, your strength, and I had to know who you were."

"Hendrix, I—" I swallowed against the tears that threatened. "I've never been with anyone before."

Silence hung between us as he reached across the table for my hand again.

"I don't care about any of that. Look at me," he said.

My gaze traveled slowly from my plate of food and up to him. My stomach clenched in anticipation of what he might say.

"I want you to feel safe with me. I would never hurt you, ever."

I nodded. "I understand now."

His thumb traced circles on the palm of my hand. His expression softened, and he took a deep breath.

"What is it?" I asked, still afraid he was going to tell me I was a freak, leave me at the restaurant, and make me find my own way back to campus.

He brought my palm to his mouth, kissing it tenderly.

"Just...just tell me how to be there for you," he said.

15

"I—I," I stammered like an idiot. How could I answer him when even I didn't know?

"Don't say anything, Gem. Please, just let me in. Don't push me away anymore."

Dumbfounded, all I could do was nod. How had I managed to find this man with such a beautiful soul? I'd never imagined a guy could be compassionate and gentle, but strong and tough when he needed to be.

"I have a few more questions before we get back on the road. And, honestly, I might have more later."

"I know, and I'll do my best to share things with you. This is the first time I'm talking about it, Hendrix."

"Thank you. Thank you for trusting me."

"Well, you can thank your sister, too. We wouldn't be sitting here together if it weren't for Mac. She's your biggest fan and your best friend. I want you to know how much she really loves you and would do anything for her big brother."

"And I would for her, too."

"What did you want to ask?" I stifled a yawn as I relaxed in the booth, the food settling in my tummy.

"Your son. Why did you want to see him now? Are you thinking of trying to get custody of him?"

A slow, smothering grief seeped into every crack and crevice of my soul.

"The evening I was thinking about leaving for Spokane, my parents received some mail that really upset them. After a little snooping, I located the letter in my dad's office. It contained Jordan's school information and a picture. The adopted mother offered to let me see him. She realized how young I was and wanted to let me know there was an option to meet him if I ever changed my mind. When I learned they were in Seattle, I considered it since I would be closer. Other than the picture, I've never seen him before, and I was curious. Whether he's in my life or not, he's still a part of me. Then yesterday you said you had a car. I knew I had a way there if you would agree to take me. Regardless of how scared I was, I trusted you enough to share my past."

I took a sip of my water before I continued.

"After the pregnancy results, I struggled for a long time with what was right or wrong. How, as a mother, I was supposed to feel about my child. I couldn't live with the fact that one part of me hated him while the other part of me loved him. It was like I had two personalities. I made the right decision, though. I could never love him the way he deserves to be loved. Every time I looked into his eyes I would wonder if he looked like the man who stole my innocence. Today he appeared happy and healthy, and I understood how love could heal brokenness. I choose to believe the laughing little redheaded boy I saw on the playground today has a good life and needs to stay there. So after seeing him for the first time, and telling you the whole story, I'm at peace with my decision."

Hendrix nodded, and a beat of silence filled the space between us.

"I won't pretend to understand what you went through, but Gem, if you ever change your mind and want to see him—I'll help you."

I drew in a sharp breath. I had no response for him. It was too much to process right now, and I needed to change the subject before I broke down again. "Why are you calling me Gem all of a sudden?"

"Because even in the darkness you radiate beauty from the inside out."

I'd never flushed as profoundly as when those words left his mouth.

Sensing it was time to go, he stood and held his hand out to me.

"I'm going to use the restroom and pay for the food before we continue toward home."

"Excellent idea. I will, too," I said, grateful for a minute to myself.

Afterward, I found him waiting at the front door for me. He smiled as he opened it, and we walked into the evening air.

"How long until we're back in Spokane?" I asked, exhaustion suddenly claiming me.

"About three and a half hours," he responded, gently brushing my hair over my shoulder before opening my car door for me.

I paused for a minute, glancing up at him.

"Thank you," I said.

His eyes were dark with need while his fingertips trailed down my cheek.

"Can I kiss you?"

"Yes, please."

His mouth swept over mine, kissing me tenderly. I hesitated, feeling shy, but when his fingers twisted through my hair, I grabbed hold of the front of his shirt and pulled him closer. My lips parted. His tongue gently caressed mine. Heat flooded my body, and an unfamiliar longing consumed me. My hand traveled lightly up his chest, my palm flattening against the muscle. His heart was beating as hard as mine. He moaned softly into my mouth while his hand protectively moved up my spine. Flashes of the awful night, of a stranger's hands on my body, blasted through my bliss, and I quickly broke our kiss.

"Are you all right?" he asked breathlessly.

"Can you be patient with me? You're the only guy I've been with since the...the rape," I managed. "I want to kiss you and be with you, but sometimes the memories barge in, and I need to see your face and recognize where I am."

"Gemma, I'll never rush you. You feeling safe is my main priority."

"You're sure? I mean, you've been with other girls and—"

"Stop, this isn't the same. You're not other girls, so don't compare yourself to my past. Ever."

"Okay, thank you." The way he had managed this whole situation filled me with gratitude.

He kissed the top of my head, and I slid into the passenger's seat and closed the door. In no time at all, we were back on the interstate.

I reached for his hand this time.

"What's going through your mind?" I asked him.

A sad smile eased across his handsome features. "I'm just concerned about you."

"Under the circumstances, I'm doing great. I suspect my moods will be up and down for a while. I hope you can deal with me."

"Don't even give it a second thought. I would be surprised if you didn't have some rough days," he replied. "Now that I can see your eyes, I can tell you're exhausted."

I shot him a dirty glance, and he responded with a low chuckle. "You're beautiful, but even the beautiful get tired, Gem. Go to sleep. It's almost eight, so it shouldn't throw off your normal sleep schedule for the rest of the night."

"Shit!" I released his hand and dug for my phone in my pocket. I'd powered it off when we'd left for Seattle, not wanting to be disturbed. I pushed the button, the phone glowing to life. Five missed calls and ten texts from Mac.

"I didn't tell Mac where I was, and she's probably freaking the hell out." I didn't even bother to read or listen to the messages. Instead, I tapped her contact info on my screen.

"Oh. My. Fucking. God. You scared the shit out of me. I thought Brandon had drugged you and carried you off somewhere, leaving you for dead!"

I held the phone away from my ear and cringed. Mac's voice was so loud she may as well have been on speakerphone. I shot a look at Hendrix, who was stifling a laugh.

"Not funny," I mouthed at him, waiting to get a word in with Mac.

The moment she paused and took a breath, I jumped in.

"I'm so so so sorry. My phone was turned off, and I'll tell you why when I'm back. I'm safe and have been with Hendrix today. I'm sorry I scared you."

"Oh, my God. You've been at my brother's place gettin' some love, haven't you?"

"What?" I screeched at her.

I held the phone away from my ear again, and my attention snapped to Hendrix. "You have your own place?" I squeaked.

"Yeah, I do," he replied, nonchalantly.

"Why didn't you tell me this?"

"You would have run the moment the words left my mouth, and I would have lost you. You weren't ready. Thanks, Mac!" he yelled, frowning.

"Wait, you're still with him?" Mac asked, incredulous.

"Yeah, and we're on our way home from Seattle. It's been a really long day, Mac."

"Girl, you've got some serious explaining to do. And Seattle? Like seriously? You couldn't have bothered to tell your bestie last night when we were plotting escape routes? Instead you hop in the car and spend eight hours alone with him? Does that even make any sense? No. Not. One. Crazy. Ass. Bit."

Hendrix's eyebrows rose.

"Mac, calm down, he can hear every word you're saying through the phone, and I don't even have you on speaker. Please, I'll explain everything when I'm there. I promise."

She sighed and lowered her voice. "Let's be clear that not only have you managed to scare the ever-living shit out of me, now that I know you're safe and with my brother, I'm pissed. So it's a good thing it will take you a while to get here. I might be calm by that time, but I can't promise anything," she said, her tone clipped.

I chewed my lip, feeling like total shit for upsetting her.

"I understand, and you can yell at me all you need to when I get there," I replied.

"No, you won't yell at her. You need to listen, Mac. No yelling. She's been through enough today," Hendrix said toward the phone.

I felt my cheeks flush hot with his protective words.

"Tell him no promises, he's on my shit list right now, too."

I moved the phone away from my ear and began to repeat what she said, but he interrupted me.

"I heard," he said, grinning. "She'll be fine, don't worry about it, okay?"

I nodded.

"See you soon," I said, dreading having to calm her down. I understood, though. I would have been scared out of my mind if it had been the other way around. I ended the call and sighed.

"I screwed up," I muttered.

"Gem, I know Mac, and the moment she sees you without your hat and glasses, she'll have a million questions about it."

I laughed. "Let's hope so. I just want her to be okay."

He raised my hand, his soft lips pressing into the back of it.

"She will be, I promise. Now try and rest, because you won't get any sleep tonight with Mac."

"Ugh, you're right. I'll try."

I willed my body to relax and took a deep breath, focusing only on the strength in Hendrix's hand as he held mine.

NOT SURPRISINGLY, I slept the entire drive to the dorm.

"Gem," Hendrix said gently. "We're here."

My head rolled against the seat, and I peered at him through sleep-filled eyes. My heart two-stepped with happiness. Contentment and happiness swelled inside my chest. Hendrix was the first thing I saw when I woke up, and I liked it.

"Hi," I said, smiling.

"Hey," he said, a lopsided grin easing across his handsome face while he brushed strands of hair off my cheek. "I love being able to do that. Please don't ever put the hat on again. At least not around me."

I nodded. "It's time to stop hiding," I said timidly. It was a big step for me, but at least with Hendrix and Mac, I no longer needed to.

I leaned forward, my fingertips tracing along his jawline, across his chin, and finally over his full mouth. "I've wanted to do that from the first moment I saw you in the library," I whispered, heated tension filling the small space between us. "And this." My hand slipped around the back of his neck, twirling the soft strands of his hair around my fingers. "It's almost like..." I hesitated for a moment, my gaze flicking up to meet his. "The night we sang together, my heart split wide open, and you stepped right inside of it. It's like you're running through my veins. Warm, safe, flowing through every part of me, my heart beating again because of you."

"Jesus," he growled, his breathing shallow. "You're going to undo me."

I tilted my chin up, barely pressing my mouth to his. He groaned when our lips met and parted, our tongues moving slowly together. His gentle touch on my neck sent shivers through my body, and for the first time, my core ached for him.

A pulsing need spread through me as his hand trailed down my spine. I arched into him, my fingers lightly traveling down his neck, his shoulder, and his chest. His hard muscles flexed beneath my palm as he continued to kiss me. Every moment with him turned into something magical, something more profound than I'd ever felt before.

He broke our kiss and placed his forehead against mine.

"I never want to push you, so you'll have to set the pace. I need you to know if I stop, it's not because I don't want to be with you. The opposite. When things get intense, I'll need a break. You also need to realize if you choose for things to progress physically, even if we're about to have sex—if you say no, it means no. I'll stop immediately."

Tears burned my eyes, and I swallowed the ball of emotions that threatened to erupt. "It's too much to ask of you. If we were that close to being together, it's mean to say no."

"No it's not. In my opinion, if a girl changes her mind, for whatever reason—fear, uncertainty, she's just not ready—the guy needs to
respect her wishes. He can go take a cold shower for God's sake. No
one has a right to cross that line."

I nodded and placed my head on his shoulder while he gently
traced small circles on my back. I slowly looked up at him, eye to eye.
"Are you for real, or am I going to wake up in the morning and
discover all of this never happened?" My stomach tightened at the
mere thought of not seeing him tomorrow, but even more at the idea
of how his betrayal could absolutely wreck me.

Then I remembered how it all started—him sitting at my table and
refusing to be chased off, sharing his music with me, and us writing a
song together. The clincher had been when he'd taken me to Seattle, no
questions asked, watched me fall apart, and had followed me to the car
and said my past changed nothing. He might not have recognized it yet,
but I was a goner, and he held my fragile heart in the palm of his hand.

He smiled at me. Each second, my heart pounded against my
chest while I waited for what he'd say next. "Gem, I thought the same
thing. Would you process things tonight with Mac and change your
mind? Would this be my last day with you? What if I never had the
chance to look into your beautiful eyes this way again? Kiss you—"
His voice trailed off, thick with concern. "I'm not going anywhere, and
I hope to God you won't be either."

I answered him with another kiss.

"I should go in and talk to Mac," I said, reluctantly.

He covered his mouth and chuckled. "Sorry, it's not funny. I don't
envy you on this one, and I know what you're in for."

"Thanks," I said dryly. "Thank you for today and handling a difficult situation so well."

"Just tell me there will be a tomorrow," he said, his forehead
creasing with concern.

I realized I'd not given him a verbal response when he basically
asked if I was going to wake up in the morning and change my mind
about us.

"There will be a tomorrow for us, Hendrix." I smiled, watching the tension melt away and his shoulders relax.

"Good. Let's get you inside," he said.

He walked around to my side of the car and opened the door for me. Although I loved being an independent girl, I liked that he was considerate and well mannered. It made me feel cherished and respected.

We strolled up the sidewalk hand in hand, taking our time, unwilling to let each other go. Despite how difficult the day had been, there were also some amazing moments, and I didn't think he wanted it to end any more than I did. Contrary to my fear, being alone with him all day had ended up a safe cocoon, and I found myself not wanting to leave.

"Guess this is it for tonight," he said, stopping in front of the door and turning toward me.

"I don't want it to end," I blurted, flushing furiously.

"Me either, but I understand Mac needs some answers."

I nodded as he wrapped his arm around my waist and pulled me to him, my hands resting on his muscular chest.

"No one said I couldn't kiss you a little bit longer, though."

Ignoring everyone and everything around us, I met him in a world that only existed of us, of his lips on mine, the heat from our bodies touching, our hearts beating wildly. He pulled me tighter against him, and I felt his full desire through his jeans. My first reaction was to break away and run, but I remained still, noting the length and hardness of him. Trembles traveled through me as fear won out.

He moved away quickly, allowing a few inches between us. "I don't know if you need me to back away or hold you." His words were raw with a mix of longing and worry. There was no way this could be easy for him.

"Space. At least this time." I looked away, regaining my footing and smiling sadly at him. "I feel bad, but I don't know what else to do."

He took one step toward me, his hands remaining at his sides. "Never, ever, feel bad, Gemma."

Chewing my bottom lip, I nodded. "Guess I'd better go." I didn't want things to end like this, though. I stood on my tiptoes, placed my hands on his shoulders, and kissed him. "I'll see you tomorrow," I reassured him.

"I'll be counting the minutes until you're next to me again," he whispered in my ear before he walked away.

My gaze lingered on him as he sauntered down the sidewalk. This time, I took him all in. Warmth spread through me as I chewed my lower lip and noted the way his jeans hugged his ass and muscular legs. How his broad, solid shoulders and back filled out his navy fitted shirt. I sighed. Was it too much to hope he really would show up again tomorrow and the day after? Unfortunately, only time would tell, and there wasn't a damned thing I could do to speed it up.

16

I drew in a deep breath and opened our dorm room door. Mac sat on the corner of her bed, studying. Her gaze slowly drifted from the book up to me.

"Hey," I said, dread seeping into me as I realized I would have to explain everything to her.

"I'm not sure I'm speaking to you...Wait, did you just walk through the dorm without your hat and glasses? Did you take them off while you were with Hendrix?" She leaned forward, her eyes widening as she stared at me. "Are you burning your hats? I mean, not the cute knit one I gave you, but the ugly denim hats? Because I think a ceremony to celebrate is in order. I mean, holy Hannah, this is huge, but wait. Did you take them off right before you walked into the room and I'm jumping to conclusions because I do that, and obviously I'm not even giving you a millisecond to say anything, but dammit, Gemma, I'm so hot pissed at you right now." She paused and took a breath.

"We can burn them," I said softly.

"Oh my God. I'm marking this on the calendar because whatever happened today, whoever you were when you walked out of this door, is not the same Gemma that is standing in front of me right now. And as your best bestie ever, I need full deets. Don't even think about leaving a single thing out, because I will stalk my brother until he tells me. I've had years of practice wearing him down, it's a skill I could seriously put on my resume."

I held my hands up in surrender. "You won't have to, but if you want to hear everything, you have to hush."

Her face fell but lit up again. "Okay, sit down," she said, patting an empty space on her bed.

My eyebrow shot up. "You cleaned up your side of the room?" I asked incredulously.

"I told you I was scared out of my head and worried sick about you. I didn't know what else to do other than put shit away. It took me hours," she groaned and smacked her forehead with the palm of her hand. "You can sit on my bed while we catch up tonight."

I pulled my glasses out of my pocket and laid them on my desk. "Guess I left my hat in Hendrix's car," I muttered and grabbed a box of tissues for us and sat down on her bed, facing her.

"Uh-oh," she said. "Tissues and you're facing me. This can't be good."

"It's a mixed bag, Mac."

She bit her lip, and I nearly laughed. At least she was trying not to ramble.

"I asked Hendrix to take me to Seattle. I swear, I thought about telling you last night, but I wasn't sure I would go through with it. There wouldn't be anything to tell you if I'd grown feathers and chickened out. Besides, you would have worried all day about it. I blew it though, and I should have at least texted that I was safe and with Hendrix. Instead, I scared you, and for that I'm so sorry. You're my best friend, Mac, and never in a million years would I intentionally hurt you."

"Best friend?" she asked, tears filling her eyes. "You've never called me that before."

"Yeah, you're the best, best friend I've ever had other than Ada Lynn," I said, smiling gently.

Mac lunged forward and wrapped her arms around my neck. I hugged her in return, my heart singing with how happy she was.

She sat back and wiped the moisture off her cheeks. I pulled a few tissues out of the box and handed them to her. "I haven't even started and you're tearing up on me already," I teased, giving her a Kleenex. "I'm not sure where to start really."

"Wherever works," she said.

"I was fourteen." Nausea swirled inside my stomach as I gathered my words to repeat everything to her. "I was brutally raped."

Mac gasped, covering her mouth with both of her hands.

"I realize you already knew something had happened to me." I bit my lip and continued. "I didn't know the man, and he hurt me really bad," I choked out. "When I finally staggered home, my hair and face were filthy, my dress was torn, my legs were bruised and bloody."

"Gemma," she whispered through her fingers.

Tears spilled down both of our cheeks as I continued. "My father is a religious man and weeks later when we found out I was pregnant..." My head dropped, the heaviness of the memory crushing me again.

Mac released the most heartbreaking cry I'd ever heard, other than my own. My best friend full-on sobbed while I struggled to not fall apart with her. She reached for me, and we grasped each other's hand as though it was our only lifeline left before we fell over the cliff.

"He made me carry to term and deliver my son." No longer able to manage my feelings, I broke down next to her, my shoulders shaking with all the grief and shock of seeing my son earlier in the day. No matter what the circumstances, he was a part of me. And there was no mistaking his red hair.

A few minutes later we'd collected ourselves enough for me to continue.

"I died inside during that time. Mom and Dad were never the same, and I was a terrified shell of a girl. I rarely left the house, I was homeschooled, and the only other person I really saw was Ada Lynn. She was the person who helped me walk out of the house when all I wanted was to never wake up again. And even then, it was only from my house next door to hers. It was like that for several years."

"Oh my God," Mac said, her heartache and pain etched into her expression.

"About seven or eight months ago, I started to chew on the idea of attending a college outside of my home. I was already taking a few online classes, but I wondered if I could leave the house and start over somewhere. The thought terrified me, but I applied to a few schools anyway. I remember the day I got the acceptance letter to attend here, Ada Lynn was outside on her porch and knew something important had shown up in the mail for me. I suck at hiding my facial expressions, it's one of the reasons I got the hat and glasses before I came out here. Anyway, she grabbed the mail from me and was elated I'd applied. She's the reason I'm here. She paid for my bus ticket and put a little bit of money in a checking account for me. We planned everything out, too. My parents had no idea I'd left until they woke up the next morning and found the note I'd left them."

"What? Gemma, sorry for saying this, but that's full-on shitty."

My jaw clenched, and guilt surged through me. "I know, Mac. My father would have never let me walk out the door, though. He would have physically blocked me from leaving. Anytime I'd mentioned moving and attending college, he'd shut me down, telling me it wasn't God's will for me to go."

A beat of silence hung in the air, and then Mac recovered. "God's will or your dad's wishes? I mean—shit. I know you grew up in the Bible Belt and probably went to church for most of your life, but I swear people hide behind religion to manipulate others or to not deal with their own shit."

I shrugged my shoulder. "I'm not going to disagree with you, Mac. I think my dad saw the remnants of what used to be his sweet little girl. Raped, broken, and changed forever. He felt as if he'd failed me. Fathers are supposed to protect their children. I think his guilt and shame controlled him, and he thought if he kept me at home forever, I would be safe." As the words left my lips, for the first time, I really understood Dad's motives. There was no way I could justify them, but at least I understood. It seemed with under-standing the situation, peace wasn't far behind. "Anyway, here I am."

"I can't imagine how hard it was for you to come out here. Weren't you scared shitless?" She palmed her forehead. "And I charged at you the second you walked into our door. Hell, even before, when I picked you up and gave you a ride." Her mouth gaped as she put everything together. "And you're still talking to me," she said, dismayed.

I laughed. "You were a little hard to stomach at first, but I wouldn't trade you for anything in the world now."

"Really?" she asked before she hugged me again.

"Really." I patted her on the back and smiled.

She released me, wiggled around on the bed, and attempted to get comfortable, then her mouth gaped open. "Holy hell! Hendrix. If he took you to Seattle, how does this all fit together?"

"Jordan is there. I went so I could see my son and tell Hendrix the truth. I did it for me, but also to see if Hendrix really did care about me and wasn't after one thing. Even though you said he wasn't, I needed to know for myself. A part of me figured if he could handle today, he was for real. But..."

"Oh God, please tell me he did okay." She covered her mouth with her hand again, waiting for my answer. Hendrix was close to perfect in her eyes.

If he had responded any differently, I think it would have crushed Mac. "It was a lot, Mac. I freaked out on him after I saw Jordan, and I had a complete meltdown. Hendrix didn't know what to do for me...suddenly, I had a kid. I told him everything, and...he just stared at me silently."

"Oh shit, Hendrix, you didn't," she muttered.

"I walked back to the car and realized it was too much for him. I'd fucked up royally hoping for anything different."

"I'm going to beat him senseless. How could he, after everything you've been through and told him today? I can't believe he treated you like that!"

"I'm not finished. Don't kill him yet. I have no idea how long I was at the car by myself, but eventually he joined me."

"You're killing me over here, hurry up," Mac said, her expression filling with anticipation while she grabbed her pillow, biting the corner of it.

I swallowed a laugh, but it was only because I knew how the day had ended.

"He said it had changed nothing between us."

Mac full on flung herself onto the bed and covered her face with her hands. Her petite body shuddered with a heavy sigh, then she sprang back up into a sitting position. "Wait, what does he mean by nothing has changed?"

"We have a date," I said, grinning shyly.

Mac released a loud whoop as she bounced on the bed. "I'm so fucking proud of you!"

I giggled while she stood and performed a happy dance on the bed. Stopping mid-step, she sank down into a sitting position. "Wait, your hat."

"Oh, yeah. After he told me everything was okay between us, and he still wanted to take me out, I slipped off my glasses and removed my hat."

Mac gasped. "What did he do?"

"Kissed me," I said, biting my thumbnail grinning.

"Shit, this is the most romantic thing I've ever heard," she cried. "It doesn't get better than this!"

"Oh, yes it does," I said, giggling behind my hand.

"Oh my God, you two are going to be like two teenagers making out every chance you can. Ugh, and I'm with you both on a regular basis." She rolled her eyes in revulsion and grinned. "So, sis, when are you two going out?" she asked, smacking me on the arm.

I blushed at her calling me sis. "I don't know yet. I think we're just taking tonight to process everything. He said nothing had changed, but I'm scared I'll wake up tomorrow, and he'll have had time to think about everything. Then...then he'll break my heart."

Mac cringed. "I wish I could tell you differently, but I can only speculate. I've never seen Hendrix like this with a girl before, though."

"What do you mean?" I asked, tilting my head in question.

"He's had girlfriends, but music has always been his real love. So girls have come and gone. I'm in new Hendrix territory right along with you."

My shoulders slumped. "That doesn't make me feel better at all. I have to admit, the only reason I've spent time alone with him is because he's your brother and you speak so highly of him."

She reached out and patted my arm. "What I can tell you is, as long as I've known Hendrix, he's a guy of his word, and I would be stunned if he changed all of a sudden. I would wonder if he was on drugs or something." Her eyebrow cocked up at me with her words.

"Thanks, but I really unloaded on him, and he reacted strongly." My mind drifted to the gas station earlier in the evening. I had no intention of sharing it with Mac, however. It was too raw and personal.

"I can only imagine how it tore him up. Hell, it tore me up."

"Now that you understand what happened, I wanted to let you know that I wouldn't have made it this far without you, so thank you. Thank you for your friendship and believing in me."

"Shit," Mac said, fanning herself with her hands. "You're going to make me cry again. But hey, no prob. It's what best friends do."

I smiled at her and nodded. "Can you tell me?"

Mac shot me a quizzical look.

"About whatever happened to you?" I asked gently, a shiver of fear shooting down my spine afraid of what she might say.

"Oh. I guess it's only fair, right?" she said twirling her braid, her anxiety apparent.

"You don't have to," I said.

"No, you need to know." She took a deep breath and expelled it. "It's like it was all a movie, like what we see on Netflix or something. I was a senior in high school, and Hendrix was already attending here. Some friends and I found out about a frat party, and I asked Hendrix if he was going. He said no, he would rather write music and record than spend time with a bunch of assholes."

Unable to stop it, I laughed. "Doesn't sound like he's changed much since then."

Mac shook her head. "We had no business there. Those guys were more experienced, and they thought if you walked through the front door of the frat house you were fair game, whether you wanted to do anything with them or not. The guy I'd been dating? Well, we were on a break from each other, so I talked my best friend at the time, Eva, into going. I swear the second we showed up, every guy's mouth dropped. She was like supermodel gorgeous. Before I knew it, we were both pretty drunk. The party was rowdy, too. We'd been to parties before, but high school parties. This was on an entirely different level, and we were rookies. A hot guy was talking to me, and while I was busy giggling and flirting with him, I lost sight of her. I didn't think much of it. She always ended up in the corner making out with some guy." Mac paused, tears forming in her eyes.

"Finally, I sobered up enough to realize it had been a long time since we'd checked in with each other and that was unusual. I excused myself from my make-out session and told the guy I needed to find a bathroom. I searched everywhere for her on the main floor, nothing. Panic took over, and I raced up the stairs and flung open every door I saw. I can't tell you how many people I pissed off doing that but finding her was my only concern. The last room..." She hesitated. "The last room was where I found her."

Her head hung down, and her shoulders shook while she cried. "She was mostly naked and passed out cold. The guy was still on top of her, screwing her, and she had no idea. I barged in and knocked him off her, beating him with a hockey stick I'd spotted in the corner of the bedroom. He ran out of the room, his jeans down around his ankles, and I locked the door behind him. I ran into the adjoining bathroom, called Hendrix, and dressed Eva. Anyway, it seemed like forever until Hendrix arrived and got us out of there. She never woke up during any of it. We finally concluded she'd been drugged."

"I'm so sorry, Mac," I said, reaching for her hand. "Did she press charges?"

Mac wiped her runny nose and nodded. "Yeah, but it didn't stick."

"Did she know him? Did you know him?" I sucked in a breath, afraid to hear the answer.

"It was Brandon, Gemma," Mac whispered.

My eyes slammed shut. Somewhere deep inside me, I'd known. As Mac was telling Eva's story, Brandon had immediately flashed across my mind. I could no longer consider his aggressiveness as immature frat boy behavior. He was truly dangerous, uncontrolled anger fueling his actions.

"Did you tell Hendrix what had happened or just that Eva was drunk?" I asked, my heart pounding against my chest.

"I told him...all of it. It's one of the reasons he was so mad at himself the night Brandon attacked you."

A heavy silence hung in the air as we sat still, understanding each other on a deeper level.

"Gemma, I know what he's capable of, and he scares me."

"Me too, but there are three of us who know the truth, and we'll stick together."

"Oh, speaking of, Hendrix wanted me to give you another pepper spray."

She hopped off the bed, opened her desk drawer, and handed it to me.

"Thanks," I said, rolling it around in my hand. "Mac?" I asked, looking up at her.

"Yeah?"

"I need your help."

17

F all had officially started. I woke to the bright morning sun peeking through our window. My bleary eyes scanned the room to find Mac bent over an art book sipping her coffee. With her ADHD, studying was difficult for her, and she had to put in more time than most people.

"It's about time you woke up," she teased.

"What time is it?" I asked, grateful it was Saturday.

"A little after ten. I didn't want to wake you since you had a hard day yesterday. However, now that you're up, I think you have a phone call to make so we can get started, right?"

I yawned and stretched, butterflies fluttering in my stomach at the thought of making the call.

"I actually have a few to make, so you'll have to share your coffee with me this morning."

She held it protectively against her chest and glared at me.

"Really?" I whined, sitting up and stretching.

"Are you always this wimpy in the morning, and I haven't noticed?" She cocked an eyebrow at me.

"Fine, I'll go grab one myself, but it will take longer for everything else."

"You're such a brat," Mac laughed. "I brought you one already. It's on your desk," she said, nodding.

"Thank you!" I groaned as I stood up, my legs stiff from all the hours in the car yesterday. I grabbed the cup and took several sips, reveling in the deep, rich flavor.

"You nervous?" Mac asked, laying her book down beside her.

"You have no idea," I replied, "but there's no time like the present, huh?"

Mac nodded. "I'm right here."

"Thanks," I said, grabbing my phone and tapping the screen. It lit up, and I located their number in my favorites. I hesitated, took another drink, and glanced at Mac. She smiled and motioned to get on with it.

The phone rang, and my pulse double-timed while I waited.

"Hi, Gemma!"

Mac giggled, and I realized she could hear even though it wasn't on speaker.

"Hey, Mom. How are you?"

"Oh, honey, it's so nice to hear from you. I'm doing okay. Your dad keeps me busy with appointments and stuff, but it's fine. It gives me someone to take care of since you're gone."

"How is he?" I asked.

"He had a doctor's appointment yesterday, and the treatment is working. I was actually going to call you today with the good news."

I slumped into my bed, a rush of relief flooding through me. "Oh Mom," I whispered, choking back the tears. "It's wonderful news. I'm sure everyone is relieved."

"We are. The treatments are really expensive, so I'm glad you're on scholarship."

My heart sank when I realized how strapped they must be right now for money. He wasn't working, and all the medical bills had to be flooding in. "We will figure it out, right?"

"You focus on your studies; don't you worry about us. We're fine."

I sat up on the edge of my bed and glanced at Mac, shaking my head no.

Her lips pursed in disappointment.

"How are classes and this roommate Ada Lynn has told me about? Do you still like her?"

"Yeah, I wouldn't trade her for the world. She's pretty great." I winked at Mac, her face lighting up as she realized I was talking about her.

"I'm so happy, Gemma. I couldn't be prouder of you."

"Thanks, Mom. It means a lot to me."

"You need to call Ada Lynn and talk to her, too. She really misses you, but she won't admit it."

"I miss all of you, too. I'll give her a call now," I said, sadness weaving through me. "I love you, Mom."

"Love you too, honey."

I ended the call and sighed. "I can't ask them, Mac. I don't know what I was thinking, but Dad isn't working, and the medical bills are piling up. On the bright side, he's doing well. The treatment is working."

"That's a huge relief about your dad!" She said, bouncing on her bed. "This also means you're not leaving." She shot me a toothy grin and then frowned. "Do we have any other options?"

"Maybe. It's going to kill me to ask, though." I tucked my hair behind my ear and tapped Ada Lynn's name on my screen.

"Well it's about time," she muttered when she answered the phone, chuckling. "It's been forever, which tells me two things. You're making friends and don't have time for an old lady, and your parents are telling you about all the good gossip around here."

I laughed. "Yeah, that's it. My parents love to gossip," I replied. "I'm sorry, it has gotten busier with classes. I'm guessing Dad told you I'm singing again, too."

"He did. I couldn't be more excited for you. It sounds like Washington is exactly what you needed."

My cheeks flushed at the thought of who was really helping me with the change. I paused, working up my courage.

"Just say it, what do you need?"

"Huh? How did you know?" I asked, my eyes growing wide.

"You always pause and sigh before something important."

I couldn't help but laugh. "Really?"

"Every single time. So, what's going on?"

"I—I need new clothes. I mean, ones that fit me properly."

Mac hopped up on her bed, standing and clapping her hands together. She knew it was one of the hardest things I could have asked for.

A gasp and silence hovered over the phone. "Did I hear you correctly?" Ada Lynn asked.

"Yes, ma'am. I can't ask my parents with all the medical bills. I'm so sorry. I'll get a job and pay you with interest for everything, I promise. I wouldn't even be here without you."

"Hush now, my blue-eyed girl. I'll transfer it over to your account, and don't you even think about paying me back. I'll just take it out of your inheritance. Everything I have is going to you anyway, so a little bit now won't hurt anything."

"What?" I screeched. "Ada Lynn," I said, covering my mouth. My head dropped, my long hair concealing my face from Mac.

"My mind is already made up, and the paperwork is all in place. There's money to bury me, and the house is paid for. You'll have a nice nest egg. I love you, girl, and when you walked out of this neighborhood and made it to Washington, I couldn't have been prouder of you. You're the daughter I never had."

Tears slipped down my cheeks at her generous heart. My chest ached with the urge to hug her and never let her go.

"Thank you," I whispered.

"Now, check your account in a few minutes. You'll have plenty of money for clothes and anything else you need for a while. I don't want you stressed out over a little cash. More comes in anyway, so spend some of it. Have some fun," she said, her tone filling with excitement. "And thank you. Thank you for giving me the gift of seeing you heal and grow. You've made an old woman so happy," she said, her voice cracking with emotion.

"I love you, Ada Lynn. You saved me when no one else could."

"Good God, someone had to, you reeked," she laughed, referring to the day she barged into my bedroom. "Now, go shop, and send me pictures. Oh, wait, I have one question."

"Yeah?" I asked timidly.

"Are you burning those damned hats and glasses I saw in the pictures you sent me?"

I couldn't help but laugh. "Yeah, Mac and I are going to have a full-on ceremony and set them on fire."

"I like this Mac character," she said. "Call me soon. Love you."

"I love you, too."

My head remained down while I attempted to stop the tears and regain my composure. I wanted more than anything to hop on a bus and see Ada Lynn and my parents, but I'd made a promise to stay here. I peeked through my hair and found Mac sitting on the edge of the bed, her fingers digging into the side of the mattress.

"Well?"

"Let's go shopping," I said, smiling.

Mac hopped off her bed, then clapped her hands while she jumped up and down like a little kid. I checked my account while she was being silly, and my mouth hung open. Guess Ada Lynn thought I needed a lot of clothes because five grand was now in my account. I signed out of my online bank app as my phone rang. Panic shot through me, and I answered quickly.

"Hendrix?" I asked.

"Hey, with everything going on yesterday, I forgot today was Saturday."

"Yeah?" My shoulders tensed while I waited for the other shoe to drop.

"We don't normally meet in the library on the weekends, and I couldn't wait until Monday to see you."

Tension slipped from my shoulders, and I smiled.

"You miss me already?" I asked quietly, trying to avert Mac's eavesdropping.

"You have no idea. All I can think about is you. I can't even write today." He blew out a big breath as though he were relieved that he told me.

"I'm sorry, I don't mean to mess it up for you." I chewed on my nail in an attempt to calm the butterflies in my stomach.

"You're not, but I do have a question." He paused.

"Okay." My nerves vibrated while I waited for him to continue.

"Remember how I said my dad used to be an attorney?" Hendrix asked.

"I do."

"Well, I guess he's gotten his shit together because he's started to practice again."

"Oh, that's awesome, right?" I asked, excitement lacing my words.

"It's fantastic. He was a damned good attorney when he was sober. So I'm hoping this is what he needs to feel like he has a purpose again, ya know?"

"Everyone needs a purpose." I glanced up in time to see Mac plop down on my bed next to me.

"His dad is returning to law," I mouthed at her. "He's been sober for a while, I guess."

She waved me off. "Yeah, I already know about it."

"So, what's the question?" I returned my attention to Hendrix.

"Um, well, in case you've forgotten we have a date to plan, and—" he paused, clearing his throat.

Oh my gosh, Hendrix was nervous. My heart swelled with the thought of him being scared to really ask me out, even though he knew I would say yes.

"Well, there's a charity event tonight, and Dad wants me to go. It's a big deal, and this is his first public appearance since he's started practicing again."

"Oh wow, you should go. You are, aren't you? I'm sure it would mean a lot to him if you showed your support."

"Go with me," he blurted.

I flinched in surprise. "What?"

"I know this isn't what we'd discussed as a possible first date, but it would be amazing to see you all dressed up and on my arm."

"As in a dress dressed up?" My pitch rose with each word I spoke.
"Yeah."

Where in the hell would I even shop for a dress? My brain scrambled for an answer, but I was terrified. This was a big deal, and I would also meet his dad.

"Gem?" he asked gently.

"Okay. I'll go with you," I croaked. "When is it?"

"Tonight, at eight."

My phone clattered to the floor. "Shit," I said, reaching down, picking it up, and ignoring the shocked expression on Mac's face.

"Yup, okay, well," I sputtered. "What time will you pick me up?"

"Seven-thirty, and I'll be in a tux."

My mouth formed an "O" and my pulse raced at the thought of how hot Hendrix would look in a tux. For the first time in my life, I might be tempted to get a guy out of his clothes.

"So, I need like a real dress and heels?" I glanced at Mac, who was sitting on her hands in order to contain herself. It was then that I realized she could hear most of the conversation.

"If you can, yeah. Mac can help you."

"Well, I'd better get busy and go. I'll see you tonight."

"I can't wait," he said before ending the call.

"I've lost my fucking mind," I muttered, placing the phone down on my bed. I swallowed excessively, attempting to clear the lump in my throat.

"What?" Mac asked impatiently.

"I said I would go with him to the charity event tonight. The one his dad is going to go to. Which means...it means I'm going to meet his dad." I could feel the color drain from my cheeks as reality crashed down on me.

"Omigosh! Come on, we needed to start planning like yesterday," she said, hopping off my bed and pulling on my arm.

"Hang on, I'm trying not to puke." Nausea swirled around in my stomach, and I folded my arms across my waist.

"Oh no. It's okay. Listen to me. You'll be with Hendrix all night long. The only time you won't be with him is when you go pee," she giggled. "And when he has to go to the bathroom, you'll be with his dad. Everything is okay. They actually have security there because a bunch of old ladies wear thousands of dollars of diamonds and shit. Like, seriously, you're a hundred percent safe. I swear."

"Really?"

"Yup. Take a deep breath, bestie. We're going shopping."

18

Shopping was hard work. I'd spent the last several years hiding behind clothes, and now I was trying on dresses that hugged my waist and pushed up my boobs.

"Mac!" I whisper-yelled while I tried to zip the eighth dress I'd tried on.

"Right here," she said, flipping open the curtain and strolling into my dressing room. She dropped her purse on the shelf, zipped me up, and I turned around slowly for her.

"Holy shit, I think we found it. Hang on a second," she said, dipping past the curtain and back in again with a pair of black heels.

"I can't walk in those," I said, slipping my feet into them, wobbling a little.

"It'll take you a minute, but I have to see this out here in the light, so come on."

She pulled the curtain aside, and I stepped into the hallway. Mac walked backward, surveying the situation.

"Holy wow," she said, bouncing up and down on her toes. "Turn." She motioned with her finger for me to spin around.

"Mac, I can't wear this. Ada Lynn would never support me showing cleavage."

Mac rolled her eyes and shook her head. "There wasn't a single dress you tried on that didn't give you a boob bump," she said, giggling. "Girl, who knew you had legs for miles? My poor brother."

I frowned. I was already self-conscious, and now Mac was concerned about Hendrix?

"What?" I asked, wringing my hands together. "What's wrong? This was a bad idea. I'm going to text him that I'm sick. I won't even be lying, I think I'm going to toss up my lunch right here."

"Stop, no puking while wearing an expensive dress. It's not allowed," Mac said sternly. "You're fucking beautiful. The poor guy is going to walk around with a massive hard-on all night," she said, giggling.

"Mac!" I scolded. "Oh my God. I don't want to do that to him!"

"I hate to tell you this, but there's not much you can do to stop it. I suspect it's not his first one since you've been around."

My nose scrunched. "You're his sister, how can you even talk about him like that. Eww."

"We're step-siblings, and I told you, we talk about a lot of shit. We're humans, and we all have a sex drive. Well, most of us do," she said, arching her eyebrow at me, and stopping herself from blurting out anything else stupid.

"I'm not dead, Mac," I said, quietly. "It's not that I'm not attracted to Hendrix. It's all just so new to me. Sometimes when he kisses me...the flashbacks..."

Mac hurried toward me and took my hands. "It was a stupid thing to say, and I didn't mean it like that. At. All."

I nodded. I knew Mac well enough now to realize when she said something stupid, it wasn't what her heart meant to say.

"Are we good?" she asked, her expression pleading with me.

"Always," I replied.

"Okay," she took a breath and backed away again. "We're missing something," she said, tapping her chin with her finger.

"What?" I looked at myself in the mirror. The short, royal-blue A-line, off-the-shoulder dress fit every curve like I'd seen in magazines. I'd just never imagined I would be standing in the middle of the River

Park Square Mall, not to mention the Nordstrom's dressing room, wearing a dress and three-inch heels.

"Okay," Mac said, breaking me away from my thoughts. "Jewelry, do you still have enough money after you buy the dress and shoes? I mean, we still have to get your jeans, shirts, and stop at Victoria's Secret. It's in the mall, too."

"Victoria's?" The pitch of my voice climbed a notch.

"Girl, you can't be wearing something that gorgeous and granny panties underneath. Work with me here."

I stifled a giggle. No one would be seeing them anyway. I glanced at the price tag and cringed.

"Mac, I've never spent this much money on one item in my life. What in the hell am I going to do with it after I wear it tonight?"

"Hmm, good point. Oh, I've got it. If you don't want to keep it, donate it. Some stores help girls go to their senior prom. Like they give them dresses."

My heart lit up with the idea of giving back to someone. "Okay, I can justify the purchase now. Let's find some jewelry."

Over the next several hours, Mac and I shopped for jeans, shirts, and everything else I needed in a size two. My cheeks were stained an irreversible shade of red while Mac picked out my new panties and bras. Several thongs and padded push-up bras made it into my basket. I kept my head down as the chatty cashier rang up my new items.

"One more stop," Mac said, glancing at her watch. "We should hurry, though. We barely have enough time."

I followed her down the mall, my bags swinging as I hurried a few steps behind her. Several store entrances later, she took a sharp turn into a salon.

"This one's on me," she said, grinning.

"Mac, you don't have to do this." My eyes widened with her generosity.

"You have the best hair I've ever seen, but it needs to be cut, shaped, and styled. You're going to feel amazing when she's done with you!" Her entire face lit up with her grin.

I sighed. There was no use arguing with her.

"Mac, honey, it's so nice to see you." A woman I guessed to be in her forties with a soft smile and red manicured nails hurried over and hugged Mac.

"Maryann, this is my bestie, Gemma."

"Oh, I see what you're saying," she said, picking up a piece of my hair. "Absolutely beautiful, and with your red, maybe we can add some soft blonde highlights?"

"Yes, ma'am," I said, shyly.

"Oh hon, no need to call me ma'am. I'm not that old," she said, laughing. "Come on back, girls. Let's get started."

Ten minutes passed as we chatted about length, shape, and what Maryann considered would be a good fit for the shape of my face. Mac sat in the seat across from us, jabbering a million miles an hour with her. Apparently they had known each other for years. Every time I tried to sneak a peek in the mirror, they scolded me. Maryann finally turned me toward Mac, so I couldn't look.

Eventually, my jitters disappeared, and Maryann worked her magic. The dead ends fell to the floor, and I stared in disbelief.

"Okay, hon, close your eyes and don't look until I tell you to."

The spin of the chair caught me off guard as she turned me around and removed the cape.

"Open up," she said, stepping away from me.

It took a moment for my brain to wrap around what I saw. My dull locks had a shine it'd never had before, and the new blonde highlights toned down the red. The cut was fantastic. Maryann had taken off a good five inches and added in some subtle layers, which made my hair fall perfectly around my shoulders. My usually wavy look was now sleek and straight. I turned slightly, admiring the length as it flowed down between my shoulder blades. I chewed my bottom lip and took it all in. This was the real me staring back at myself. I'd shed the façade and finally gained the courage to show myself again.

"I love it," I whispered. "I love it." A smile eased across my face, and I touched my newly styled strands gently, not wanting to mess it up.

Mac turned spun me around and hugged me. "I'm so glad you like it. Thanks, Maryann, you're the best!" She hugged her and paid the bill. Twenty minutes later, we were pulling into our dorm's parking lot. A few girls gave us open-mouthed stares as Mac and I carried all my bags inside. The attention was new to me, and I wasn't sure how to handle it. I'd kept myself hidden ever since the pregnancy, trying to avoid anyone really seeing me. Now? Here I was wearing clothes that fit me, and my hair was no longer a mess.

"I'm going to do your makeup," Mac announced, as she pushed open our room door.

"Oh, I forgot about the makeup we bought."

"Yup, and we're about to use it. Helping you get ready will give me something to do, anyway." She smiled while she set the bags down on my bed. I followed suit behind her and sank down on the edge, my feet throbbing.

"I'm tired already, Mac. Wow, who knew shopping was such hard work?"

"I know, right? Now listen carefully. Go wash your face, brush your teeth, scrub your pits, and freshen up all the lady parts," Mac said, wiggling her brows at me. "Do not in any way, form, or fashion get your hair wet or near the water. I do not want it to frizz."

I did as instructed and returned to the room. Mac grinned as she flipped the lamp on, rolled out the desk chair, and patted the seat for me. She rifled through my bags and pulled out the makeup she'd helped me choose at Sephora.

"You don't need much, just a little."

I moaned from exhaustion and moved from the bed and into the chair, allowing her to apply the foundation, eyeshadow, and mascara. She touched up my eyebrows and stepped away, a thoughtful look on her face. I hoped she was admiring her work.

"Poor Hendrix," she muttered behind her hand.

"Why do you keep saying that?" Panic crept up my throat, and my heart pumped wildly in my chest. "What's wrong with me?"

Mac laughed, placed her finger near her crotch, and raised it, thrusting her hips forward. I couldn't help but giggle and remembered her earlier comment about him walking around with a hard-on. My hand lifted toward my face, and she shot forward, pulling it away.

"Do not touch the perfection," she said, nodding at me. "Hands off the face."

Mac reached for a mirror on the desk and held it to her chest. "Are you ready?"

I nodded, and Mac flipped it around. Startled by my reflection, I stared in disbelief.

"Holy hell, Mac. Is that me?" I asked, leaning toward my image.

"Yup. I kept it light and natural to accent your cheekbones and the shape of your eyes. It was effortless, really. You have no idea how beautiful you are, do you?" Mac asked, shaking her head. "Eva did. She used it to her advantage, too. She manipulated the poor guys, and they followed her around like she was a goddess, and to them she was. You're not like her. You would never hurt a guy on purpose. Tonight was the first time I wondered if your new look would change you, though. If Gemma, my bestie, would become someone different if she ever realized how gorgeous she was." Mac's voice was threaded with sadness, and I suspected something similar had happened with Eva.

I turned my chair slowly, taking her hand in mine and smiled. "I can't say what the future holds, but from what I've seen in my nineteen years, family sticks together no matter what."

"Sis?"

"No," I said, grinning. "Not in the sense that I'm marrying your brother, but I do consider you my sister."

Before I knew it, my chair rolled across the floor and smacked into the desk when Mac yanked me up and wrapped me in a huge hug.

She pulled away, her eyes misty with tears, and hurried to the garment bag that held my dress.

"You have fifteen more minutes until Hendrix arrives. He will show up at this door tonight instead of meeting you outside, and he will be on time. So let's get you dressed."

My nerves hummed as I stood and approached the dress.

"Don't forget to change your drawers for God's sake. Wear one of the new pairs we got you. You won't need a bra since it's off the shoulder."

My eyes grew wide. "Shit, I hadn't considered that. What if it's cold and I nip! I don't have five layers of clothes to hide behind anymore."

Mac giggled. "The dress fabric has a lining in it. You just didn't notice. You're fine."

"Oh my God. All of this is so over my head, I would be completely lost without you."

In a matter of minutes, I stood in front of the full-length mirror that hung on Mac's closet door and stared at myself.

"This is so stupid, but I feel like fucking Cinderella," I muttered.

"Mm, I don't think Cinderella would ever say the word fucking, but by all means, it's a new world." Mac burst into giggles. "All right, he should be here any minute. When he knocks, open the door wide so I can watch his expression."

"What expression? I mean, why would he view me any different —" I didn't finish my sentence as I realized he would be seeing me for the first time, just like I had in the mirror a few minutes ago. My stomach did massive backflips, and I sank on Mac's bed, my hands trembling.

"Breathe," she said, rushing over to me. "You're never alone and look—" She got up, grabbed something from the pocket of my old, oversized jeans, and held up my pepper spray. "See this?"

I nodded.

"Don't trip out on me, but it fits right here." I gasped as her fingers pulled the material away from my breasts and slid the pepper spray into a thin piece of material and readjusted my top again. "This brand of dress has a place for women to discreetly hide pepper spray between their cleavage. Cool, huh?"

"Is it why you kept bringing only this brand to me?" I asked, shocked. Mac continually amazed me with her ability to constantly think ahead.

"Yup. See, I've got your back bestie, even when I'm not around. So if Hendrix needs to step away, you're still protected."

A light knock sounded against the door, and I sprang out of my chair, nearly stumbling over my feet in the heels.

"Careful," Mac said. She grabbed my arm and stabilized me. "Deep breath and open the door."

My eyes closed, and I inhaled sharply. It was just Hendrix. I'd spent the entire day with him, alone, in a car. I could do this.

One step at a time, I managed to walk to the door.

"Open it wide," Mac whispered loudly.

My fingers wrapped around the doorknob, and I held my breath while I swung it open.

19

Time stopped as my attention landed on him. My breath hitched in my chest while I took in every inch of him in his tux. He was striking, his hair above his shoulders, his eyes dancing. My heart skipped a beat. He looked amazing—every single bit of panty-dropping amazing.

Hendrix's mouth gaped open, and his cell phone clattered loudly to the floor. I remained quiet as his focus traveled down my body and back up to my face again. Neither of us spoke.

"You might want to make sure your phone didn't break," Mac snickered.

Hendrix bent down, grabbed it, and held it up.

"The phone is fine," he said, grinning, his eyes landing on me again. "Wow! Gemma...you're stunning." He peered around at Mac. "Thanks for helping her. You did well. I think you could start a styling business and get rich."

"I thought I did pretty damned good myself. All right, you two have fun, and let me know if you're not coming home tonight, please."

"Mac!" I hissed.

Hendrix shook his head and chuckled as he extended his hand to me. "Ready?" he asked.

I nodded, grabbed my cell phone, and looped my arm through his. The second my dorm door closed behind us, Hendrix took a deep breath.

"Jesus, you're so beautiful," he said softly.

"Thanks. You're pretty hot yourself," I replied, blushing. "It was all Mac really." I pulled on his arm and stopped him before we reached the steps. "Hang on." I bent down and slipped my heels off. "I don't have the stairs mastered quite yet," I said, giggling nervously. We safely descended the stairs to a noisy group of girls on the first floor. I crouched down and slipped my shoes back on. When I straightened, my gaze locked on Gigi, her mouth slack. All the girls in her group fell silent while Hendrix and I passed them. A bit of pride swelled in me as we walked out the front door.

We strolled to his car in silence. He reached for the handle and paused.

"No, Gemma, it wasn't all Mac. You're breathtaking. And you're going to have a lot of eyes trained on you tonight, including older men. I need to know before we go any farther if you're doing okay. I understand that this change is from the inside out, and what you've been through—what you're trying to leave behind. With that in mind, I can't take you tonight if I even think you're going to be scared or hurt." His jaw clenched after he said the last part.

"I know you'll be with me. Am I safe with your dad?" I asked.

Hendrix nodded. "As long as he's sober, he's your go-to guy if I'm not around. If he starts drinking again, I'll let you know. He stopped drinking over a year ago, though."

"Okay, I can stick close to him if you're not with me. Mac showed me how much she loves me today." I smiled. "You have to take a few steps away, so I can show you what I mean."

Puzzled, Hendrix released the door handle and walked backward, his dress shoes smacking lightly against the sidewalk.

"A few more," I made a shooing motion with my fingers for him to keep going. When he was a safe distance, I pulled the top of the dress out a bit and slipped the pepper spray out. He grinned. "As I said, Mac showed me some major love today." I slid it into my dress and readjusted myself.

"Can I move closer now?" he asked, his voice low and husky.

I nodded. Goosebumps suddenly dotted my skin, and I shivered. In two long strides, he reached me, wrapped his arm around my waist, pulled me to him, and crashed his mouth down on mine. His hands traveled up to my shoulders, and I gasped as his fingers danced across my bare skin. His desire was evident as he kissed me until I was breathless and heady.

To my disappointment, he pulled away slightly, holding me at arm's length. "I told you I would show up today and wouldn't take off on you. I'll tell you again and again until you can trust me with every fiber of your being."

"Thank you," I said.

Hendrix gave me his sexy smile and rested his forehead against mine. "We better go, or we won't make it at all."

I smiled shyly.

I nodded and ran my fingers along his jaw. "You look amazing tonight," I whispered, breathing in his woodsy cologne.

He growled and took a step back.

"Oh, sorry, we should go, huh? Your dad won't think very highly of me if I hijack his son for a make-out session." I wrinkled my nose at him while he opened the car door for me.

"If it were any other night, you could sure as hell hijack me."

I laughed, and he slipped into the driver's side, leaned over, and kissed me again. "Maybe we'll sneak out early instead?" he asked, his brows rising in hope.

"Hendrix Harrington, I'm not that kind of girl," I chided. "For you, though, I'm willing to give it a try." At this point, I would give just about anything a try if Hendrix asked me.

His chuckle filled the car as he turned the ignition, the engine purring to life.

He touched the power button on the stereo, and our song filled the car.

"What? It's finished?" I asked with excitement.

"Yeah, do you like it?" he asked, his fingers tapping nervously on the steering wheel.

"You sound fucking amazing," I said.

"So do you. This couldn't have happened without you. And, I finally nailed down a name for it. What do you think of 'Couldn't Love You More'?"

My eyes widened as the song repeated, the lyrics and harmonization consuming me, taking my thoughts to the first time we met, his concern and protectiveness for me even then. He glanced at me, his expression gentle while he reached for my hand.

"It's perfect," I replied, suddenly overwhelmed with a feeling I'd never experienced before. My head throbbed as the terrifying realization began to fully form inside me. Not just in my mind, but my heart, my body, and every fiber of my being.

Although I was almost in a full-blown panic attack, I casually turned to stare out my passenger's window. I took a deep breath and focused on the city lights. He couldn't know. I cleared my throat and sang with the song, and before I knew it, he'd joined me, and my nerves settled down to a dull roar.

"Here we are," he said, pulling up to the parking lot of the Riverside Place.

"Holy hell, this is beautiful. Look at the architecture!" I scooted forward in my seat while I released the seat belt, opened the glove compartment, and tossed my phone inside. It had never crossed my mind to purchase a handbag for the evening. Hendrix hurried around to the other side and opened my door, extending his hand to me.

I slipped my hand in his and stepped out of the car. "The columns are magnificent," I said, scanning the building as we walked toward the entrance.

"There are eighteen total. President Theodore Roosevelt shoveled some of the dirt during the groundbreaking, too," he said.

"Oh my God, Hendrix, don't let me trip and bust my butt while we're here. This place way outclasses me and showing my ass would be mortifying."

Hendrix coughed. "Depends on which side you're on," he mumbled under his breath.

My cheeks flamed as I realized he'd literally pictured me on the floor with my ass in the air.

"I'm going to ignore you even said that," I said, punching his arm playfully while we strolled through the hallway and into the ballroom. I automatically backed away and fumbled with my fake pearl necklace. Panic coursed through me as I realized there were easily three hundred plus people in the room. Hendrix grabbed my hand and pulled me to the side of the door, leaning me up against the wall.

"You say the word, and we're out of here," he whispered in my ear. "Look at me, Gem."

My legs shook as I focused on him. "Take a breath. I'm right here." His hand caressed my cheek before tucking a piece of hair behind my ear. "You have pepper spray on you, and we are going to walk straight over to my dad. You're going to hold onto my arm the entire night. I won't leave your side, all right?"

I swallowed my fear and grabbed his hand. "I didn't know," I stuttered. "I had no idea there would be so many people."

"It's no different than campus really. You did fine at the concert with Mac, right?"

"Yeah, until Brandon." Panic hitched in my throat with the sound of his name.

"Brandon won't be here tonight or anywhere around. I promise. It's you and me, babe."

My legs steadied, and he kissed my palm, my body shivering from his touch instead of fear.

"I can do this."

He nodded. "Yes you can. You're the strongest person I've ever met. This is a cakewalk compared to what you've already conquered."

I frowned, staring at his bowtie, and up to gorgeous eyes. "You're right. Even compared to yesterday."

"That's right." He leaned in for a quick kiss. "You ready? We can stand here until you are. We have all night. There's no rush."

"I'm okay, thank you."

Hendrix turned and extended his arm. I looped mine through his, and he placed a strong, warm hand over mine. Classical music played in the background while waiters offered champagne and hors d'oeuvres. He guided me through the crowd, and we approached the back of a middle-aged gentleman.

Hendrix patted him on the shoulder, and an older spitting image of him turned around, beaming at his son. This would be Hendrix in thirty years. I released his arm as he hugged his dad. An awkwardness settled over me while Hendrix took my hand and pulled me next to him.

"Dad, this is Gemma. Gemma, this is Franklin Harrington, my father."

"Sir," I said, extending my hand and smiling. "It's a pleasure to meet you,"

He took my hand in both of his, then tilted it up, and kissed the back of it.

"A true southern belle," he said, flashing the same smile as Hendrix. My heart leaped out of my chest.

"I see where Hendrix gets his good looks from," I said politely. Oh my God. What the hell was I saying? Maybe my brain simply couldn't handle two gorgeous men this close to me. I felt like a hormonal teenager.

Franklin grinned, and we engaged in small talk about Louisiana, music, and how I met his son. The tension eased from my shoulders as Hendrix slipped his arm around my waist. His presence steadied me, no matter where we were.

Before I knew it, a few hours had passed quite pleasantly. So far, the only thing I regretted was wearing these damned shoes. I silently swore at Mac while I tried to wriggle feeling into my toes. Franklin and Hendrix introduced me to several people, including the mayor and multiple attorneys. From the looks of it, everyone was rolling in money. Even though my dress was expensive, in my opinion, I was glad I spent the money.

The event also gave me some insight into another piece of who Hendrix was. He effortlessly mingled and talked with everyone. The money never seemed to matter, and he was as comfortable with influential men wearing Rolex watches, their wives dripping in diamonds, as he was with people his own age. Franklin was rubbing elbows with the city officials and some of the top attorneys in the country, according to Hendrix. Suddenly it dawned on me. Hendrix came from money, yet he'd never said a word. He never treated me less than him even when I wore oversized clothes and threadbare tennis shoes. Not once did he ever look down his nose at me. In fact, it was the opposite.

Seconds later, my earlier realization and the fear that accompanied it reappeared.

20

"I need to speak to you, Hendrix. Right now."

Hendrix stopped mid-conversation with Mrs. Beasley, his hand immediately moving to support the small of my back.

"Excuse us, please," he said to her, then quickly navigated us through the crowd and out the front door. The chill of the night air slapped me in the face as we stepped outside.

I pushed his arm off me and hurried away from him as fast as I could in my heels, gasping and tears blurring my vision.

"Gemma! Wait!" I heard his dress shoes smacking the pavement while he jogged after me. I rounded the corner just in time to fall apart. His hand braced my elbow as the tears came down my cheeks.

"Gem, what happened? Talk to me," he coaxed gently.

"I can't believe this. How in the hell have I been so stupid?" I glared at him. "What other secrets are you keeping from me, Hendrix?" His face fell with the realization of why I was upset. "How am I supposed to trust you if you're lying to me?" I asked, hiccupping through my tears.

"It's not like that. Please," he said, his shoulders sagging. "Let me explain."

"No more lies," I spat. "Goddammit, quit jerking me around and tell me the fucking truth for a change. I mean, first, it was 'I don't sing,' then you didn't tell me Mac was your step-sister, and now this?" My voice climbed in pitch, and I wiped the tears away, no longer caring about my makeup.

"No, it's not like that. Please, listen to me."

I hesitated. Pursing my lips into a thin line, I wondered if he would lie to me again. "Talk fast," I snapped and bit my lip.

"First, I never admit to anyone I can sing. I got teased about it for years. I was one of the few guys in choir and competitions. Other kids picked on me, which is why I got into boxing. So it's a habit, and I would sound like a total dick if I walked around and said, 'Hell yeah, I can sing.' I'm sorry it came off like I was hiding it from you. It was never my intention. And Mac? I had no idea you two were even room-mates until the night of the concert when I helped bail you out of trouble. Up until that time, she'd never mentioned you. Mac and I talk plenty, but lately, it's been mostly about Asher. When Brandon popped up again, I spoke to her about staying safe. So that night, walking you two back to the dorm, that's when I realized you were her roommate. Tonight? Sure, be mad at me if you need to be, but let me explain. Yeah, I come from money. A lot of fucking money, actu-ally. None of it matters, though. The girls who know throw them-selves at me, and I'm never sure if it's because I sing, I'm rich, or if it's because they actually like me as a human being." He paused, running both of his hands through his hair, glancing upward at the starlit sky, then at me. "I don't care about your clothes or any of that shit. I wasn't joking. All I care about is your heart and how you treat other people. You're my sister's best friend, and now she never shuts the hell up about you. You can do no wrong in her opinion and honestly? Not in mine either," he said, his voice trailing off, his gaze locking with mine.

His expression, the pain, the fear—it wrecked me. I placed my hand against the wall of the building, steadying myself. His words, the raw emotion behind them, left me weak.

"Goddammit, Gemma, don't you get it?' he asked, breathlessly. "I love you."

I drew in a sharp breath of cold air at his words. Suddenly, all the events from the last two days hit me, overpowered me, and threatened to bring me to my knees. In one step, Hendrix caught me before I hit the ground.

"Shit," he said. "You're shaking. Let's take you to the car where you can get warm."

My head buzzed with anxiety as he removed his tux jacket and wrapped it around me. In a daze, I let him lead me to the car and put me in. He ran to the side and started the engine. My teeth chattered while the air blew cold.

"I'm sorry. I'm such a dick," he said, pulling his jacket tighter around me. The hot air began to blow from the vents, but I continued to shiver.

He pulled out of the parking space and headed toward campus. My mind struggled to work through everything he'd said. In my heart, I knew he was telling me the truth. I'd just gotten angry, thinking he'd lied to me, and then absolutely terrified when he told me he loved me.

I swallowed, my throat dry and scratchy as I turned toward him.

"Take me to your place," I whispered.

21

Hendrix suddenly swerved the car over to the shoulder of the road and shifted into park.

"What?" he asked, confusion dancing across his features.

"Take me to your place, Hendrix."

He shook his head. "No. Not tonight. You've been through too much. And if I take you there, I'm going to want to wrap you in my arms and make love to you all night long."

Cars passed us and honked. I ignored them as I stared at him and absorbed every beautiful thing about him.

"Did you mean it? You love me?"

He turned in his seat, facing me. "Yes. I love you. I love you so fucking much it's tearing me in two. More than anything in this world, even more than music, I love you. I want you by my side. I want to kiss you, and laugh with you, and show you how beautiful life can really be."

A tear slipped down my cheek. "I love you, too, Hendrix."

His eyes widened. "You do?"

"I realized it tonight, and it terrified me way more than you having money. I'm not mad about you not providing full disclosure about your finances. I understand why you didn't. I was angry with myself for being so scared of what I'm feeling."

He stared at me, and I reached for his hand. "So please, take me to your place tonight. I'll text Mac."

He searched my face for a long moment, nodded, shifted the car into drive, and pulled back onto the street.

I opened the glove compartment and pulled out my phone. In a few taps on my screen, I texted Mac I was staying with Hendrix.

My screen filled with love emojis seconds later. I pushed the fear aside when I realized I was on my way to his place. He squeezed my hand.

"It's on the Spokane River, the view is amazing," he said.

"I bet it's great for writing music, huh?"

"There's nothing like it."

"Why in the hell were you always sitting in the college library then?"

"You. I'd never set foot in there until the day you had your panic attack. I was actually sitting outside working on a chorus when you showed up."

"You're telling me the only reason you even walked in there was for me?" I asked, surprised, and still confused about what he saw in me.

"Yeah," he said, signaling a right turn on North Upriver Road.

We pulled into a curvy driveway and meandered up a hill to his house.

"Shit, you don't even live in an apartment?" I asked, peering through the darkness at the two-story home. Large picture windows spanned the front and were partially hidden behind tall pine trees.

"No, I own it, Gem."

"What? You're a junior in college and own a house? On the river? I might be from Louisiana, but I know water property is seriously expensive."

"It's Dad's way of trying to make up for being a drunk, shitty father."

"So it's free and clear?"

"Yeah."

I stared at him, the fact slowly sinking in that he had more money than I'd ever imagined.

"Let's go," he said.

The indoor and outdoor lights automatically turned on as we approached. He punched in a code and opened the door, allowing me in first. My heels clicked against the white marble entryway, breaking the silence between us.

"Take a look around, and I'll show you every door and every window in case you feel the need to take off running."

I laughed, but he knew me well enough to know what would ease my mind and make me feel safe. My eyes scanned the living room with the massive stone fireplace, and the black leather couch that looked like you could sink into it and never get out. A 65-inch TV hung on another wall.

"Let me show you the kitchen," he said, taking my hand and leading the way. The moment his foot reached the kitchen floor, the room lit up.

"This has to be custom, right?" I asked, scanning the marble countertops and cherry cabinets in awe. I'd never seen a kitchen so beautiful.

"Yeah. It was fun designing it. Are you doing okay?" he asked, rubbing my back.

I nodded, scanning every inch of his space.

"Come on. This is why I bought this place."

I followed him out of the kitchen and to the sliding glass door. The patio lit up as we walked outside.

"Oh my God," I whispered. Although I couldn't see the river in the darkness, I could hear the rushing water. The scent of the fresh air tickled my nose, and I inhaled deeply, soaking in the peaceful surroundings.

"You're so beautiful," he said.

My pulse skipped a beat, and I took a step closer to him, slipping off my heels.

His fingers traced down my neck, and I leaned into his touch. "Are you sure you're ready?"

"Yeah, I'm sure."

"I love you so much," he said before his lips gently brushed against mine.

"I love you, too."

Heat traveled through my body as he kissed me softly, each touch of his hand sending shivers down my spine.

"Let's take you inside." He opened the slider before he led me up the stairs.

My eyes widened when we entered his bedroom. A modern, dark brown, four-poster California king bed sat in the middle of the room with a plush navy-blue comforter and matching pillows. A cozy sitting-area was tucked into a spacious corner. The floor-to-ceiling windows, no doubt, displayed a beautiful view in the daylight. A full-sized matching dresser was against the opposite wall.

I stood speechless while he undid his bow tie and removed his tuxedo jacket from around my shoulders.

"Man, that feels so much better," he said, cracking his neck. "The only time you'll catch me in a tux is for an event like tonight."

I smiled shyly, my legs quivering as my focus rested on his bed. Was I really ready to do this?

22

My body shuddered with fear and excitement, my stare glued on him.

"The moment you're not okay, tell me. Promise?"

"Yeah," I said, and then his mouth was on mine. I locked my fingers around his neck, and we simultaneously took several steps toward his bed.

"Can I unzip your dress?" he whispered.

I nodded, unable to say anything, fear and need intertwining themselves inside me. He turned me gently, my back to him. The rasp of the zipper broke the silence. I kept my elbows pinned to my sides, preventing my dress from dropping to the floor. Butterflies erupted inside my stomach as his fingertips trailed down my bare arms.

"I think you should look at me, and let's keep the lamp on. I want you to know you're safe in here with me every second," he said.

"Thank you." In one quick motion, I lifted my elbows, brushed the fabric from my shoulders, and allowed my dress to drop to the floor. My nipples hardened against the cool air, and I trembled, exposed in front of him.

"Holy shit, you're more beautiful than I could have ever imagined." His voice was hoarse, his eyes dark with desire as his focus traveled over my near nakedness, only my thong left in place. His gaze lingered briefly on my light c-section scar.

"Can I touch you?" he asked, cautiously.

"Yes," I said with more confidence than I felt. He needed to understand I wanted this, too. I wanted to make love to him. I wanted to replace the memories of that horrible night. I had the choice this time, and I chose him.

He placed his hand on my chest. "Your heart is racing. We don't have to do this."

"I realize that. I know I can pick up my dress right now and walk out of your front door. I don't want to, though. I want to be here with you. I want to feel you inside of me, I want to take back everything that was stolen from me, and I want to do it with you."

He reached up and unbuttoned his shirt, removing it and tossing it on the floor. I scanned his muscular chest, arms, and thick, corded shoulders. His abs rippled as he flipped the button open on his slacks but didn't remove them.

"I want to show you how much I love you," he said, pulling me flush against him. My breasts brushed against his hot skin, and a rush of heat pulsed between my legs.

"I want to show you what it should be like when someone loves you. Tonight is all about you." He kissed me and stepped away.

"Get comfortable on the bed," he ordered.

Embarrassed, I sat down and scrambled backward awkwardly on the giant mattress.

"You have nothing to be shy about. You're so beautiful it's hurting me. I'm going to lie down next to you if it's okay?"

I patted the bed next to me, my heart pounding so hard I thought I might pass out. The mattress gave under his weight, and I rolled into him, my back arching and my breasts flattening against his chest. He scooted away enough to allow some space between us and gently caressed my cheek. His hand cupped my breast and I gasped, his touch scaring and electrifying me at the same time.

"Does it feel good?" he asked, gauging my reaction before taking me into his mouth, his tongue flicking across my nipple. My body melted, the sensation on my skin was so intense I was afraid I might blackout. I rolled over onto my back and threaded my hands through his hair, holding him to me, while he stroked my sensitive bud with his tongue.

His fingers trailed down my stomach, lingering on my scar. My body tensed, and he immediately stopped and lifted his head, searching for any signs I wasn't handling the situation.

"I'm all right," I whispered.

"I don't want to do anything to hurt you or trigger bad memories. Please be honest with me so we can stop if we need to."

"I will," I assured him.

He nodded but held my gaze as his fingers trailed down to my thong, quickly dancing over the fabric and across my core. I gasped.

"If you know nothing else about me, don't ever doubt you own my heart, Gemma."

His fingers traced my sensitive skin through the thin material, igniting an intense desire between my legs.

My eyes closed briefly as he continued. I moaned and raised my hips to meet his hand.

"Everything you lost, I want to return to you. Let me love you," he whispered in my ear.

My hand moved tentatively over the dips and valleys of his muscular shoulders and back, his bare skin sparking electricity beneath my fingertips.

"Can I take off your thong?" he asked, his voice husky.

Nerves shot through me at the idea of him seeing me completely naked.

I nodded and watched while he stood at the edge of the bed, his need bulging against his slacks.

"Raise your hips," he requested.

I did as he asked, and he slid them down my legs and dropped it to the floor. He ran his hands from my ankles up the inside of my thighs and pushed my legs apart. "You're so beautiful, so wet." He moaned.

Using the pads of his thumbs, he gently massaged the inside of my thighs.

"Keep your eyes open, and tell me if we need to stop."

The next thing I knew, his head dipped between my legs, his rough tongue flicking across my sensitive skin. I moaned and bunched up the comforter in my hands. He gently sucked my clit, and I arched off the bed as he claimed me. He slid his hands underneath my ass cheeks and lifted me off the bed, his mouth licking and sucking me.

"Hendrix," I whimpered. "Oh my God, what are you doing to me?" I gasped, closing my eyes.

His finger traced my entrance, and I cried out. My eyes flew open, searching wildly around the room until I remembered I was with Hendrix. With the realization of who I was with, I didn't want him to stop. My gaze traveled down between my legs, watching him, his hair tucked behind his shoulder, his intense stare locking on me while his tongue flicked across my center. Heat swirled through me, and a strange sensation began to build. My attention never left him while I held onto his hair, my body burning with new sensations.

He sucked me, his fingers digging into my ass cheeks, my breaths short bursts of hot air. He moaned as he gently bit me, taking my bundle of nerves into his mouth, sucking slowly, rhythmically. My head tilted back, and I shattered, drowning in waves of pleasure, coming apart and being remade at the same time.

"Hendrix," I cried. The moment his name left my lips, he stopped and was next to me, his hands cupping my face.

"Gemma?" His voice carried a hint of panic.

I grabbed him and dug my nails into his shoulders as I broke down and sobbed against him, my tears spilling onto his bare chest.

"Babe, I'm sorry. We can stop. Shh, I love you," he said, wrapping his arms around me, allowing me to break down against him.

Finally, my body shuddered with its last cry, and I lifted my head to look at him.

"You didn't do anything wrong," I said, tracing his jawline. "Since that night, I've carried around so much shame about my body. But this, you—you made me feel beautiful—no longer dirty."

He placed his forehead against mine. "Never. I don't want you to ever feel dirty again."

"Hendrix?"

"Yeah?"

"Make love to me. I need you inside of me," I said.

His breath quickened while he stared at me for a long minute, then he reached over the bed and into the nightstand drawer. I averted my attention as he removed his pants and tore open the condom. I knew if I saw him, saw the size of him, I would chicken out. This was almost more than I could handle already.

He laid next to me again. "Eyes on me please," he said, stroking my cheek. "I need you here with me while we make love for the first time."

I spread my legs, and he slowly lowered himself over me, bracing his body on his strong, muscular forearms.

"I wish this wasn't going to hurt you. This part is going to kill me, but I don't know what else to do."

I slid my hands around his neck and pulled him down to me, kissing him. His hand cupped my breast, teasing my nipple, and heat coursed through me again as he placed lazy kisses down my neck.

He raised my hips a little, and I felt him push slightly at my entrance. He lifted his head and brushed the hair away from my face.

"I love you," he said, and with one thrust, he slipped deep inside of me.

My head tilted back, and a scream ripped from my throat. Everything in me snapped the moment he entered me. The hands no longer belonged to Hendrix. His mouth belonged to my rapist. His intrusion speared my soul. "Gemma!" Hendrix said firmly, remaining still. "Look at me. Look at me, goddammit." His hand cupped my cheek.

Forcing myself to focus on him, my breathing came in short bursts. "Don't stop," I cried. "Jesus, don't fucking stop."

A tear streamed down Hendrix's face as he moved gently in and out of me.

"This isn't worth it, Gemma. I can't do this," he choked. "I love you too much."

My legs wrapped around his waist, squeezing him, not allowing his body to leave mine. My nails dug into his lower back while I timidly arched up to meet him. "No, you're already here. Don't stop."

My eyes widened as the guilt and sadness flickered across his features. With each move, the pain lessened, and I calmed down, my gaze never leaving his.

"I love you, Hendrix. I love you so much."

Tears streamed down my cheeks, and I began to move with him, slowly, gently, his body inside me, filling me with everything good in this world, stripping away all the pain and all the shame. All my guilt.

"Talk to me, babe. Should I keep going?" he asked, desperation in his voice.

"Yes," I said, flashing him a quick smile. "Keep going. It's starting to feel better. You feel good inside me," I hiccupped through the tears.

He placed kisses on my forehead, nose, and gentle, passionate ones on my lips as he thrust in and out of me. With every stroke, he gave a piece of my heart and soul back to me.

I moaned as he picked up his pace.

"Is this what you wanted, Gem?"

"Yes," I responded, breathless, the pleasure outweighing the physical and emotional pain.

He shifted over me and slid his hand between our bodies, teasing my clit. My eyes widened while he continued stroking and teasing, moving deeper inside me.

"Oh my God," I said. "You feel so amazing."

He smiled as he continued, and a familiar sensation began to swirl in my abdomen. I bit my lower lip while my head tilted back.

"Are you with me, Gemma?" he asked.

"Yeah," I moaned.

"I need you to come for me again." He panted. "I need you to come before I can."

His fingers caressed my sensitive flesh, his pace quickening.

"Oh," I groaned and dug my nails into his shoulders. "Oh."

"I love you, Gemma. Come with me," he urged.

Although I didn't want him to stop, my entire body tensed, and jolts of pleasure rippled over me.

"Shit," he said, "I can't hang on," he said, coming with me, his body shuddering.

Moments later, he gently collapsed against me and stilled. I stroked his hair as he remained inside me, my pulse beginning to slow, my heart awakening.

He lifted his head, searching my face for my reaction.

"Thank you," I whispered. "Thank you for setting me free."

"Dammit, you scared the shit out of me. If I hurt or scarred you— I would never forgive myself."

"You didn't," I said, my fingers skimming lightly across his chin.

He kissed the tip of my nose. "I need to take care of this condom," he said.

I nodded, grieving the loss of his body heat while he sat up and pulled out of me. I watched him as he walked into the bathroom, his leg muscles flexing with every step he took. A moment later, he returned, climbing into bed with me again. He kissed my cheek and placed his forehead against mine. "As much as I want to be with you, Gemma, I can't do that again."

23

My heart sank. "What do you mean?"

"The sheer terror on your face, it was too much. Sex isn't worth losing you over."

"I didn't feel good to you?" I gasped, shoving away from him.

He reached out and grabbed me before I could move farther away.

"Stop, I didn't say that. You're amazing, and there's no place I'd rather be than inside of you. However, I love you, and you being present with me mentally," he said, gently tapping my forehead, "and here," he said, tapping my heart next, "and spiritually," he said, tapping my lower abdomen, "is more important than getting off. I need all of you with me, not just your body."

My heart softened with his words. He was choosing me over the sex. He wanted what was best for me. The emotion that lingered in his expression, and the love I felt from him in this moment, washed over me, taking all of my darkness with it. I'd never felt this close to someone, loved someone as deeply as I did Hendrix. Before I knew it, I'd rolled on top of him, my legs straddling his waist. I laughed at the wide-eyed look of surprise he gave me.

"Gem?" His hands gripped my waist as he stared at me.

"Who knew all you had to say was I love you, and I'd happily give you all of me?" I asked, grinning. I flipped my hair over my shoulder as I sat on top of him, my breasts exposed, realizing my body was ready for him again. This time, I wanted to see him. He'd already been inside me, now I wanted to look at him, admire every muscle, every inch of the man who loved me enough to tell me no.

I moved off him, my hand on his stomach, my attention traveling down his chest to the light brown hair trailing below his belly button and down to his erection. I let loose a small gasp when I saw how long and thick he was.

"How did you even fit in me?" I asked, my brows knitting together.

He grinned. "It was very tight," he said, chuckling.

"Is that a good thing?"

"Oh yeah, you have no idea."

Once again, I took in the sight of Hendrix's body, so perfectly sculpted and masculine, and I frowned, frustrated with my lack of experience. "I don't know how to make you feel good," I said.

"Yes, you do," he said, his eyes darkening with longing.

"Will you help me?" I asked, wrapping my fingers around his shaft.

He took in a sharp breath, his hand moving to my back.

"Like this?" I grasped him firmer.

"Yeah," he said.

"What else?" I blushed, suddenly shy. "Show me."

His eyes opened, and he wrapped his hand around mine. He moved my fingers up and down his length, then let go. I continued on my own. The pleasure was evident in his expression. Without thinking about it, I moved down, hovering over him as I continued. I cautiously kissed the tip of him.

"Shit," he said, his head popping off the bed while he peered at me. I licked his sensitive head, and his eyes rolled back. I assumed from my own experience this was a positive thing.

I eased more of him into my mouth, sucking him slowly. His fingers threaded through my hair, grabbing a fistful. My body ached for him again as he moaned and moved his hips.

"Grab a condom," I said and moved, allowing him to get into the nightstand. This time I watched while he opened the packet and rolled it over his length.

I straddled him, positioning myself on top, and sat down, slowly taking him in inch by inch. He grabbed my waist, and I settled in.

"You're so beautiful," he said as I sat still, allowing him to fill me.

I rocked against him, timidly, the palms of my hands on his chest. "Like this?" I asked.

"Perfect," he said, tucking a stray hair behind my ear.

My pace quickened, my soreness subsiding as we found our rhythm together. I shifted my weight back, the feeling different than when I leaned forward. His fingers slipped between my legs and began massaging my bundle of nerves. I released a soft moan while he teased me.

"So wet," he whispered. "I want to see you when you come, and you're wrapped tightly around me."

I moaned, my body waking up from a long sleep, my breasts bouncing with each movement.

"Hendrix," I whimpered. "What are you doing to me?" I panted. "Harder." I slammed down on him as he lifted his hips off the bed, our need taking over from our emotions. His grip tightened as he guided me, and I slid up and down his shaft.

"Oh yeah," he groaned.

My fingernails dug into his chest as delicious sensations swirled through me. A loud groan escaped me as I released, my core tightening around him. His eyes slammed shut while he thrust deep inside me again and again until his body tensed, his muscles rippling as he came inside me.

Satisfied and happy, I collapsed on top of him. He played with my hair as I listened to his heartbeat.

"Maybe you on top is a safe way for us to be together for now," he said, kissing my head.

"What do you mean?" I asked, looking up at him.

"You can see me, you have control. Maybe it will help you feel better emotionally."

I nodded and lifted my head off his chest. "I did like it, I felt safer this time. No flashbacks, either."

"Tell me you love me, Gem."

I smiled as my heart nearly exploded, finally free to admit it. "I love you, Hendrix Harrington, and everything about you."

"How did I get so damned lucky?" he asked, cupping my cheek.

I laughed. "It's the other way around. You took the time to look past everything I was hiding behind and somehow managed to see me."

"I've loved you from the moment you told me it was your table." He chuckled.

"I was pretty territorial. Sorry."

"No, it was a good thing, just be that territorial with other guys and not me."

I giggled.

"How about we get under the blankets, and you let me hold you while you sleep?" His arm tightened around me. I didn't want to let him go either.

I peeked at the clock. It was after midnight, and exhaustion seeped into my weary bones.

"I'd love to," I said, giving him a quick kiss before I got off the bed.

He got up, flipped the covers back, adjusted the pillows, and crawled into the bed. I slipped in next to him, turning on my side and sliding a leg over him.

"Sweet dreams, Gem."

"You too, Hendrix." And for the first time since I was fourteen, I slept peacefully.

24

I woke to a soft kiss on my forehead and peered at Hendrix through a sleepy haze.

"Morning, gorgeous," he said, his fingertips trailing little circles on my forehead. "How are you doing?"

"Sore," I said, smiling up at him.

"You know what people recommend for that?" he asked while his hand slipped beneath the blankets, down my stomach, and between my legs. My breath hitched as he gently slid a finger inside of me.

"I think I'm addicted to you," he said softly.

A smile eased across my face while I reached under the covers and wrapped my fingers around him. His erection throbbed in my hand while his mouth took mine in a hungry kiss.

"I should start on the pill," I said, stroking him. "So we don't have to deal with condoms every time, and we can just be together," I whispered in his ear.

He growled and slid underneath the blankets, his tongue dancing across my core. I spread my legs, welcoming him, his mouth, his finger inside me. My hands dug into the mattress as he licked and sucked me. Finally, I flung the covers off us and grabbed his hair, lifting my hips, grinding against his hand and mouth.

"It's working. I'm not sore anymore," I gasped, giving in to the overwhelming sensations, my body tensing in pure desire.

He moved over me, grinning and fumbling around in his night-stand for a condom.

I bit my lower lip when he entered me, slowly sliding inside until he could go no farther.

We rocked against each other, our bodies and hearts synchroniz-ing, blending, harmonizing while we made love to each other. Never in my wildest dreams had I ever thought I would be in a man's arms, devouring every moment of him touching me, loving me.

Hendrix raised our joined hands above my head, our fingers intertwining, our gazes locking. He shifted his hips in a circular motion, touching every sensitive spot inside me. My eyelids fluttered closed as I moaned.

"That's my girl," he said, continuing.

I wrapped my legs around his waist, pulling him deeper. He groaned, picking up the pace.

"Shit," he muttered.

Our breathing sped up, and we continued to rock together, our bodies moving in unison. Sweat beaded lightly across his forehead, his arm muscles flexing with every thrust.

"Hendrix, you will always have my heart," I whispered in his ear. "Forever."

He began to tense, his pace quickening. My body automatically reacted to his pleasure and the realization I could make him feel this good.

"Gem, I can't hold on. You feel too amazing," he panted. My body tingled with his words. I tensed in response, my core tightening around him as we released together.

He collapsed next to me, both of us panting, grinning at each other like idiots.

"Better?" he asked.

"Much," I replied, laughing.

Life had changed so much in the few months since I'd left

Louisiana. It was almost as though by leaving, I'd begun to shed my past like a cocoon.

"I love you," he said, tilting my chin up.

"Love you, too," I said softly before he kissed me.

"As much as I don't want to say this, it's after nine, and you should probably call Mac. I'll make us some breakfast while you do."

I groaned and slapped my hands against my forehead. "What am I going to tell her? She's going to have a million and one questions. I don't talk about—this," I said, pointing between us. "It's private."

He chuckled. "Mac and I have talked and shared a lot, but I'm with you on this one. She knows we're together, but it doesn't mean you have to give her details."

My cheeks flushed at the thought of even attempting to answer her questions. "Maybe I'll just text her that I'll be home later today. If you have time, I would love to see outside again now that we have daylight."

"Anything you want," he said. "I'll give you one of my shirts since you don't have anything else here except your dress. Maybe that should change?" he asked, eyeing me.

"What? You want me to keep some clothes here?"

He shrugged. "Why not? I have this big closet and plenty of drawer space. The nights you stay over, you don't have to worry about packing an overnight bag. You'll already have stuff here. We can keep it simple and spontaneous."

"Simple? I'm not sure this is simple, Hendrix."

"I know," he said, kissing the palm of my hand. "Sometimes it's less scary if we just say it is. And technically, because you like to think things through at every angle, keeping a few things here isn't any different than if you packed a bag to bring. It's easier not to have to think about it, and if we end up here, you're already prepared."

"Guess it makes sense when you put it that way."

"Yup," he said, grinning.

"I need to find a doctor, too. I can't get pregnant. I'm not sure if I'll ever want kids, but especially not right now."

Hendrix's eyebrow arched, and sadness flickered across his features. "Never?" he asked, his voice hoarse.

"I'm not sure," I said, propping up on my elbow. "Honestly, I never wanted any to begin with. Hendrix, this is all too new for me to make any life-changing decisions at this moment."

"Yeah," he said, his attention drifting away from mine. He sat up on the side of the bed, his shoulders slumping.

"Hendrix," I said, my hand gently rubbing his back. "I love you, but that's the only thing I can say for certain right now."

"I understand," he said, reaching for my other hand. "I think about it sometimes, what a life would be like with you. Would we have brown-haired or red-headed babies? Obviously they would have blue eyes, but—"

I kissed his shoulder. "I'm only nineteen, and I've lost so many years. I need to learn to adjust to all the changes. To you. Don't give up on the idea, but I can't talk about it right now either. We're so new —" I said, my words trailing off.

He turned toward me, sadness flickering through his eyes. "I realize we're new, Gem. But I want you to know, you're the first woman I've met that I could see myself with long-term."

"Really?" I gasped. I'd never considered the future or anything long-term after the pregnancy. I couldn't see past all the pain.

He nodded. Suddenly, a ball of darkness exploded inside of me. I couldn't think about it right now. I couldn't entertain the idea of a future with him.

Hopping off the bed, I wrapped a blanket around my naked body and made a mad dash to his bathroom.

He swore as I closed the door on him and locked it. Without asking, I turned on his shower. Startled, I backed away while the water shot out of multiple showerheads. I dropped the blanket and stepped into the warm stream and let it ease my mind. Scanning the ornate tile of his colossal shower, I wondered if we were too different to make this work.

He came from money, I came from brokenness. A tear slipped down my cheek as I placed my hands on the shower wall and shut out everything around me. Inhaling the steam, my mind flipped through every moment I'd had with him. Never had he treated me differently for my insistence on wearing baggy clothes, tinted glasses, and a hat. He'd stood up to Brandon for me more than once. He'd even asked me out before my physical transformation, but most of all, he'd loved me while I relived the darkest time of my life and shared my past with him. How could I not love him? And we had our entire life to plan our future, kids or no kids, what we wanted to do, where we wanted to live. None of it was relevant now, only him. Only us.

After analyzing everything while I washed my hair, I concluded I wanted to be with him. I loved him, and nothing else in this world mattered.

Twenty minutes later, I finished my shower, grabbed a towel from the rack, and dried off. Maybe I was just tired, or I was on overload, but after the shower, I felt calmer. Wrapping the plush fabric around me, I unlocked the door and stepped into his bedroom. He wasn't there, though. My bare feet padded on the silky soft carpet, down the stairs, and toward the smell of breakfast. He stood in the kitchen, wearing only jeans and no shirt. He had his back to me, cooking.

"Hey," I said, "I'm sorry."

"Don't apologize, Gem," he replied, turning toward me. "It was my fault. Sometimes I get so caught up in us, and I forget this is your first relationship. You've come so far. I don't want to ever be the person to send you flailing backward again."

"I know," I said softly. "I love you, and now that I realize you can also cook, I'm in even more trouble," I said, smiling. "I'm starving."

"Me too. And, as much as I would like to see you walking around in my towel all day, I should find you a shirt and some sweats or something." He moved the pan off the stove and rounded the counter.

His hands cupped my chin, tilting my head up toward him. "I'm so glad you're here," he said, kissing me.

He took my hand and led me to his walk-in closet. We laughed when his initial choices seemed to swallow me, but soon I was snuggled up in one of his long-sleeved T-shirts and sweats. They were still way too big, but thank God for an elastic waist and a drawstring. We sat down at his table and enjoyed our first breakfast together.

"You're all of my firsts," I said, stopping mid-chew.

His gaze traveled up from his food to me while he reached for my hand.

"I'm honored," he said. "You're my first, too."

My brows raised. "Uh, I don't want any details, but it's obvious you've slept with other women. Which hopefully means you took them out on a date, too. So I don't really see how I'm your first for anything."

"I've never been in love before," he said, placing his fork down on the side of his plate.

"You haven't?" I asked.

"No. I've never felt anything remotely close to it. I think after I lost Kendra—" He hesitated for a minute, pain and regret flickering in his eyes. "I didn't think I could really take care of someone or protect them like I should."

"No, it's not true," I said, shaking my head. "You've already protected me from Brandon, and you've protected Mac, too. Kendra wasn't your fault."

"I shouldn't have left her alone, and I find the same fear is creeping in again. I'm afraid to leave you, afraid I'll fail you, too."

Tears formed in my eyes as I scooted my chair back, walked over to him, and slid into his lap. His arms wrapped around my waist, and he held me tightly.

"No one can be with me twenty-four hours a day, seven days a week. Not you, not Mac, no one. This is something I think we all need to work on together, Hendrix. I need to feel safe, Mac needs to feel safe, and you need to know we're okay when we're not with you. If it's not Brandon, it would be someone else. If I could, the one gift I would give every woman, every girl, is a way to protect herself—" My voice trailed off, and I leaned my forehead against his. "This is what I do know, we're stronger together. You've given me the gift of life again, and no one else has been able to do that."

He searched my face. "When you leave, just come back to me," he whispered.

"Always." Even as the words left my mouth, even with everything I'd lived through, I knew there was no real way I could promise him tomorrow. There were never guarantees.

25

A little after five o'clock, I swung the door open and cringed, waiting for the rapid-fire of questions from Mac. Instead, I found her sitting in the corner of her bed, studying.

"Hey," she smiled and gave me a small wave.

"Hey?" I asked, stepping in and sliding off my heels. I changed into some boyfriend jeans and a long-sleeved green flannel shirt and flopped down on the side of her bed.

"How's it going?"

"Good," she said, glancing up at me. "You?"

"Fine," I said cautiously. What was happening? This certainly wasn't what I'd anticipated. "Well, I've got some studying to do before classes tomorrow."

"Me too," she replied, not looking up from her book.

Unsure of what was up with her, I grabbed my books off my desk and settled on my bed to study. I was flipping through my playlists when a text flashed on my screen.

I hate being away from you.

I grinned, keeping my head down, my hair enclosing me in a small blanket of privacy while I texted Hendrix back.

I miss you already, too.

How's Mac?

Strange.

I hit send, and my fingers tapped the keyboard on my screen.

She's acting like I didn't spend the night with you. She didn't ask a single question.

The black dots indicated he was typing, and I impatiently waited for his response.

What? Is she sick? Did you check her for a fever?

I muffled my giggle and glanced over at her.

No. I've never seen her like this, so I'm not sure what to do other than act like it's not a big deal.

It's a huge deal. You own my heart.

I chewed on my bottom lip with his last text.

I meant Mac being a big deal. LOL. I promise I'll take care of your heart, though. I love you.

I can't take this anymore. Not being with you is awful. I'm coming to get you.

My eyes widened. He'd only dropped me off at the dorm twenty minutes ago. I knew what he meant. I ached for him in every way possible when he wasn't with me, too.

I wish I could be with you tonight, but I have to study, or I'll flunk out and have to go back to Louisiana.

That doesn't work for me. Guess I won't see you tonight. If you change your mind, let me know, and I'll be there in a few minutes.

Smiling, I tapped out my reply and then set my phone down. Not a minute later, Mac's phone vibrated. She grabbed it off her desk and strolled out of the room, never saying a word.

"Shit," I muttered. This wasn't how I figured she would take the news of Hendrix and me at all. Was she jealous? Upset? I couldn't figure her out. I sighed and situated myself against the wall, crossed my ankles, and forced myself to focus. My thoughts continued to ping-pong between Mac and Hendrix, though.

Flustered and unable to concentrate, I slammed my book shut, hopped off the bed, and walked out the door. I stopped short when I located Mac, sitting at the top of the stairs, crying.

"Mac?" I asked, running toward her. "Hey, what's wrong?" I sat next to her and put my arm around her shoulders.

"Asher," she wailed. "He's getting married!"

"Oh Mac, I'm so sorry. I've been in my own world and never even realized you still had feelings for him."

"It's okay," Mac said, wiping her nose. "I usually talk to Hendrix about him, but he was busy last night so—" She attempted a smile at me through her tears.

"You can talk to me now, too. I'm okay. Well, better at least."

"Yeah? That's good, right?" she asked, tilting her head.

"Yes, it means I can be there more for my best friend when she needs me," I said, squeezing her shoulder. "Come back in, tell me what's going on, and then we'll study together. My concentration is shit right now anyway."

"Tell me about it," she said, rising.

Back in our room, we settled on my bed, sitting Indian style and facing each other. I almost felt like a little kid again, hanging out with my best friend, Fae. I pushed the memories away and chided myself. Fae was no longer a part of my life. Now that I was older, I realized how horribly she'd treated me after the rape. This wasn't about me, though. This was about Mac.

"Deets," I said, smiling at her.

"It sounds funny when you say it," she said, laughing through her tears. "Must be the southern drawl."

"Thanks, I'll work on it."

"I got an email from him," she said, her shoulders slumping. "Which brought back all kinds of emotions and shit, because he told me he still loves me, always will, and in the next sentence said he's engaged," she cried.

"What? He said he still loves you?"

"Yes! Like what the fuck? Isn't it bad enough he's getting married without making it worse and telling me he still has feelings for me? Does he want me on the side?"

"Well, I'm confused," I said, pondering.

"Makes two of us," she said, twirling her braid around her finger.

"If he still loves you, why is he marrying someone else?"

"Daddy," she said.

My mouth formed an "O." I had no clue how to respond, so I sat quietly, waiting for her to tell me more.

"So, uh, you're used to me sticking my foot in my mouth, but you've already figured out your boyfriend is seriously rich, right?"

I shrugged and nodded, unsure of what it had to do with Asher.

"Okay, so Hendrix's dad, my ex-stepdad, has like a lotta, lotta, lotta money. He and Asher's dad put together this ginormous deal and BAM, just like that, Asher's dad pocketed millions and was now playing in the same circles. Like, even though ex-stepdad fell from grace, he never lost his money. It was still working for him in the background, so when he got his shit together and decided to be there for Hendrix, he bought him the house and car. Hendrix wanted a better relationship with him, but he figured he shouldn't be stupid and turn the gifts down since life could change in like a nanosecond."

A grin spread across my face. There was my Mac, rambling on a million miles an hour.

"What?" she asked, raising her hands in question.

"I was worried about you earlier, but keep talking, I think it's helping."

She eyed me and then continued. "Asher and I dated part of our sophomore year and all of our junior and senior year. Well, we split up once for a week, but it didn't really count. Anyway, as I've mentioned before, he was my first, and I do mean my first, like Hendrix is yours."

I flushed crimson red with her comment.

"You're gonna have to get over it because besties discuss this stuff," she said, pointing at me. "And you look absolutely magnificent in that green shirt. It's so nice to see you wearing some color and not those other drab clothes. Anyway, shit, where was I?"

"Asher's dad and the circles they ran in," I reminded her.

"Yes, so Asher's dad introduced him to some super-rich girl after we split up, but what Asher didn't know was that there was another business deal going on with her dad."

"Oh," I said, linking the pieces together. "So the marriage is a business deal? People do that shit?"

"Girl, please, you would be shocked at what happens behind the closed doors of the rich."

My eyebrows shot up.

"So when is he getting married?" I asked.

"This is the only part that made me feel any better, two years. Since they're young, both dads want them to graduate, blah, blah, blah. It sounded like they'd get a mansion for their wedding gift, too. Ugh, what the hell?" she asked, falling backward on my bed and smacking her forehead with her palm.

"Mac, have you talked to Hendrix yet? He knows everyone, right? What does he think?"

"Yeah, he texted me. I talked to him when I stepped out of the room. I didn't want to upset you."

Guilt washed over me. I'd not been a good friend to Mac. I needed to change that. She'd been nothing but amazing to me, holding me up when I didn't think I could stand on my own two feet anymore.

"Don't keep things from me anymore. Besties talk about this stuff, right?" I asked, reminding her of her own words.

"Yeah, we do. Anyway, I told him, between bawling my head off."

"What did he say?"

"He told me a lot could happen in two years, and maybe Asher would come to his senses and not let his father control him."

"Why did you two break up?" I asked gently.

Mac stared up at the ceiling and back to me. "You and I have a lot in common, but at the same time, not a lot in common." She bit her lip. "I got pregnant."

"Mac!" I gasped, slapping my hands over my mouth. "You've never said anything about it."

"I couldn't," she whispered. "First, I didn't know you, but obvi I do now. Second, there was serious hush money along with the abortion."

"Mac?" I cried. "Did you want the baby?"

"No. I mean, I love Asher, but we were kids. And I swear it was in the water at the high school. I think I was the sixth girl that year to get preggers."

"So his dad stepped in and ended things?"

"Yup. Neither Asher nor I wanted to split up. However, if it had gotten out that Asher knocked me up, Daddy was afraid it would tarnish his reputation and business."

"Ugh, such absolute shit," I said, my jaw clenching with the injustice. "Is he why I've never seen you interested in anyone else?"

Her nose wrinkled at me, "Yeah, I can't get over him, and apparently, he feels the same."

"I'm so sorry," I said, taking her hand in mine. "I guess I lived behind my walls for so long I didn't realize what other girls were going through, too. I know you said you didn't want the baby, and I totally understand it. Believe me, I do, but it still changes you."

"Yeah, it did. It fucked us both up for a while," she said, quickly glancing at me, then toward her bed.

"You're right. We do have a lot in common, but my parents forced me to carry Jordan."

"Do you want custody of your—" Mac asked, blurting it out quickly.

I shook my head. "No, and we can talk about it some other time. Tonight, it's about what you need. All right?"

I laughed as Mac tackled me with a bear hug, and this time I hugged her in return just as hard.

She settled down, peering at me through her long dark lashes. "I want Asher back, Gemma. It's been over a year, and there's not a minute in the day I don't think about him."

"Well, he obviously feels the same way, but maybe there's something we can do about it in the meantime," I said, wiggling my eyebrows at her.

26

I was lucky. I had friends in my life that I would do anything for.

My fingers danced across my keyboard as I texted Hendrix my plan.

Even though this was for Mac, my heart sang, realizing I was about to see him again so soon.

"Are you all set?" I asked her, eyeing her cute skinny jeans and a blue V-neck shirt.

"Yeah. I can't believe I'm doing this. I think you might have a little bit of villain in you," she said, giggling. "It's a good thing."

Ten minutes later, my phone buzzed. "Let's go," I said, hopping off my bed. Mac and I slipped on our coats. The end of October brought with it what I considered winter.

We hurried down the stairs as fast as we could and ran down to the front door.

"Hey," Hendrix said, reaching for me and giving me a quick kiss. "A few hours was too long not to be with you," he whispered in my ear, delightful shivers traveling down my spine.

"Ready, Mac?" he asked her.

"I'm so fucking nervous, you guys. I can't believe I'm doing this."

"There's nothing to it really," I said, nudging her.

None of us said a word as we all walked toward Hendrix's car and got in. The engine purred to life, the warm heat filling the inside.

Hendrix reached for my hand after he'd pulled out of the parking lot and headed toward downtown Spokane.

"You two are gonna kill me. You haven't even been apart for more than a few hours."

"What?" I asked, confused.

"I know it was him texting you less than five minutes after you returned to the room. Your entire expression lit up like it was Christmas."

"Mac," I chided her, embarrassed. Hendrix's chuckle filled the car while he squeezed my hand.

"Are we there yet?" she asked from the back seat.

I laughed. "I have no idea where we're going, so I can't help you."

She glanced out the window, her leg bouncing incessantly.

"I can't believe you talked her into it," Hendrix said quietly.

"Makes two of us," I replied.

"When I drop you off tonight, why don't you let me come up and take a few things to my place for you?" Hendrix glanced at me, then returned his attention to the road.

"Seriously?" I asked. "I mean, I know you mentioned it, but I wasn't sure if you were just being nice."

Hendrix laughed and raised my hand, a soft kiss landing on the back of it.

"I want you with me tonight. This being apart shit sucks. I can't even write. I need my muse."

"I can't leave Mac alone, and I have to study." I groaned as it dawned on me that Mac and I weren't studying at all like we needed to.

"Fine. She can come. I have a guest bedroom. She's used it a million times."

"She has?" I peeked at her over my shoulder and smiled.

"Yeah, before you came along, anyway. Guess you're the first roomie she's liked because she hasn't stayed the night for a while."

"Isn't that the damned truth," she chimed in from the backseat.

"The other roommate was awful. I was at Hendrix's every time he offered, which was a lot. The girl lucked out and basically had a room to herself."

"We had a lot of fun," Hendrix said. "A few drunk nights." He laughed.

"Yeah, and a bitch of a hangover the next day, too." Mac giggled.

Hendrix and Mac chatted about old times, and I realized he was keeping her busy while he drove. It was nice to see a brother and sister get along so well, even if they were only step-siblings. I'd learned that family was who you chose, not necessarily because you shared a bloodline.

"Okay, we're here," Hendrix said, parking the car. I searched around the near-empty, well-lit parking lot. "You know the rules."

"Yeah, yeah. I do," she huffed.

"Good luck," I told her.

"Just pray I don't get so nervous I blow chunks all over him," she said, opening the car door and hopping out.

"So gross," I muttered to Hendrix while we watched her from the car.

"She's terrified," he said. "She does the leg bouncing thing when she's really scared."

"I hope this helps, but I don't know. Maybe it was—" I didn't finish my sentence.

My mouth dropped as a tall, blonde, good-looking guy ran toward her, picked her up off the ground, and twirled her around. Her giggle broke through the parking lot.

"Is that Asher?" I asked, peering through Hendrix's side window.

"Yeah. He's a nice guy, too."

Asher placed her feet back on the ground, and I flushed as they shared a deep kiss.

"Wow," I said, looking away quickly.

"They're intense," he said, glancing at me. "What you see right there is exactly how you make me feel."

"Me too," I said quietly. "I hated being away from you today."

"Come home with me, then," he said, leaning forward and kissing me tenderly.

"But Mac," I whispered.

Our mouths parted, and he slipped his tongue inside. Every second he touched me, my body craved him.

"We're fogging the windows up," he said between kisses.

I giggled and broke away.

"Is she doing okay?" I asked, pointing at my best friend.

"Happiest I've seen them since this whole shit thing happened."

Sadness taunted me with the thought of not being with someone you loved that much. How Hendrix had become the very air I breathed, how he possessed my heart and body. Everything I had, everything I was, he held in the palm of his hand. It scared me to realize how much he could hurt me.

"So it's a yes?" He turned toward me, anticipation filling his voice.

"What's a yes?" I asked, tearing myself away from my thoughts.

"You'll stay with me tonight, and I'll take us all to school in the morning?"

"Let's see how Mac is doing when we're done." I wanted to be sensitive to her feelings. "Sometimes we need girl time, ya know?"

"You're killing me over here, Gem." He flashed me his smile, and I almost came unglued.

"Is it going to be a while?" I asked, running my fingers up his jeaned thigh.

His eyes widened as I cupped his crotch. He pushed the button on my seatbelt, flipped it away, and reached for me. I giggled as he pulled me over the center console to straddle him.

"We can give them all the time they need. I have a suspicion they will be in his car in a few minutes, doing what we are," he said, his fingers slipping underneath my shirt and running up my spine.

"If I were on the pill already, I'd slide you inside me right now," I said, kissing him, nipping on his bottom lip with my teeth.

He raised his hips and groaned. "You're definitely coming home with me tonight. We'll just have to be quiet," he said breathlessly while his hand slipped into the cup of my bra and teased my nipple.

"Hendrix," I gasped. "You're turning me into a sex fiend."

"As long as you're riding me and only me, I'm totally okay with it," he growled and flicked open the top three buttons of my shirt. He moved the material out of his way, his warm mouth covering my breast.

My head tilted back as pure pleasure flooded my body.

"Is this normal?" I asked between gasps.

"What?" he asked without slowing down.

"Wanting you so bad I feel faint."

He stopped and stared down at me. "Are you okay? Are you sick? What about flashbacks?"

My fingers trailed his jawline, my heart overflowing with love for him.

"I'm fine, Hendrix. I didn't mean for you to stop. I've never felt this way before, I don't know if my reaction to you is normal. I guess I'm afraid that the scars of my past have left—have left me—broken. What if something is so wrong with me it can't be fixed?"

27

Time stood still while I waited for him to answer the one question I'd had for the last five years since the rape. I'd dared to think for just a little bit I was wrong, but then there were moments with him, the fear was so intense I couldn't fight it.

"Gemma," he whispered, stroking my hair. "You're perfect, don't think otherwise for a single moment."

The back door flung open, and I fumbled to fix my top, hop off Hendrix, and in my seat. The dreaded flush crept up my neck as Hendrix rubbed his jaw and glanced out the window.

"You've gotta give us some warning, Mac," he said, frustration thick in his tone.

"Sorry, he didn't have much time."

"How did it go?" I asked.

"I miss him so much," she said, breaking down in tears. "He said he still loves me, but the only thing we can do right now is sneak around. And...and, I can't be the other woman! I recognized I was tonight, and I can't do it."

"Mac," I said, reaching for her hand. "We will figure something out, okay?"

She sniffled again and attempted to stop crying. "I just want to go to the dorm."

Disappointment tugged at me, but there was no way I would go with Hendrix and leave her alone. Not when she needed me the most.

I turned around in my seat and reached for Hendrix's hand.

"I know," he said, solemnly. "And I love you for it."

SADNESS SEEPED deep into my bones as I watched Mac cry. I'd quickly said goodbye to Hendrix when he dropped us off. The moment the door to our room swung open, Mac ran to her bed, curled around her pillow, and broke down all over again. I lay down next to her and remained still. Since I'd not had a best friend my own age, I was unsure of how to help her, so I did what I would have needed, and provided her quiet support.

After some time, she turned toward me, and we turned toward each other, propping up on our elbows.

"This is what sisters do," Mac said, sniffling and wiping her nose on her sleeve. "We hang out in the bed and cry about guys."

"I'm here, Mac. I think I hurt you more than helped you tonight, and it's screwing with me. I guess I thought that if you two saw each other, even for a few minutes, it might help you say goodbye, or even better, he would break off the engagement."

"You did help me, Gemma. You did. I realize I'm completely wrecked right now, but it was worth it, and I would do it again. I know I can't be the other girl while he's engaged to someone else, though. Tonight was bad enough, and it took everything inside me to walk away." The tears began again, and she rolled on her back, placing her the palms of her hands over her face.

"They're not getting married anytime soon, so let's see what happens. After seeing you two together and the love between you, I can't believe it's over, Mac," I whispered.

She peered at me. "I don't know if it's good or bad, but until he's married, I'm going to hope he comes back to me."

"Me too. Everyone deserves to be loved like that."

She popped up into a sitting position.

"Gemma, you're loved like that. Don't ever walk away from it either because you might lose it forever," she hiccupped through her tears.

Nausea rolled in my stomach at the idea of losing Hendrix now that I'd opened up to him, given everything to him. He had the ability to crush my soul, but I was so far gone there was no turning back.

"I'm going to do my best," I said and released a heavy sigh.

28

The weeks flew by as winter settled in, and the snowflakes began to fall. Somehow, I was managing to pass my classes even though I spent a lot of time with Hendrix. Mac had taken me to see a doctor, and I was now on the pill.

After some cajoling, Hendrix had finally talked me into keeping some clothes at his place, and on the weekends, Mac and I stayed with him. It was better for her not to be alone at the dorm, and we wanted to be available if she needed to talk about Asher. I fought the urge to strangle him a few times after texts or emails swearing he loved her, because with each one, I watched powerlessly as her heart broke all over again.

Tonight, we all sat at Hendrix's kitchen bar while he made us some drinks. Mac was in a funk after another message from Asher, and I was exhausted after pulling an all-nighter studying for an upcoming criminal justice test.

"Are you sure?" Hendrix asked, making the screwdrivers for us.

"Yup, if I'm going to try some alcohol, this is the best place to do it, right? You both know my secrets, and I'm already sleeping with you, so it's not like you'll push me when my guard is down," I said, giving him a small smile.

"I didn't put very much vodka in yours, so just take it slow. If you feel sick, we'll grab you some water."

After he slid our drinks toward us, Mac raised hers. We followed suit.

"To family," she said.

"To family," Hendrix and I said, clinking the glasses.

I took a small sip and smiled. "Tastes like orange juice."

Hendrix laughed. "Give it a few minutes, and it'll sink in."

I smiled and took another taste.

"I can't believe it's November already," I said. "The holidays are around the corner, and this will be the first time in my life I'm not in Louisiana—" My words trailed off, and I took a gulp. "I'm going to miss them terribly, but if I were there, I'd miss you guys. So I guess there's no winning."

"Are you going back?" Mac asked, her eyebrows arching in question.

Hendrix put his screwdriver down and walked around the bar toward me. Anticipation flickered across their faces. I guess none of us had thought about it. I should go home to see Dad, but they'd made me promise not to unless they called. I also knew Mac and Hendrix had their own families to be with, which would leave me at the dorm alone. My heart sank with either possibility.

"No," I whispered. "I'll stay here at least for Thanksgiving. I might visit over Christmas break."

Hendrix's jaw clenched, and Mac's lips pursed.

"We'll talk about this later," he said, his tone gruff. He kissed my forehead, then walked around the bar, taking a long pull from his drink. His shoulders slumped, his head hanging down while his hair fell around his face. I wanted to go to him and kiss him long and hard. The idea hadn't occurred to me it would be our first Christmas together. I hadn't thought much past each day.

He straightened up, his expression softening. "I wanted to tell you we're singing next weekend."

If my glass had been in my hand, it would have dropped to the floor and shattered.

"What? So soon?"

"Yeah, and we had a deal, so you can't talk your way out of it," he said, grinning.

Was he enjoying watching me fidget and freak out?

"This is going to be so amazing!" Mac grinned at us, her expression filling with excitement.

I winced at the volume of her tone. Although I'd gotten used to how loud she was, sometimes it snuck up on me. Especially if I was stressed.

"I'll help you get ready, and this is going to be so awesome. Omigosh, I haven't even heard the song, but even the one time outside, ya know, the night Hendrix fell in love with you, like I watched it happen. The moment your voice blended with his, he was a goner. I've never seen him like that. Like ever."

"Thanks, Mac," Hendrix said, sarcasm threading through his tone.

"Oh, yeah, well a girl needs to know these things. Right, Gemma?" she asked.

My cheeks flushed, not only with her directness but for Hendrix.

"I wouldn't have had any idea if you hadn't said anything," I said and reached for his hand.

Hendrix took a breath, "Mac's right. The day behind the library was the beginning, but the night after the concert, that was it for me. There was no turning back, it was a done deal."

My eyes widened. It was one thing to know a guy loved you, but when you found out the second it happened...my heart melted. If Mac hadn't been with us, I would have taken him straight upstairs and showed him how much I loved him in return.

Hendrix held my gaze, his thumb tracing circles on my hand.

Mac cleared her throat loudly.

"Back to music, you two. Gemma, you know this song, you've been practicing and recording with Hendrix for weeks now. You've got this."

"Plus, the fact she won't be on stage. Well, she'll be behind the curtain, so she won't faint on me," Hendrix reminded her.

I groaned and mentally reviewed all the awful possibilities that could happen. I took a long drink of my screwdriver and sighed. Suddenly, a tingle shot through me, my shoulders relaxed, and a calm washed over me.

"And there we have it, folks." Mac pointed at me and giggled.

Hendrix chuckled while my fair skin betrayed me again with a full body flush.

"So, this kinda feels good," I said, laughing. "I've only had like one drink of moonshine, and I thought it was going to set me on fire."

"Oh my God, moonshine? Like, straight up moonshine?" Mac said, barking out a laugh.

"The night before I came up here, Ada Lynn broke out her stash," I said, grinning at the memory. I slid my glass toward Hendrix. "You can add a little more."

His eyebrow arched. "Fine, only a little bit, though. I want to make sure you're not puking on me in a few hours."

"*Ew*, no. I don't want to get drunk, it's just nice to relax."

"Not me, I'm happy to get absolutely ripped. It's one of the rare times I'm quiet," she laughed.

Hendrix chuckled and nodded in agreement.

We talked about the upcoming performance next weekend. I wasn't sure whether or not I was happy that we would perform on campus again. At least I was familiar with the area, but the mere idea of singing in front of that large of a crowd scared me.

Mac was drunk within an hour, and I settled into a comfortable lull from the alcohol. Hendrix seemed fine and paced himself. Maybe he figured he might have to drive or didn't want to let his guard down. I wasn't sure, but he stayed in control, and then it registered in my fuzzy-headed brain. Franklin. From our conversations, I knew Hendrix didn't want to go down that road. My pulse raced with the overwhelming urge to wrap my arms around him and hold him.

I peered at the kitchen clock and realized it was almost midnight.

"Mac, you okay?" I asked.

"Yup never felt better," she said, slurring her words.

"She'll be fine, probably have a headache in the morning, but she'll pass out soon," Hendrix said, winking at me.

Although I didn't want Mac to pass out, I knew we were ready to have some privacy.

A soft snore interrupted my thoughts, and I glanced at Mac, sound asleep, her head lying on the countertop.

I giggled. "Just like that, huh?"

Hendrix laughed, "Just like that. Let me put her to bed."

I watched as he walked over to her and gently nudged her awake. Well, if that's what you could call it. He wrapped his arm around her waist and guided her up the stairs. A few minutes later, he was beside me, spinning the barstool toward him.

"I wondered if she would ever pass out," he said, his lips landing on mine. His fingers smoothed down my cheek, tucking my hair behind my shoulder while he trailed kisses down my neck. I scooted forward in my chair, wrapping my legs around his waist as he pressed his hips into me. I moaned and tilted my head, allowing him access.

I fumbled with the button on his jeans, unzipped them, and slid my hand inside. My fingers wrapped around his erection and gently stroked. I wasn't sure if I wanted him in my mouth or inside me.

I yelped as he pulled me off the chair, my legs remaining wrapped around him while he carried me upstairs to his bedroom. He shoved the door closed with his hip and turned me, so my back was against the wall. His hands cupped my ass as he leaned into me. Pressure built up between my legs, my body tingling with every kiss. He shoved my shirt up with one hand and moved my bra out of the way, his tongue flicking across my nipple.

I whimpered as he gently caressed me, my desire growing with every touch.

"You've got to get rid of these clothes, they're in the way," I said.

I laughed while he lowered me, and my feet touched the floor.

"Arms up, please," I said, tugging his shirt over his head. I bit my bottom lip as I took him all in. His thick arms, broad chest, and abs were the most perfect I'd ever seen. I kneeled and tugged on his jeans, removing them along with his boxer briefs. His erection throbbed with need, and I wrapped my lips around the tip.

"Jesus," he moaned as I glanced up at him, sliding his length into my mouth. His fingers grabbed a handful of my hair while his hips shifted forward, my hand and mouth stroking him. The more excited he became, the more my body responded, my panties growing wetter by the minute.

I stood and kissed him. "I need you inside of me," I whispered.

His hands ran up the sides of my stomach, and he removed my shirt. His finger skillfully flipped open the clasp on my bra, and it fell to the floor. My jeans and thong were next, and I kicked them off, leaning against the wall.

He dropped to his knees and placed my left leg over his shoulder. His hungry mouth latched onto my clit, sucking and teasing me. A finger slid inside me, and I grabbed his head, fisting his hair, as my hips tentatively moved with him. His other hand ran up the back of my thigh, kneading my ass cheek.

My eyes closed, and I allowed myself to sink into my desire, into him. A warm sensation began swirling in my core, building.

"Hendrix, I—I," I panted. His mouth left me as he stood and wrapped my legs around his waist and kissed me.

"I need a condom," he said, breathlessly, his tip pushing at my entrance.

"No, you don't," I said. "I'm on the pill now."

With one swift thrust, he was deep inside me, and I released a moan of raw desire as he took control.

"Good God, you feel amazing," he moaned.

I touched my forehead against his, holding his gaze as he held me against the wall and quickened his pace.

I nipped at his bottom lip and pulled gently. My eyes fluttered closed, and I leaned my head against the wall, my moans growing louder while his pace quickened.

"I love you," I gasped. "Come inside me, Hendrix," I said softly in his ear.

He growled, his eyes darkening with need.

"Nothing is between us, just you and me, baby," I coaxed.

"Gem," he grunted and tensed. "Shit, I can't, ah!" My own desire peaked as I watched the pleasure spread across his face, his body shuddering with his release.

Breathless, he relaxed on top of me, my legs still wrapped around him.

Light kisses feathered across my forehead.

"You're my garden of Eden," he whispered. "I can't imagine my life without you."

My breath hitched. "If this is Eden, I don't ever want to leave," I replied, tears threatening again, but this time from contentment and happiness.

29

The next week was consumed with classes and band rehearsals. The performance was at the Spokane Arena, indoors. I'd also decided it was time to tell my parents and Ada Lynn I was performing. Although I caught the hints of sadness in their tone for missing it, they were supportive and overall excited. Dad had continued to make progress and was on the upswing, which made my heart lighter. I'd updated everyone on the new clothes, too. If they'd doubted my decision to attend college in Washington, the changes made it obvious the move had been a positive thing for me. However, I kept mine and Hendrix's relationship under wraps. I wasn't ready to share anything yet.

"Are you ready?" Mac asked, excitement bubbling in her voice.

"Yeah, I think so. I don't think he suspects anything, and the other guys have been really good, but am I making a mistake?" My jitters were turning into full-blown trembles, and I rubbed my clammy hands on my skinny jeans.

"Breathe, and don't forget, you don't have to go through with it. The guys understand what to look for. I'll be right there, too," she reminded me.

I nodded, realizing once again how hard I'd fallen for Hendrix. I would have never considered anything like this a year ago, and here I was, about to sing in front of a crowd of people. I'd not even done that in our small community choir, where the concerts might have included thirty-five parents and a few extra kids.

"All right, time to go," Mac said, grinning.

"What if I pass out or blow chunks or something else to embarrass him?" I asked, fiddling with the hem of my dark green sweater.

"Girl, please, the second you hear his voice you'll join him, and everything else will slip away."

I nodded, hoping like hell she was right.

Twenty minutes later, Mac hugged me goodbye, and I walked up on the back of the stage. I peeked around the curtain and waved to Hendrix.

He hurried toward me and picked me up, twirling me around.

"You showed up," he said, chuckling and setting me down.

"I promised you I would. I'm not sure how to deal with the nerves, though."

"Close your eyes," he instructed. "Feel my arms around you right now, my breath against your skin, my lips on yours." He paused and kissed me tenderly. "And my heart, every time it beats, it's for you," he said, placing my hand on his chest.

My breath hitched. "How did I get so lucky?" I asked, my chest filling with more love than I thought I would ever be capable of.

He smiled and squeezed my hand. "Worst case scenario, the nerves overtake you, and I can sing it on my own. No one will know the difference."

My gaze fell. "I don't want to let you down."

"You could never let me down, Gem," he said tenderly, tucking my hair behind my ear.

"Hendrix, we're about to start," the drummer, John, announced. "Hey, Gemma, good luck tonight."

"Thanks," I replied, my hands visibly shaking.

Hendrix kissed me on the forehead. "We're the second song, so you can pass out right after it's over," he said, a lopsided grin spreading across his handsome features.

"Not funny," I hissed and shook my head at him. I stood on my tiptoes and gave him a quick kiss before he left me alone backstage. I hurried to the dressing room and changed out of my jeans and sweater, preparing for the performance.

A few minutes later, the cymbal rang through the night, and the crowd began to scream.

"Welcome!" Hendrix's voice broke through the noise. The high pitch of girls screaming rang in my ears. "We've got a special show for you tonight," he continued.

I flinched, realizing it was my cue, and if John heard the piano, he knew we were moving forward. My heart pounded against my chest as I sat down, my fingers on the keys. Hendrix had no idea I played. I'd always wanted to surprise him with it. I inhaled deeply while Hendrix continued to work the crowd, then a moment of silence hovered in the air. My eyes slammed shut, my fingers poised, and I cleared my throat quietly. My mind floated to Hendrix, his lips, his arms around me, the strength he'd given me. I could do this. For him, I could do anything. The middle C note sounded through the mic.

"This is for you, babe," I said softly and began to sing "At My Weakest" by James Arthur.

The curtain slid open, revealing me sitting at the piano playing, facing the audience and singing. John nodded at me as my focus fell on Hendrix, his face full of surprise while he stepped aside, listening. My confidence grew as I continued.

I smiled when I spotted Mac in the front row, bouncing up and down.

The guys in the band sang background, our voices blending effortlessly. I stood when the song neared the end, and I sauntered up to Hendrix. His mouth gaped slightly when he noticed my blue dress and heels from Franklin's event.

Gasps echoed through the crowd as they began to recognize who I was. Although I'd sported my transformation for several weeks, I'd only been seen around campus and in my classes. My social life consisted of only two people—Hendrix and Mac.

I took his hand as we turned toward each other, and the song ended. He moved toward me and kissed me passionately. The crowd went wild, and for a moment, no one else existed except us.

He backed away, raised his mic, and grinned.

"My beautiful and amazing girlfriend, Gemma Thompson!"

Catcalls and cheers rang through the stadium. Even though my nerves were on high alert, the love in the crowd was exhilarating.

"Ready?" he asked.

I nodded, the band began, and we sang, "Couldn't Love You More." The more we sang together, the more the crowd slipped away, the more my heart belonged to him, and I willingly gave it to him.

When our song ended, I gave the crowd a little wave. Hendrix kissed me, and I exited the stage as the clapping and cheering continued. The curtain closed behind me, and I hurried toward the piano, sinking onto the seat, lightheaded. I'd done it. I wasn't sure how, but I'd sung to Hendrix Harrington.

My chest ached from my heart pounding so rapidly. I smiled as I realized Ada Lynn and my parents would have been proud of me. Hell, I was proud of myself. I placed my forehead against the top of the piano and allowed myself to relax. An hour passed as I listened to the band, still resting on the piano.

I was humming along to Hendrix's vocals when suddenly my head was roughly jerked back. The sting of my hair being pulled brought tears to my eyes as a gruff hand slapped over my mouth. Another hand slipped into my dress, grabbing my bare breast.

"I knew you were a sweet piece of ass underneath those ugly clothes," Brandon hissed in my ear. "If I had time, I would bend you over this piano and fuck you senseless, but the concert is about to end. I just wanted you to know when the time is right, I will come for you, and I mean it literally."

My body trembled against him, his fingers pinching my nipple and his teeth biting my earlobe. I screamed against his hand. And as quickly as he appeared, he disappeared.

Tears flowed down my cheeks, and I frantically searched for him, but he was nowhere to be found. He must have known how to get on and off the stage without being detected.

Trembling, my body collapsed, and I slid off the piano stool, hitting the floor on my hands and knees. Revolted from his touch, my stomach heaved, and I puked. Sobs wracked my body as arms wrapped around my waist and pulled me up.

A scream left my lips, and I pounded my fists against whoever had me.

"Gem! Gem, it's me, Hendrix. I've got you. It's okay."

"Brandon," I choked out before I collapsed on him.

30

It was an odd sensation to wake with multiple faces staring down at me.

"Shit," I said, swallowing and realizing I was lying flat on the floor.

"Hey, be still for a second," Hendrix said, his hand squeezing mine.

"Are you all right? You scared the shit out of us," John said, concern heavy in his expression.

"Can you sit up?" Cade asked. "My sister passed out the day of her wedding, and I remember my mom sat her up slowly. I think she was really dizzy, but she was pregnant, so it was probably why she passed out in the first place."

Fear shot through me. Is that why I'd passed out? Worry lines creased Hendrix's forehead. He knew, to me, nothing worse could happen.

"Brandon found me," I said.

"What the hell?" Cade said. "I thought we had some security tonight, dude?" he asked Hendrix.

"We did, but they can't be everywhere at once." His jaw clenched.

I knew him well enough to understand he was trying not to lose his shit.

"We can talk about this at home." He draped his coat over me and scooped me into his arms. "No one can touch you now," he whispered.

I leaned my head against his shoulder while he walked me off the stage and through the back door of the arena. He didn't set me down until we had arrived at his car, and I settled into the safety it provided.

"Mac," I said as he got in and started the car.

He nodded, pulled his phone out of his back pocket, and tapped the screen.

"Hey, Gemma is with me. I'm taking her to my place tonight." He fell silent, and I could hear Mac reply but not make out what she was saying.

"Yeah, she was amazing tonight. Apparently, Brandon thought so as well." His voice was low. Haunted. Guilt clung to every word. He gripped the steering wheel, his knuckles turning white. "She's okay, but I don't know everything that happened yet. I'm sure she'll update you when she's ready. Have Cade and John take you to the dorm and walk you up to the door. You understand me?" he asked, his tone firm. "Text me when you get there."

He ended the call and pulled out of the parking lot. I curled up in my seat and stared out of the window while he drove, Brandon's words ringing in my ears. This had been my biggest fear about shedding the oversized clothes. I seemed to attract unwanted attention.

"Tell me what happened," he demanded.

"No," I whispered.

Hendrix didn't push the issue, but I knew it wasn't over yet.

He sped through the back roads toward his house as silence fell between us. It was heavy and loud, or maybe it was just in my head.

With each passing moment, I could feel myself slipping away. I should have never sang tonight, I'd left myself open and vulnerable to every Brandon in the audience, and as much as I wanted to think he was the only threat to me or any other girl, I realized I would be lying to myself.

We arrived at his house, and I walked through the front door, dazed. The moment we were locked inside, I stood in his living room, unzipped my dress, and allowed it to drop to the floor. I stepped out of it and kicked off my heels. My body tensed, warning him not to touch me. Hendrix remained still, not attempting to move any closer.

I held his gaze. "Burn this fucking dress. I don't ever want to see it again," I said, my voice laced with venom.

I walked away and proceeded up the stairs, leaving Hendrix standing alone in the living room.

31

No longer needing permission, I walked straight into his bathroom and locked the door behind me. I slipped out of my thong, kicking it to the side while I turned the water on. Opening the door, I stepped underneath the hot spray. Unwilling to contain them any longer, sobs shook my body. I slammed the sides of my fists against the shower wall and screamed. My legs rebelled, and I slid down onto the floor, the water flowing over me as I released another gut-wrenching scream.

"Gemma!" Hendrix yelled, pounding against the door.

Blackness swirled across my vision, and every painful memory came flooding back—rough hands tearing at my clothes, his member shoving inside of me, ripping me apart, the morning sickness. And then it flashed to Brandon's hands on me. His threatening words rang through my mind. Then—nothing.

"Babe, Gem, talk to me."

My eyes fluttered open to find Hendrix fully clothed, kneeling in the shower next to me. "I think you passed out again. You're scaring me, Gem, talk to me." Anguish twisted his expression as he attempted to reach me.

No words formed, nothing except blankness. He stood and turned the water off, his attention never leaving me. He bent down and scooped me into his arms, both of us soaking wet. He carried me to his bed and laid me down gently. He disappeared briefly and returned with towels and a blanket. He sat me up and gently dried my hair.

"Please, baby, say something," he pleaded, his eyes clouding with fear. "I can't lose you." His words caught in his throat. There was nothing I could say. I wasn't sure I hadn't lost myself tonight. This time, I didn't think anyone would be able to bring me back.

He laid me down again, carefully drying my skin. I stared at him, expressionless, while he covered me with his blankets and laid down next to me.

"Can you look at me?" he asked.

I knew I needed to give him something, but there wasn't anything else to offer. Turning my head toward him, a tear slipped down my cheek. "No matter what, I love you," I whispered, feeling nothing, but having enough comprehension to realize he needed some hope.

His head dropped to my shoulder, his body shaking with a deep breath. A few minutes later he glanced up at me, his eyes rimmed with red.

"Did he—Did that motherfucker—" His words trailed off, his hand balling into a fist, unable to finish his question.

I turned my head away from him, searching for any strength left inside me, even if it was from hatred.

"No," I said, looking at him again.

Hendrix expelled a deep sigh, his head hanging down.

"But."

His head snapped up, fear flickering across his face.

"He slid his hand down the front of my dress and swore he would find me and fuck me. He said he was watching my every move."

The moment the words left my lips, anger shot through him. Hendrix hopped off the bed and paced across the room. Rage rippled through him, and his eyes glowed with fury. Every vein in his arms and neck popped to attention. I'd never seen him so furious.

"I wasn't there to protect you," he whispered. "I didn't protect you!" he roared.

I realized that even though what I'd experienced tonight was awful, there was one person who could bring me back, and he was standing in front of me. Grief split me in two as I watched him blame himself.

"No," I said, holding the covers over me and sitting up in his bed. "No, it was my fault. I shouldn't have sung with you tonight, I shouldn't have bought different clothes, I shouldn't—"

Hendrix rushed over to me and sat on the side of the bed, cupping my chin and turning my head toward him.

"Stop. This has nothing to do with your clothes or you performing on stage. Brandon is a sick bastard who gets his kicks from hurting people, women, in the worst way possible. We will figure this out. I'll figure this out. For now, you're back with me. I thought you'd slipped away for good."

"Me too, but seeing you blame yourself, thinking you had failed me—Hendrix, you're the only reason I'm even here. Every time I think I can't go on or I've checked out inside myself, I somehow find my way to you. You know how to love me."

"I love you so goddamned much," he whispered.

"Promise me. Promise me you won't blame yourself. Brandon is sneaky, he understands how to work around things, and he's obviously watching me. For a little while, being with you, I was able to forget about him. I felt safe with you and Mac, but I should never have let my guard down."

"I want to kiss you so bad. I don't want to scare you, though."

I glanced up. His eyes held so much love my heart skipped a beat. Leaning over, I kissed him.

"Would you hold me tonight?" I asked.

"Anything you need."

I MISSED classes the next morning, and so did Hendrix. He'd chosen to stay with me and cook breakfast. I'd stepped out on the deck, listening to the wild, yet calming sounds of the Spokane River rush by. A part of me wanted to immerse myself in the water, let the darkness surround me, and claim me. The old as well as the more recent demons pulled at me, taunting me to return to Louisiana where I could hide. However, my heart was here in Spokane with Hendrix, and he would be the reason I would push forward and stay.

He opened the sliding door and joined me.

"It's freezing out here, but it's beautiful," he said, wrapping his arm around my waist and kissing the top of my head. "Can you eat?"

I nodded as he guided me into the house, grabbed a blue, green, and white Seattle Seahawks blanket from the closet, and draped it over my shoulders.

Nibbling mindlessly on the bacon, my thoughts drifted back to last night.

"I need to buy a pregnancy test. My period is late, and I was so caught up in preparing for the performance I hadn't realized it."

His shoulders and arms tensed, his forkful of omelet hovering in mid-air.

"Maybe I messed up taking the pill," I said. "I don't think I did, but I passed out twice last night. I just need to know." The bacon dropped from my hand onto my plate.

"What kind do you want? I realize most guys wouldn't know anything about it, but I picked up Mac's when she—"

I nodded. He didn't need to finish the conversation.

"Let me call her and ask. I have no idea. The last time, I went straight to the doctor. I'll be right back," I said, excusing myself from the table, then climbing the stairs to the bedroom. Somehow, with all the commotion, I'd lost track of my phone last night but found it on the nightstand next to my side of the bed.

My heart sank as everything dawned on me. What if I was? I chewed my bottom lip while I called Mac.

"Bestie, are you okay?"

"I don't know... Mac, what kind of pregnancy test should I buy?"

Silence filled the phone.

"Shit. No fucking way, you're on the pill, right?"

"Yeah, but what if I hadn't taken it for long enough before...Well," my voice broke off embarrassed I was sharing so much with her.

"Early Response is what I used."

"Thanks. I'll keep you updated."

"Okay," she whispered. "I'll be waiting, so the second you find out, please let me know."

"I will." I ended the call, headed downstairs, and joined Hendrix.

"I'll go, you stay here and try to relax," he said, kissing me on the top of my head. "And eat something for me."

TIME STOPPED while he was gone, every second away from him felt like an eternity. I was left with my own darkness, my own thoughts. What would I do now that I was almost twenty and in love? What if I was pregnant? Would I keep it? Panic rooted itself inside me, and I stood up from the table and paced through the living room, my heart pounding with each step.

The front door finally flung open, and Hendrix approached me with a brown paper bag.

"Can I be with you?" he asked.

My brows shot up, "Um, not while I pee, no," I said, taking the bag from him. "The minute I'm done, you can sit with me, though," I said, my tone softening. He wasn't the only one worried about the outcome. His life would drastically change as well.

I took his hand, and we walked up the stairs and into his bedroom. The click of the bathroom door closing behind me sent my pulse racing into overdrive.

Pulling the pink and white box out of the bag, I opened the top and carefully read the instructions. Thank God I had to pee, so we didn't have to wait any longer than the dreaded three minutes for the result that had the power to once again change my fate.

I followed the instructions to the letter, put some tissue on his counter, and placed the stick that would reveal my future on top of it.

After I washed my hands, I opened the door, set my phone timer, and joined him on the edge of his bed.

"No matter what the results are, I'm here. I'm not going anywhere," he said quietly.

I took his hand in mine and leaned my head on his shoulder, waiting as the seconds ticked by, my heart pounding, my mind growing foggy.

My alarm sounded, and I jumped. Tapping the screen to turn it off, I stood and stared at him.

"One line means no, two lines means yes," I said, my hands trembling.

He nodded and led me into the bathroom. Everything from the night before with Brandon slipped into the background with each step we took together toward the results. We stood next to silently, and my focus dropped. A cry escaped me as I fell into Hendrix, my arms wrapping around his neck, the tears flowing.

His hand threaded through my hair while he held me, and we took a moment to catch our breath.

"Do you still love me?" I asked, peering up at him.

"Pregnant or not, my feelings for you aren't going to change," he said.

"Are you disappointed I'm not?" I already knew he wanted kids, and I wasn't sure if it was something I would be able to give him.

"No, not now. We have our whole lives in front of us to figure this out."

"Our whole lives?" I asked, my heart swelling at the idea of spending forever with him.

"Our whole lives," he said and hugged me.

32

Relief washed over me as I texted Mac the results. After a few messages, I promised I would see her later after classes. Until then, I needed to figure out my next steps concerning Brandon. Although a part of me wanted to take care of it myself, I also realized there was strength in numbers, and I needed Hendrix's and Mac's help.

I reveled in the silence and safety of my boyfriend's arms as we watched the fire flicker to life in the fireplace.

"I've never actually sat in front of a fireplace before."

"Really?" Hendrix asked incredulously.

"Nope. It's too warm in Louisiana, and most homes don't even have one."

"Will you take me someday?"

"To Louisiana?" I peered up at him. "Why in the hell do you want to visit there? It's hot, muggy, and the swamps are full of gators."

He chuckled. "Because it's a part of who you are, and I want to see where you're from, meet your family, see where you grew up."

My gaze returned to the crackling flames, sadness seeping inside me.

"We're poor, Hendrix. Dad's cancer has left him with only some disability income, and Mom has stayed home with me since I had Jordan."

He tilted my chin up, and I met his stare. "If you have a good family who loves you, then you're the richest person in the world."

"I'm really rich then," I whispered.

His lips brushed against mine, and I rested my head against his chest, the fabric of his sweatshirt soft against my cheek. As much as I wanted to be with him, the pregnancy scare and Brandon's brutality had left me gun shy. Thank God Hendrix understood.

Our lazy afternoon came to an end, and Hendrix drove me to the dorm. Instead of leaving me at the front door, he walked me upstairs. Out of respect for Mac, I knocked lightly and peeked in.

"Hey, your brother is with me. I wanted to make sure you were decent."

Mac hopped off the bed, grinning, motioning us to come in.

She embraced Hendrix and me. We sat down on my bed while Mac plunked down in the chair and faced us. She flipped her braid behind a shoulder and straightened her red and black flannel shirt.

"So, I'm not an aunt, huh? Bet that scared the shit out of both of you. Hell, it did me. You would have thought it was me taking the damned test again. I just stared at my phone, waiting for your message. Oh my God. You can't do that again, Gemma. Like, what happened to make you think you were?"

Hendrix shook his head at Mac's rambling and nodded toward me to tell her. He took my hand while I told her how my period was late, but more importantly, I'd passed out twice.

"What?" she asked, her leg beginning to bounce.

"I'm fine, everything is okay. Well," I said, shooting Hendrix a look. "I wasn't okay at first, but I'm working toward figuring things out."

"I don't understand. Why did you pass out?" Mac pinned me with an intense stare.

"Brandon assaulted me again during the concert."

Mac shot straight up out of the chair, sending it rolling across the floor. Her cheeks flamed red, her tiny hands balling into fists.

"Someone has to stop him!" she cried. "Hendrix, what are we going to do?"

"I'm working on it. After talking things over with Gem, I think it's going to take all three of us, though."

Mac stomped her foot against the floor and paced the small room.

"Okay, this is how it's going to go down. I'll start following him. I'll be discreet, so he has no idea. After I figure out his routine, Gemma can meet him, and the second he pulls her off around a building or somewhere isolated, Hendrix, you slip a bag over his head and put him in a sleep hold. You'll need to park your car somewhere close, so we can drag him and put him in your trunk. I'll buy some rope, and we'll tie his hands and feet together. When he wakes up in the back of your trunk, unable to see or move, maybe then he will understand what he's doing to us. How terrified and powerless we feel." She paused for a second and continued. "We can take him out on Elk Chattaroy. There's a ton of acreage out there, not to mention it's wooded. Hendrix, all those years of boxing, you need to put it to use on him. Hell, I even want to get a few good jabs in while I can. Since it will already be dark, we'll leave the motherfucker there, and he'll either figure it out or freeze to death." She stopped, folded her arms across her chest and waited.

My mouth hung open in shock. She wasn't kidding. She was completely serious about every word of her crazy plan.

I shot Hendrix a look, his face paled, and he swallowed hard.

"Mac, how do you really feel about him?" he asked, his tone filled with sarcasm. "All the years I've known you—you've never talked about hurting someone. This, you've thought about—a lot. The plan is too detailed."

Her face clouded with a combination of shame and anger.

She sank onto the edge of her bed, her shoulders slouching in defeat.

"The night I found him with Eva..." She glanced up at the ceiling briefly. "He was still raping her, but when I barged through the door, the hatred in his eyes terrified me. He's not a guy just looking to shoot his wad, he's looking to instill fear, and not only rape a girl's body but her mind and soul, too."

I flinched at her words, understanding exactly what she was talking about, the residue of my own experience still lingering everywhere I turned years later.

"I've seen it too, Mac. I'm so sorry about Eva. I know what it's like to lose your best friend over something like that," I said.

She stared at the floor, her leg still bouncing. Hendrix nudged me with his shoulder. I turned to him, seeing the concern in his expression.

"Mac, I'm not excited about breaking the law, and as shitty as it sounds, I have no doubt Dad would try to get me out of it," Hendrix stated.

"Hendrix," I gasped. "Seriously? You're going to break the law and pull the daddy card?"

"Gemma, you don't understand. Hendrix has never even considered something like this before," Mac said, protectively.

Relief washed over me. I couldn't be with someone who didn't have a moral compass, but apparently, Brandon was pushing him over the edge. We were all seriously considering something awful in order to stop a monster.

"Mac, as great as your plan sounds, and I won't lie, there's a part of me that would love to carry it out, watch him piss his pants from fear, and beat the shit out of him, but I have to keep in mind there's a bigger picture. Dad has barely started his career again, and I can't be the one to ruin it for him. Something like this could really tarnish his reputation. He's worked hard at climbing out of his dark hole, I can't send him back to it." Hendrix frowned with his words.

Mac's shoulders sagged further.

"Don't worry, though. You've given me another idea. One that will keep you and Gemma out of it. And, honestly, the band is picking up momentum, and I don't want to write new songs from prison."

My brows shot up as it dawned on me no matter who his father was, Hendrix could end up with a record if we moved forward with Mac's idea.

"We're all in agreement he needs to be stopped, so if you two will trust me, I won't let you down this time," he said, holding my gaze. "This time, I'll protect you."

"Ugh, is this what Asher and I looked like? I might be sick," Mac teased.

"Yes," Hendrix replied, his expression serious. "So you can't flip me any shit."

He kissed me and turned to Mac.

"Do you trust me? Can you give me one more chance to make this right?" he asked, his attention bouncing between Mac and me.

"You know I trust you. I also realize you're human, and we all make mistakes. It's not that your heart isn't in the right place, but you can't be everywhere at once," Mac responded.

"I know, but I have to try."

"I trust you," I whispered. "I trust you with my life."

Sadness flickered across his face as his fingertips touched my cheek. "I better not screw this up again, then."

The three of us sat in silence for a few minutes, each of us lost in our own thoughts. Exhaustion seeped through me, and I knew I needed to stay with Mac tonight, but I longed to be in Hendrix's arms.

"I should go and let you two catch up," he said, standing. I stood with him.

"I'll walk you down. Mac, I'll be right back."

She nodded, and we headed out of the room and down the stairs. The main floor was bustling with activity as we made our way outside.

The chill of the night air shot through me, and I shivered. "I didn't grab my coat."

He glanced at me and squeezed my hand.

"Let's go to my car for a minute. I need to talk to you."

33

My heartbeat screeched to a halt. What was wrong? Had the last few days been too much?

We slipped into the car, and he turned it on. He waited in silence while the heat blew through the vent. Every second was agony. Whatever was about to come out of his mouth was big, and I wondered if things were too much for him to handle. I couldn't blame him. I was a mess and a handful, and the shit just kept coming.

He turned toward me, his expression growing more serious.

"You're scaring me," I whispered.

He didn't move to hold my hand or reassure me.

"Hendrix?" I asked, attempting to contain my tears.

He inhaled and blew out a sharp breath. "Move in with me," he blurted.

Shock slammed into me, knocking the air out of my lungs. "What?"

"Move in with me. I can't stand leaving you. I can't stand not having you next to me, watching you sleep."

"You watch me sleep?"

He nodded. "Please."

I tried to wrap my head around what he was asking me, but more importantly, the changes it would mean for myself and not to mention, Mac. I would share his home with him, his space. Even though I didn't own the dorm room, it was still the one thing I could call mine. And Mac. I couldn't leave her alone when she was trying to deal with Brandon and Asher. On the other hand, how could I tell him no when my heart wanted to pack my things tonight?

"Say yes," he said, his eyes pleading. "We can give you some time and do it over the Thanksgiving break. I realize you don't have a lot to move, but maybe we can do some shopping and pick out some new furniture or pictures or whatever you want so you have no doubt in your mind it's also your home. It belongs to you as much as it does me."

"I love you so much it hurts sometimes," I said, taking his hand. "What about Mac? I can't leave her right now."

"And I love you even more for it. In fact, I wondered what you would think about her moving in as well? The house is plenty big enough for us all. It will save both of you some money, too."

"What?" I barked out a laugh. "I should have known you wouldn't have forgotten about her."

"She's my sister, and you two are the most important people in my life."

My eyes filled with tears at his words. Day after day he continued to show up for us no matter what shit he had to wade through to get there.

"Yes," I said. "Yes, I'll move in with you."

Relief washed over his face right before his mouth came crashing down on mine.

"I love you so fucking much," he said, between kisses.

I giggled and replied, "Not near as much as I love you."

His kiss deepened, and my body responded to him.

Breathless, he pulled back and kissed the tip of my nose.

"I don't want to rush anything, okay?" His expression softened with his words.

I nodded. It had only been twenty-four hours since Brandon had threatened me, and I was still attempting to process everything.

"I'll walk you to the dorm now." He hopped out of the car, walked around to my side, and opened the door for me.

I smiled as he extended his hand to me and helped me out. Shivering, we ran up the walkway. We hurried into the warmth of the dorm, and he pulled me against him. I gasped as he kissed me deeply in front of everyone. Some of the girls even started cheering.

"Soon, I won't have to tell you goodbye," he said before he opened the door and walked away, leaving me lightheaded and breathless in front of an entire hall filled with clapping girls.

Flushing, I kept my head down and hurried up the stairs. Mac and I had some things to talk about.

Barging through the door, I flung myself on my bed and sighed. She burst into giggles at the silly grin on my face.

"My how shit has changed from the first day you walked through the door."

"I know, right? Anything else from Asher?"

Mac hesitated. "I—I."

I sat up, she had my full attention. "Yeah?" I motioned for her to hurry up and tell me everything. The moment I saw those two together, I knew they had what Hendrix and I had, and from what I could tell, it was rare. Maybe he was with someone else right now, but I was rooting for them a hundred percent.

"I talked to him on the phone," she admitted.

"Oh Mac, don't feel bad about talking to him for a few minutes."

"Phone sex," she blurted.

My skin flushed hot with her confession.

"Oh, well, no judgment here," I said, attempting to cover my surprise. "Is he sleeping with his fiancée?" I asked, anger rising inside of me at the idea he might be playing Mac.

"He says no, but he's a guy, so I'm not sure if I can believe him. This whole thing is a convoluted shit fest."

Even though the topic was serious, and Mac was quickly becoming the other woman, I laughed at her comparison. She wasn't that far off.

"You don't have to say anything. I understand I have to break it off.

It's taking everything I have in me not to text him or meet him so we can steam up the windows in his car."

For the first time, I totally got it. There wasn't a minute that didn't pass by that I wasn't mentally thinking about Hendrix in the bedroom.

"We have a lot to figure out, huh?" I sighed, reality crashing down on me again.

"Well, not really. I mean, it sounds like Hendrix has a plan for what to do about Brandon. I hope he can make it happen before the asshole hurts someone again. Like, I don't want you going anywhere alone again. We're like fucking glue, you and me. And if we aren't near each other, then Hendrix better be beside you. I don't think he'll leave you alone again, honestly. Who the hell thought Brandon would go backstage, though? What a sneaky bastard," she spat.

"He definitely surprised me," I said, remembering him slipping up behind me, never making a sound. Dread crept over me at the realization that I'd been such an easy target even while I was surrounded by people.

"I'll block Asher on my phone," Mac said, sighing.

"And your email?" I asked. She could block him on her phone all she wanted, but there were still plenty of ways to communicate.

"I'll delete them the minute they show up in my inbox."

I hesitated for a moment, selecting my words carefully. "I think, if you're really honest with yourself and me, you won't follow through with it. Even if you block him, it will only be a day or two before you unblock him. He's your drug, Mac."

She groaned and flung herself onto her bed.

"And there's no judgment in that because I would totally be the other girl with Hendrix, just to have any part of him. Eventually, though, I would gain my senses and realize I don't deserve to be second, ever. And if he loves you, he won't put you in that position. So, do what you need to do, and I'll love you and support you in your decision."

Mac's shoulders tensed, and she released a heavy sigh. "I don't want to be the other girl, and I do have morals, I swear.

And you're right. Neither of us deserves to be second to anything or anyone. You don't have to worry about that with my brother, though. He's already put you before everything. Even his music."

"Shit, he can't do that."

"I don't think you have a say in it, it's just the way it is. If you asked him to never perform again, he would do it."

"I would never ask him to give it up. I mean, I would fully support him and his dreams, whatever the future might look like."

"Even if he travels?"

My stomach clenched. It'd never crossed my mind he might go on the road more than just in Washington. It was more than I could handle, plus he'd asked me to move in with him. I didn't think traveling was on his agenda at the moment. Or was this his way of keeping me safe while he was gone? Providing me his home along with a roomie so he would feel comfortable about leaving? Wouldn't he have talked to me about it?

"Hello," Mac said, snapping her fingers at me. "You totally went down a dark road on me. He has no intention of leaving you. He's not mentioned one thing about performances outside of Washington and Oregon. And those, he'll want you with him, singing if he gets his way."

Suddenly, I felt stupid at second-guessing his intentions. I really didn't think I would have made it this far without Mac keeping me on the right path, soothing my fear.

"You swear?"

"Swear to you," she said, covering her heart.

"I believe you." My worry subsided, and I recalled his expression when I'd told him I would move in with him. The one thing I hadn't thought through was if Mac said no.

"Sup, bestie? You're thinking so hard over there I can actually hear the wheels turning."

There was no use torturing myself any longer. "You and Hendrix are pretty close."

"Yeah, he's my best friend. Other than you I mean."

"Is it true? What he said about you staying with him a lot last year when you had the bitchy roomie?"

"Ha! She was one of those girls who had a resting bitch face. Like all the time, it never changed. I don't know if she was getting Botox shots or what."

I laughed while she continued on about the old roommate.

"Anyway, now I have you, and I wouldn't trade you for anything. We have the perfect set up."

My heart sank. She wasn't going to want to do this, and honestly, I completely understood. Why in the world would she want to share a place with her brother and me?

"He asked me to move in with him," I blurted.

"Wow! Shit!" She paused, her eyes widening "Wow," she repeated again. "What did you say?" In a rare moment, I had her undivided attention.

"I told him I couldn't leave you."

Stunned, she jerked back a little in surprise. "You what?"

"Mac, I can't leave you when you're going through everything with Asher, and we're both on high alert with Brandon. What kind of friend would I be?"

"Do you know what I would give to move the hell out of these tiny, noisy-ass dorms? Do you have any clue of how much I struggle with ADHD and all the ruckus?"

"You'd move out if you could?" I asked, hope rushing through me.

"Hell yeah. Please. Although I'm deeply touched, and I love you for being so awesome, you need to move in with him."

"Well, I've finally admitted to myself he really does love me."

Mac barked out a laugh. "A little slow, aren't you?"

I shot her a dirty look. "Thanks, Mac." I paused for a minute. "When I said I couldn't leave you, he said he wanted you there, too."

"What?" she asked, hopping off her bed, scurrying over to mine, and plopping down, staring at me intently.

I turned toward her. "He said you were there a ton last year anyway, and your room is already ready. He said we could move in a few weeks, over Thanksgiving break."

"Oh my God, seriously?" she squealed. "Yes! Yes! Yes!" She bounced on my bed and gave me one of her bear hugs. "We're going to be so tan over the summer, too. Oh, and the nights of drinking and laughing. This is the best thing ever!"

I laughed, grateful she was excited, which meant I could also allow myself to feel happy.

She sat back down, grinning.

"He said he would take me shopping, and we'd do some redecorating, so I'd feel like it was my place, too."

"Oh my God, he's so fucking whipped!" She yelled and laughed.

"Mac," I chided her as my cheeks flushed. It would be odd having sex with her brother while she was down the hall, but we'd already done that. She'd just been passed out. At least there was another room between ours. And there would be times she had classes, and we could sneak home and make love anywhere we wanted. Heat spread through me as I thought about making love to him in front of the fireplace or on the kitchen counter. Maybe he'd bend me over the kitchen table when I felt safer, spread my legs, and enter me from behind, his hand teasing my sensitive flesh while he pumped in and out of me.

I swallowed hard, realizing I was having a full-on sex fantasy in front of his sister.

"Well, I guess it's settled. We have a few more weeks, so we need to tell housing we're moving out."

"Done," she said. "I'll take care of it tomorrow. I'll need to find a few boxes. We don't have a lot, but you definitely have more clothes than you did when you moved up here."

"Except for the dress. I told Hendrix to burn it after Brandon."

Her expression hardened. "Excuse me while I mentally inflict horrendous amounts of pain on Brandon." She paused and sighed. "You were beautiful in that dress. I'm sorry he ruined it for you. I hope you'll consider buying another one. Now that you and Hendrix are together, you'll need a few dresses for events with his dad."

"Franklin goes to a lot of them? I mean, I guess it makes sense. I hadn't asked Hendrix how many he goes to, honestly."

"Well, I don't know about now, but before his dad took a career downturn, he attended one a month."

"Oh shit," I muttered. "One was enough for me, how am I going to deal with so many?"

Mac giggled. "You'll get used to it. And Hendrix is such a natural with everyone, I'm sure you noticed at the last one."

"I noticed a lot of women checking him out, even the cougars."

Mac barked out a laugh. "You're jealous," she said, pointing at me.

"I am not." I picked up my pillow and whacked her upside the head.

"Fight's on, girlfriend," she said, hopping over to her bed and grabbing her pillow.

Before we knew it, feathers were flying around the room while we lovingly beat the shit out of each other, jumped on our beds, and laughed as loud as we could. What was gonna happen? We'd get kicked out? It no longer mattered. Nothing mattered except that I could finally see a glimpse of a future that made my heart sing.

34

Classes passed by slower than Mom's molasses dripping from the jar. My focus sucked ass while our moving date grew nearer. Mac was as excited as I was. In the meantime, we stuck close together. Some nights I stayed with Hendrix until around midnight, but then I went back to the dorm, so I could be with Mac.

Asher had continued to reach out to her, and she hadn't been able to shut the relationship down yet. I knew where her heart was, but I had also started to question his motives. Granted, my experience with guys was zilch, but I knew enough to understand he was most likely having sex with his fiancée, which wasn't fair to her or Mac. I was quickly learning I had to keep my mouth shut and my opinion to myself. It wasn't worth the risk of alienating my best friend. She felt bad enough as it was without me adding to it.

After the baby scare, Hendrix agreed to continue to wear a condom while I took the pill. My doctor had a long talk with me after I shared about the rape and c-section and that Hendrix was my first active, consensual sexual relationship. She sat down next to me, tears in her eyes as she took my hand and told me what an amazing young woman I was. I didn't feel anywhere close to amazing, but I also wasn't blindly grasping for something that made sense in my life anymore, either. Somehow, the universe had opened its arms wide and blessed me with Hendrix and Mac, not to mention I was singing on a regular basis again.

Sex with Hendrix had continued to get better with time. And I wasn't worried about becoming pregnant anymore, which allowed me to relax and enjoy him. We took advantage of every minute we had alone. Even though we would be sharing a bed every night, Mac would be with us more often as well.

Excitement swirled inside me with the idea of waking up in his arms every morning.

MY LAST CLASS of the day ended, and I hurried toward the library. Even though we'd agreed I would never walk anywhere alone, it hadn't worked out exactly as we hoped. My fingers wrapped around the pepper spray, my head up, alert, and aware of everyone around me.

Sighing with relief, I opened the door and hurried through the library. My heart swelled when I saw him, his hair hanging down over his face. I waved at the librarian as she smiled broadly at me. I often wondered what she'd seen the first day I walked in here and what she thought now, the remarkable difference in me. Sometimes butterflies are just ready to be born.

"Hey, babe," I said, sitting next to him.

He dropped his pencil and pulled me to him, kissing me. A slow torturous ache spread through my body.

"Hey," he said, his eyes hooded with desire.

Apparently, his mind was in the same place mine was most of the time.

A soft giggle escaped me while I trailed my fingers across his jawline.

"I finally did it."

"What?" I asked, eager to hear about his day.

"I wrote our next song."

"What? Ours?"

"Yeah. I talked to the guys, and they agree, you should join us. I don't mean on one or two songs, I mean on at least half, if not all. We can take it slow, write some together, record in the studio, and see if we can get onto Spotify. Dad already made a connection and sent our song in."

"What?" My jaw dropped. "You did all of this without talking to me first?"

Hendrix blanched. "I thought you would be excited. I—I wanted to surprise you. I guess it was a bad idea on my part. Nothing is in stone, Gem. We don't have to make any other changes other than moving you in."

Sadness clouded his features, and guilt seeped through me for snapping at him. My fear of him leaving me while he performed had turned into something different. The last time I'd sung in front of a crowd I'd been threatened and assaulted. How could he not have talked to me about such a big deal? Franklin should have suggested Hendrix speak to me before he sent in a recording of our song. Of my voice.

Anger swelled inside me.

"You should know by now that I don't like big surprises. You had no right sending our music in without my consent." I stood quickly, sending my chair skidding across the floor.

"Gem, babe, I'm sorry," he said, grasping for my hand. "I'll stop the whole thing, and we can talk about it whenever you're ready."

"Well, you were wrong." I bent down. "Did you forget what happened the last time I was on stage with you?"

Hendrix pursed his lips, guilt etched on every inch of his face. "No, I didn't forget. How could I ever forget what happened, and I wasn't there to protect you."

"I'll talk to you later. I need some space." I scooped my backpack up from the table and hurried out the door, not bothering to glance over my shoulder at him.

The cold air greeted me as I pushed through the doors and

hurried outside. Unfortunately, the sun set by four in the afternoon during winter. I pulled my coat tighter around me while I made sure to stay on the well-lit sidewalk, but sometimes not even the light could save someone from the darkness.

It was so cold few people were outside, which made me even more nervous. Fear shot down my spine, footsteps growing louder behind me. I glanced over my shoulder, but I couldn't see very far. Was it Brandon, or was my mind screwing with me? Picking up my pace, I screamed as a hand landed on my shoulder and twirled me around.

"Hendrix? What the hell?" I cried.

"I realize you're pissed at me, but there's no way you're walking to the dorm by yourself. I called out, but you didn't hear me, so I figured I needed to catch up to you."

He wrapped his arms around me. Even though I was mad at him, I loved him and felt safer when he was next to me.

"I'm sorry," he said, kissing my forehead. "Not only for scaring you now, but not thinking about my dumb ass move with the music. I got excited and lost my head I guess."

"I'm sorry, too. I shouldn't have gotten so angry about it. I just—I'm not sure I'm ready to come out of hiding some more. It didn't work out too well last time."

"Come on," he said, taking my hand.

I smiled at him, grateful he loved me enough to not let me walk alone even when I was mad at him.

"Let's get through the move, let me settle in, and we can talk about it afterward, okay? Sometimes you move faster than I do, and it really is one day at a time for me most days. I look at the last several months, and I'm in utter shock how much my life has changed. Sometimes it seems like I'm on a crazy fast rollercoaster with all of these hills, and I'm barely hanging on."

"I understand. Just remember, you're no longer alone."

I smiled at him. Somewhere along the way, I'd lost the ability to be mad at him for long.

"Okay," I said as we approached the front doors of the dorm. "Do you have practice tonight?" I asked.

"Yeah, but if you need anything, let me know. We're across town, so stay where you're safe. I'll be about forty-five minutes away."

This had been something new to adjust to as well, knowing his schedule and where he was. Since we'd agreed to live together, he'd been an open book. Not that I suspected he'd ever lied to me, but he wanted to let me know there might be times he couldn't answer the phone right away and to stay close to Mac or in public where Brandon couldn't hurt me.

He leaned down, his lips gentle against mine.

"I love you," he said. "We're okay? I need to know before I leave, or I'll stand here with you until you're not mad at me anymore and be late for practice."

I laughed. "You don't need to be late. We're good," I replied, kissing him in return. My hand slipped between us, and I cupped him through his jeans, massaging him for a moment until I knew I had his attention. "Think about me tonight," I whispered and stepped away, grinning.

He rubbed his jaw and shook his head, smiling as I gave him a small wave and walked into the dorm.

I sighed and made my way up the stairs. Tonight would be my last night here, and as excited as I was about living with Hendrix and Mac, it would also be different. I'd not told Ada Lynn or my parents yet. In my mind, until I'd settled in and we knew it was going to work out, I didn't think it was worth getting yelled at over.

I opened the door, dropped my backpack on the floor, and flopped down on my bed. Mac wouldn't be out of her evening class for a while, and it was the first alone time I'd had in weeks. Since Thanksgiving break had officially started for me, I had nothing to study either.

My thoughts replayed Hendrix's words about the music, and I sighed, grabbed my phone, and turned on Spotify. I tapped my screen and closed my eyes as I listened to "Garden" by Dua Lipa, allowing myself to sink into the music and dream again. I missed it, quiet time, and the opportunity to lose myself in it.

Finally, I allowed myself to think about my future and what I might really want. I'd lost so much over the last five years that I'd never given myself the opportunity to plan like other girls had. By the time they'd started high school I'd lost my innocence and delivered a baby. My world looked nothing like first dates and prom. Things had changed, though. Hendrix had found me, and Mac had helped make it happen.

Contentment and happiness washed over me, and before I knew it, I drifted off to sleep.

My phone vibrated, breaking through my music and my sleep. Puzzled, I held up the phone. It was after ten, and Mac hadn't made it back yet, but it wasn't her. Ada Lynn's name flashed across my screen. It was midnight there, and Ada Lynn never stayed up past nine or nine-thirty. Then it hit me. Dad.

"Ada Lynn?" I asked, sitting up in bed. "What's wrong?"

"Honey, you need to come home."

35

M y heartbeat skidded to a stop. There was no mistaking the fact Ada Lynn had been crying, and I knew she would never tell me to come home unless something had gone horribly wrong.

"I've booked you a plane ticket, so you'll need to hurry. You don't have much time."

"Ada Lynn, is he? Is Dad? Did he?" My pitch rose with each question.

"It's not your dad. He's fine. Your mom's been in a terrible accident," Ada Lynn choked on her words, breaking down in sobs.

"No! Dammit, tell me she's okay. Tell me she's alive," I said, sinking to my knees, tears flowing down my cheeks.

"I can't, Gemma," she said, her voice barely audible.

Time stopped. My mind frantically scrambled for something to hold onto. Mom? It couldn't be true. I'd just talked to her... Shit, I couldn't remember when the last time had been. A few days? A week? I'd been so submerged in Hendrix and singing I'd not even called as often. Now she was...gone.

"No!" I screamed through my sobs, my phone dropping to the floor.

Ada Lynn let me cry for a minute, and somewhere in the back of my head, I realized she was talking again. I picked the phone up and tried to listen to her.

"Now, you need to get ahold of yourself and go to the airport. Throw your clothes in your bag and call for a ride. I booked the next flight out, and I'll email you the details as soon as we hang up. You'll have enough time to get through security, but you'll have to run in order to board in time. If you miss it, you'll be there for another six hours."

"Okay," I muttered in shock, already throwing my clothes into my bag. "I'll see you soon." I hung up the phone, scurrying to pack my bag. I glanced around the room and realized I hadn't packed everything. Maybe Mac could grab the rest and take it to Hendrix's tomorrow.

Hendrix.

A shudder shot through me as I grabbed my phone. How could I leave him? Unfortunately, I had no choice. I set up my Uber and called him. After four rings, it went to voicemail. I swore as I disconnected the call and checked the arrival time for the Uber. It was less than five minutes.

I called him again, this time leaving a message to meet me at the airport the minute he got this. Hopefully, he would get the news in time. There was no way I was telling him Mom had died over a voicemail or text. My brain scrambled to make sense of what had happened. In minutes, my world had turned upside down and crashed down on me.

The door flew open, and Mac practically danced into the room. She stopped short when she saw my bag and face.

"Gemma?" she asked, tears immediately forming in her eyes.

"I have to go, Mac."

"Your dad?" Her expression filled with fear.

"He's fine. It's Mom. She—she," I struggled against my tears. "She was killed in a car accident tonight," I hiccupped. "I can't get in touch with Hendrix, either."

My phone buzzed with the alert that my Uber was here. "I have to go."

"I love you," Mac said, grabbing me in a hug. "I'm so sorry," she whispered. "I'll tell Hendrix, and we will move your stuff for you tomorrow, okay? Although I should tell you to stay in Louisiana for as long as you need to, I'm not. Hurry the hell back." She swiped at her tears and attempted a smile.

I nodded. "Thank you," I said, hugging her again.

My phone buzzed with another reminder, and I dashed down the stairs and out the front door. I spotted my ride and lugged my bag as quickly as I could.

"Gemma!" I turned, wondering who had called my name. "Hey, I'm Andrea Wallace. We met at the student center concert, remember? I'm the one majoring in nursing."

"Oh yeah. Sorry, I never caught your name. I don't mean to be rude, but I have a ride waiting for me. I'm headed home to Louisiana for a little while."

"Oh." Her attention darted around at a few other students making their way to the dorms. "It's probably for the best."

"What?"

"I uh. You're dating Hendrix Harrington, right?" She glanced around nervously.

"Yeah? So?" I peered over my shoulder to make sure my Uber hadn't pulled off. I waved to it and held up a finger, hoping they would understand I would be there in a minute.

"Andrea, I don't mean to be rude, but I really have to go."

"If you're smart, don't come back," she gushed.

"What in the hell are you talking about? Are you all right? This is sort of strange. I mean, you and I met for maybe five minutes."

"I know, and I can't tell you how awkward this is, but some things are going on at this campus. Well, you're better off never returning."

"Yeah, no shit. I've already seen a lot. I have to go, have a good evening." I spun on my heel and began to walk toward my ride.

"Wait," she said, hurrying after me.

I sighed, my patience draining fast. I turned toward her again, my eyebrow arching.

"I wanted to tell you to have a safe flight."

"Are you fucking kidding me right now?" I snapped. "Not that it's any of your business, but I just got a phone call that my mother was killed in a car accident tonight. So whatever it is you're dealing with, I'm really sorry. I have a plane to catch."

She wrung her fingers together; her shoulders shook as she inhaled sharply. "I'm so sorry. Oh, my God, I'm going to make it worse." Tears spilled down her cheeks. "It's the right thing to do, though. It's the right thing to tell you."

"What?" I growled, finally losing all my southern manners.

"I'm pressing charges against Hendrix Harrington for raping me."

CONTINUE HENDRIX'S and Gemma's journey in **Love & Deception and Love & Redemption** are available individually or in the Gemma and Hendrix Collection **boxset**. Just click here.

GEMMA & HENDRIX are back in 2 new books! Click here for Love & Vengeance and here for Love & Retaliation.

ALSO BY J.A. OWENBY

Bestselling Romance

The Love & Ruin Series

Love & Ruin

Love & Deception

Love & Redemption

Love & Consequences, a standalone novel

Love & Corruption, a standalone novel

Love & Revelations, a novella

Love & Seduction, a standalone novel

Love & Vengeance, a standalone novel

Love & Retaliation

Bestselling Romantic Mystery

The Wicked Intentions Series

Dark Intentions

Fractured Intentions

Coming of Age

*The Torn Series, **inspired by True Events***

Fading into Her, a prequel novella

Torn

Captured

Freed

Standalone Novels

Where I'll Find You

JOIN MY ARC TEAM

If you're interested in joining my ARC team, then email me at jenowenby@frontier.com and include links to the Amazon reviews for my books.

I appreciate your help in spreading the word online as well as telling a friend. Reviews help readers find books they love, so please leave a review on your favorite book site.

You can also join my Facebook group, J.A. Owenby's One Page At A Time, for exclusive giveaways and sneak peeks of future books.

Love & Ruin

J.A. OWENBY

Edited by: Deb Markanton

Cover Art by: iheartcoverdesigns

Photographer: CJC Photography

First Edition

ISBN-13: 978-1-949414-14-1

Gain access to previews of J.A. Owenby's novels before they're released and to take part in exclusive giveaways. www.jaowenby.com

ABOUT THE AUTHOR

International bestselling author J.A. Owenby grew up in a small backwoods town in Arkansas where she learned how to swear like a sailor and spot water moccasins skimming across the lake.

She finally ditched the south and headed to Oregon. The first winter there, she was literally blown away a few times by ninety mile an hour winds and storms that rolled in off the ocean.

Eventually, she longed for quiet and headed up to snowier pastures. She now resides in Washington state with her hot nerdy husband and cat, Chloe (who frequently encourages her to drink). She spends her days coming up with ways to torture characters in a way that either makes you want to throw your book down a flight of stairs or sob hysterically into a pillow.

J.A. Owenby writes new adult and romantic thriller novels. Her books ooze with emotion, angst, and twists that will leave you breathless. Having battled her own demons, she's not afraid to tackle the secrets women are forced to hide. After all, the road to love is paved in the dark.

Her friends describe her as delightfully twisted. She loves fan mail and wine. Please send her all the wine.

You can follow the progress of her upcoming novel on Facebook at Author J.A. Owenby and on Twitter @jaowenby.

Sign up for J.A. Owenby's Newsletter:
BookHip.com/CTZMWZ
Like J.A. Owenby's Facebook:

https://www.facebook.com/JAOwenby
J.A. Owenby's One Page At A Time reader group:

https://www.facebook.com/groups/JAOwenby

ACKNOWLEDGMENTS

To my husband, you are my forever. Thank you for being my biggest supporter.

To my community of authors and readers, thank you all so much for your support.

A NOTE FROM THE AUTHOR:

Dear Readers,
*   If you have experienced sexual assault or physical abuse, there*
is free, confidential help. Please visit:
*   Website: https://www.rainn.org/*
*   Phone: 800-656-4673*

This book may contain sensitive material for some readers. Gemma and Hendrix's story is considered a dark romance with language, sex, and violence.

Lightning Source UK Ltd.
Milton Keynes UK
UKHW040716170123
415494UK00001B/36